THE
LIST

THE LIST

MICHAEL BRISSENDEN

This is a work of fiction. Names, characters, places and incidents either are the product of the author's imagination or are used fictitiously. Any resemblance to actual persons, living or dead, events, or locales is entirely coincidental.

Published in Australia and New Zealand in 2017
by Hachette Australia
(an imprint of Hachette Australia Pty Limited)
Level 17, 207 Kent Street, Sydney NSW 2000
www.hachette.com.au

Copyright © Michael Brissenden 2017

This book is copyright. Apart from any fair dealing for the purposes of private study, research, criticism or review permitted under the *Copyright Act 1968*, no part may be stored or reproduced by any process without prior written permission. Enquiries should be made to the publisher.

 A catalogue record for this book is available from the National Library of Australia

ISBN: 978 0 7336 3742 1 (pbk)

Cover design by Luke Causby/Blue Cork
Cover photographs courtesy of Arcangel
Author photograph courtesy of ABC/Andrew Taylor
Text design by Bookhouse, Sydney
Typeset in Sabon LT Pro by Bookhouse, Sydney

*For my father,
R.F. (Bob) Brissenden,
1928–1991*

Afghanistan

HE WOULD ALWAYS REMEMBER THIS SMELL. THE CRUSHED MUSTY undergrowth beneath the pines, the last hint of summer on the breeze, the taint of rocks and earth from the river water on the clean mountain air. It was the smell of the beginning of things and of a long journey to come.

This was the Afghanistan he would recall.

Not the dust, the blood, the fear and heat of the desert battles. From up here in the mountains, looking down over the ripening corn crops and the valley, Afghanistan almost looked benign: an ancient, ordered, predictable place. But like beginnings and rivers, what lay around the next bend may not be what was expected. A good soldier knew that.

Did the soldiers snaking their way down the valley now in their American Humvees and Australian Bushmaster armoured vehicles know? Did they know the bridge they were heading towards was a mess of splintered wood and rubble? Could they sense something was up? The smarter ones might have noticed there was no one in the fields. They might have wondered why a rusty pickup was parked at an angle off the side of the road; obscuring the view of the broken crossing around the corner and of the first Taliban fighters perched on the rocky incline. They might have. But they hadn't and now it was too late. Now there was no chance to turn back. The ambush was upon them.

He didn't underestimate them. Particularly the Australians. They were good soldiers and had been working with the Americans up here, searching out his local commanders and cutting down small groups of his fighters. He had been picking them off whenever he could with carefully placed IEDs. When it came to explosives, he had a reputation as a great improviser. The Australians called him 'Sabre'. He had become their number one target. They'd come close to finding him. Their intelligence was good but not good enough. Their last operation targeting him had left four of the brothers dead.

That day, his jihadis had joined with a local guerrilla group on an ambush mission only to be ambushed by the Australians. He had survived only because he'd stayed behind at the last minute to recover from an infection that had left him feverish and disoriented. The special forces team had struck quickly and decisively. Only one of the bodies – a young boy – was unspoiled. The others had been fouled – their right hands hacked clean off and taken away. Their arms bloodied stumps.

It wasn't fingerprints the Australians were after. No records of him existed as far as he knew. Perhaps they were looking for chemical residue from the bomb making? Anything that might prove they had finally made the kill they wanted so badly. He was lucky he hadn't been there then. But he was here now. The Australians were tough, well disciplined and well trained, but they died the same way everyone else did.

From beneath the pines on the top of the rise, he watched the vehicles round the corner.

They crawled to a stop. Tentative. Now they knew something was wrong. It was still 150 metres to the bridge but they were sandwiched between the impassable river and his fighters who had quickly taken up positions on the road, wrapped in their dust-coloured headwear, brandishing an assortment of guns and rocket-propelled grenades. Other fighters were holding positions across the river. Some remained with him under the trees up the hill. The infidel soldiers were surrounded. His collection of Afghanis and foreign jihadis – some from Saudi, some from the battles in Chechnya and southern Dagestan, and a few others from as far as Copenhagen, Berlin and other parts of Europe – could only imagine what was going through the minds of those inside the little air-conditioned boxes. But he knew how they thought. He knew how different the Australians were from the exuberant, brash Americans. The Australian SAS soldiers would be amped up in there. They'd be sweating and swearing quietly, but they'd be falling back on their training. Calm. Professional.

He had played cricket with boys just like them. He'd stolen bicycles and cars with them, he'd fought with them, laughed with them, played practical jokes with them. He'd done all the usual things that preoccupied boys who grew up in the rough end of Greenacre, Lakemba and Punchbowl in Sydney's western suburbs. When he was a boy he'd even liked some of them, but he'd never been one of them. In the last few years, he'd made it his mission to kill as many of them as he could. And now he was going to send them a message.

•

'Fuck!' Mick Harrison was the first to realise they'd been ambushed.

In the last few missions, they'd deliberately set themselves up as ambush targets. Luring the Talibs to a fight only for them to discover they were the ones surrounded. An easy trick for a while. But the Taliban had got smart to the double ambush and had done their homework. There were no tricks now.

It had been Harrison and Aaron Wappington's turn to ride with the Americans in one of the heavily armoured Humvees today. They were in the lead vehicle, followed by the two Bushmasters and another heavily armoured Humvee bringing up the rear.

'The cunts have got us caught,' Wappo said from the other side of the dual cab just as rocket-propelled grenades and bullet rounds started raining in on them. A huge explosion seemed to suck the oxygen out of the air and then blow it back, like standing too close to the side of the road as a B-Double road train roared past. Outside, a ferocious whirlwind of shrapnel blew through the convoy. One of the vehicles had either taken a big hit or run into an IED.

The Humvee's American driver, Big Jim, was wrestling with the lumbering vehicle, trying to move it into a defensive position. He couldn't see much and he was starting to panic. A round hit the Yank patrol commander next to Jim as the comms shrieked to life. The American attack controller in the other hummer was calling in air strikes. Everything was moving fast.

Harrison armed himself with an 84-millimetre rocket launcher and scrambled out. Someone needed to get an eye on where the fire was coming from and hit back. One of the Bushmasters must have taken the hit. The second hummer had pulled alongside and the soldier in the front gun turret was cutting crazy with the 7.62 calibre machine gun, firing all over the place, making a lot of noise but shooting at nothing.

Wappo tumbled out after Harrison with a 60-millimetre mortar just as a volley of heavy machine-gun fire strafed his position. Some of it hit the mark. Big Jim slumped across the steering wheel. He wouldn't live. Behind him, his commander was screaming as blood poured from what was left of his left leg.

Harrison moved beside the bulk of the hummer, which was giving him and Wappo some cover. Most of the fire was coming from behind the pickup truck they'd had to negotiate their way past just a few minutes earlier but they were also taking fire from the steep verge above them that ran along one side of the road. Harrison took a bead on the pickup and let a round from his rocket launcher loose. It blew the front off the vehicle. Shrapnel and black smoke flew into the sky as the fuel tank erupted in another suctioned whoosh of noise and chaos. It was answered almost immediately with more machine-gun rounds and RPGs. Shrapnel and bullets bounced off the vehicles and screamed past him, kicking up dust; a frenzied hail of sharp-edged metal. Harrison and Wappo had known each other a long time. Combat to them now was second nature. They knew when they were in trouble. They were in trouble now.

An F-18 roared overhead and unleashed a burst of fire into the Taliban position behind the pickup. The Yank calling the directions must have given the pilot a good lock because the strike shut the storm down for a good few minutes. Then the plane peeled off ... mission over. More would come soon, surely, but this one had at least given Harrison and Wappo enough time to get better cover and survey the wreckage.

The two Bushmasters had taken direct hits. It didn't look like anyone could have lived. Inside each armoured vehicle were five of their own. Mates. Blokes they'd trained with for years and fought alongside on this rotation for the past six months. That was war. They drill you for it. They give you the counselling. But you never get over it. Losing your friends. Never. Now wasn't the time to dwell on it though. They drill you for that too. How to put it away in a box to deal with later. Trouble is the box gets full. They don't tell you how to deal with that. A female AFP investigator was also along for this ride. Harrison didn't know her well but he'd seen her around. Nice looking. Youngish – early thirties maybe – a bit aloof but nothing new in that, most of the women here were.

The gunner in the other hummer was still firing at shadows. Wappo crawled in and calmed him down. Somehow got him to focus his aim onto the position above them. For a moment, it seemed the gunner was having an impact but then another storm of metal from heavy AK fire rained down onto his position. When it stopped, there was no more crazy spray coming from the other hummer.

'Wappo, you all right?' Harrison called out, already fearing the answer.

Nothing. Dust and smoke hung in the air. A fierce and cloying quiet settled in.

'Oi!' he shouted. 'Anyone else there?'

Nothing.

Jesus. Fuck. He was on his own.

He lay on his back on the dirt beside the bullet-riddled hummer for what seemed like hours but was probably little more than a few minutes. Nothing moved. No one groaned. Bits of metal pinged and cracked as they contracted from the heat of the battle. Then he heard them coming. The crunch of boots on gravel, voices carried on the breeze here and there. Louder now. Closer. They were talking in low grunts. What could he do? Crawl under the smoking hummer and hope they didn't find him? Not likely. Sit up and meet them with a smile – hands in the air? Or fight and try and take out as many as possible before they killed him? The last option seemed the only choice. They'd most likely kill him whatever he did. But if he was going to fight, he had to find something other than the spent rocket launcher that was lying beside him. There were guns in the hummer. He leveraged himself up and crawled over the body of a nearby American. His M4 was lying on the other side of the cab. Harrison reached across.

'Don't touch it, please.' The voice came from behind him. An Australian accent, cultured, but unmistakably Australian.

Harrison turned, hoping to see a friendly face. But there was no welcome grin. No smiling, bearded sunburnt Aussie in special forces desert gear.

Instead half-a-dozen Taliban in tawny brown robes stared back at him, bristling, with weapons pointed in his face. The man in the middle had no gun and was dressed head to toe in black. A black scarf wrapped tightly around his head. A long, flowing black beard spilled from a lean dark face. Black eyes, a sharp almost feminine nose. The impact was menacing. No doubt it was supposed to be.

'Who are you?' Harrison asked.

No reply.

The black jihadi addressed the others in Arabic not Farsi, Harrison noticed. His Arabic was rudimentary and he could only catch bits of what was being said. None of it was encouraging. Two of the Talibs dragged him out of the hummer by his boots. He landed with a thud on the dirt, his helmet clanging against the chassis on the way down.

'You're an Aussie?' Harrison asked.

Again, there was no reply. Instead the two manhandlers propped him up against the car. A rifle butt smashed into his helmet, sending his head careening off to one side. A searing pain engulfed him. Mick Harrison felt a warm trickle of blood run down from his ear. Were they going to kill him? Surely they were. Please get it over with quickly.

He was still wheezing and coughing when they came in for him again. This time one pinned his shoulders to the vehicle. The other one took a belt and began wrapping it around his right arm – just above the elbow. It was tight. Harrison could feel it restricting his blood flow. His arm began to throb almost immediately. After a few more grunted instructions from the man in black, the fighter stretched Harrison's arm out to one side and pushed it down so his forearm was lying flat on the ground.

He saw one of them pass a small tomahawk-style axe to the man in black.

The mysterious black-clad Aussie jihadi leant in close, almost putting his lips to Harrison's ear. Mick could feel the damp, fetid breath on his cheek. The man spoke. A whisper in that unmistakable accent.

'Out here they call me Scorpion. Back home they call me something totally unremarkable. You can kill us one by one but you'll never defeat us. And this? This is for all the brothers in Lakemba.'

'*Allahu akbar*,' he said quietly.

'*Allahu akbar*.' The others shouted enthusiastically.

The man stood back. Harrison saw the axe. He saw the man raise it high. He saw it come down in a sickening slow motion arc and he saw his own hand lying in the dirt. Pumping. Twitching. Unattached. A scorching pain coursed up his arm. Everything went black.

1.

By the time Sidney Allen fought his way through the heavy traffic heading west from the city and parked the pissy little Hyundai he and Haifa had been issued from the car pool, the NSW uniforms had the barriers up across the footpath and the entrance taped off.

The shopfront was little more than two metres wide, with a glass door and a panel advertising haircuts in English and Arabic. Ten dollars for a standard clip. Kids nine dollars. The shop was wedged between an old-fashioned haberdasher – selling school uniforms and cheap sports clothes in local team colours – and a grocer's that sold just about anything and everything and doubled as a Vodaphone agent.

The 'Jamal Taha' barber shop was a humble little business among dozens of other humble little businesses that lined Auburn Road. It looked like it'd been there long enough to pay off someone's immigrant dreams, or at least keep the children fed and launched into a new life tens of thousands of kilometres away from the homeland they'd fled.

The body was slumped in the barber's chair – a bullet through the left temple – blood splattered in an arc across the mirror. So much for the promised better life.

The shop had been sectioned off into two spaces. There was police tape and a checkpoint outside. Sid and Haifa both showed their credentials and signed in. Standard crime scene investigation procedure. Inside, more tape cordoned off the area around the chair with the body. No one could cross that line without wearing a forensic suit, gloves and a face mask. Sid recognised Cavan Maskey. Despite all the gear he had on, he hadn't yet crossed the tape. Cavan lifted his mask when he saw them coming.

'Kebab wars,' he said.

'What?' Sid hadn't heard death called that before.

'Kebab wars. That's what they call this around here. The Sunnis and the Shias have been at each other's throats for ever but since the Syrian stuff started it's become really bad. Bit like the Micks and the Prods back in Belfast in the old days.'

Sid had known Detective Sergeant Cavan Maskey since they both went through Goulburn together back in the early nineties. Maskey had never been able to shake his Falls Road burr. He still sounded just like he did when Sid first met him, back when he was a nineteen-year-old cadet fresh off the plane – a refugee from 'the Troubles'.

But to be fair, it was always going to be hard for Cavan to shake off his past. His family was so nationalist his mum named all the kids after Irish towns: Cavan, Derry, Ennis and Sligo. The first three were okay, but Sligo . . . Poor bastard.

In the last few years, Cavan had traded his uniform for a suit and joined the Middle East Organised Crime Squad and immersed himself in the gang wars of the western suburbs.

'It's not a straight up B4L hit that's for sure,' Cavan said. 'Hamzy's Brothers for Life wouldn't have been so neat.'

He ambled towards Sid and Haifa and started to carefully remove his disposable nitrile gloves.

'How's things, Sid? I'm guessing this one must be one of yours. They don't send the Feds out just for one of the brothers.'

'Yeah, he's one of ours. Not a biggie. But he's on the list.'

Sid took his old friend's outstretched hand. It was a bit softer than he remembered. But then a lot about Cavan Maskey had become a bit softer in the past few years.

'The jihadi list?' Cavan asked.

Sid nodded. There was only one terror watchlist.

'So, what are we looking at, Cav?' Sid fell back into the easy familiarity he'd had with Maskey all those years ago.

'I'm not so sure. Doesn't look like the regular drive-by you see out here. Drugs probably. Retribution certainly,' Maskey said. Then he changed the subject. 'You're still in good shape by the looks, Sid.'

In comparison to Cav's steady, careless, burger-fuelled decline, Sid reckoned he was still looking okay. For a copper anyway. If that's what he still was. These days he spent most of his time working on counter terrorism, in the shadows with the geeks and the hardheads in national security. He wore a better cut of suit than the NSW boys, nice shoes too.

If anything, Sid was struggling to keep weight on. He'd noticed his face thinning out over the last few years but he still looked the right side of forty. A good head of hair helped even if a sprinkle of grey had started to creep in at the temples. Well, that's what the women would say, although there hadn't been much of that sort of action in his life since Rosie. That was years ago now. Still seemed like yesterday.

Some of his colleagues had already jumped to conclusions about him and Haifa, but as far as Sid was concerned she was a colleague.

'Hi. Cavan Maskey.' Cavan thrust his hand out to Haifa. 'He's not going to introduce us so let's be bold.'

'Sorry,' Sid said. 'Haifa, Cavan – Cavan, Haifa Hourani.'

'Hourani. That's Lebanese, right?'

'Yes, that's right.' Haifa stared Cavan down as if to say 'So?'

'Haifa's with our counter terrorism group,' Sid said, looking at Cavan. He knew instantly what Cav was thinking.

Haifa was good looking – tall, fit, jet-black shoulder-length hair, a nose you'd best describe as 'proud' and unusually light, striking, smoky grey eyes. Brain the size of a planet too. Specialist in Arabic and Farsi, she knew more about what was happening out here between the Sunnis and the Shia, the real jihadis and the internet warriors, than anyone.

'It could be sectarian I suppose,' Haifa said. 'But if it is, it's bold. Killing a Sunni boy on this street? That's asking for all-out war.' She walked across to the other side of the room, careful not to lean over the cordon tape. But she peered in as close as she could get, examining the victim's head wound.

Too close for Sid. He could mostly cope with bodies once they were dead but he still didn't have the stomach for a detailed inspection when not much time had passed between the violence and the death. Even after years of trying to work through it with the psychs it shook him up. It was because of that very first time – a dark freezing night and a busload of sixth graders run off the road – the worst anyone had seen on the Barton Highway for years and that really was saying something given the notorious reputation of that road. When he and his shift buddy got out of their patrol car they could hear the screaming coming from inside the bus. The kids couldn't get out. Some were already dead, others soon would be. It took some time for the ambos and the cutters to come in from Canberra and it was the waiting that did it to him. They couldn't do anything – just talk to the ones they could see. They tried to calm things down. But there was panic inside. Kids screaming and crying. Some of them knew they weren't going to make it. When they finally did cut them out they found seventeen kids dead. Others wouldn't make it through the night and still others would carry the wounds forever – including Sid. He'd seen plenty worse since then – especially in Iraq during his tours there: IEDs, market bombings and the like – but that bus crash was first and it stuck with him. Every new body dragged him back to that cold night on the Barton Highway.

And then there was Rosie. At least he hadn't heard her scream.

This one wasn't screaming either – not anymore.

'So how do you know he's Sunni?' Maskey's question was directed at Haifa but it dragged Sid back to the here and now. 'These guys don't make it easy. They don't wear Pope rings.'

Haifa shot Cav a look that was part disdain and part benevolence. As if to say 'How the fuck have you got this far in the force?' Sid had seen that look from her before.

'This place,' she said, gesturing around the room, which was full of black-and-white photos of outdated hairstyles that no young Leb would be seen dead wearing, along with posters for Lebanese community organisations and quotations in Arabic that Sid recognised were from the Qur'an, 'it's Sunni. The shop is named after Jamal Taha, probably Lebanon's most famous footballer. Played for Al-Ansar, which has a fanatical Sunni following that stretches all the way from Beirut to Lakemba. Believe me, as the only girl in my family with three older brothers, I know. Also,' she pointed to the body, 'no tattoos – it's *haram*, at least for the really true believers. Gang members don't care. They'd tattoo the IS flag on their foreheads if they thought it might give them some street cred. But the real boys – the fanatics – no tatts.'

'*Haram* – forbidden,' Cav said trying to prove he wasn't totally outclassed. 'Proscribed under Islamic law. Yeah, I know about *haram*.'

'And his name –' Haifa looked down at her notebook. 'Omar al-Naimi. No Shia would ever be called Omar.'

'Okay, so he's Sunni. Just about everyone on the list is. What's the motivation?' Sid asked, still unable to look closely.

He watched as Haifa walked to the other side of the room, her gaze flicked from the arc of blood streaked across the mirror back to the body. Then she stopped and took a careful step forward.

'I'm not sure. But I think this has something to do with it.'

'What?' Sid and Cavan both said at the same time.

'Someone's hacked off his right hand.'

2.

THE LOCAL UNIFORMS HAD CLOSED OFF THE STREET AND THE traffic had been thrown into chaos. It didn't take much to cause gridlock in Sydney these days. It was only two o'clock, well before what used to be the rush hour, and it was stinking hot.

Sid turned the car into the barely moving queue of overheating vehicles. Haifa was flicking through her notebook with one hand and checking something on her phone with the other. She looked vaguely concerned, or perhaps it was just concentration, Sid thought, like she was cramming for an exam. She'd been with the team less than six months but she'd already established a reputation as a thorough and meticulous investigator.

On the radio news, the prime minister, Brian Williams, was talking about a major national security address he was due to give when the parliament resumed in Canberra the following week. Politicians loved national security – particularly prime ministers who couldn't deliver on much else. The leadership rumours were circling around Williams and most of the pundits thought one more misstep would undo him. But his one hope, his one strand of credibility, was national security. That's what he thought anyway. That's what the focus groups and the pollster spivs would have been telling him. They always believed that shit.

A few months ago another so-called 'lone wolf' had attacked a post office in Sydney armed with a shotgun and an IS flag. He was taken out by a police sniper after a short three-hour siege. No one else was hurt but it was all adding to the fear. Copenhagen, Boston, London, Paris, Jakarta, Manchester, Sydney – again. It was the third lone wolf siege in two months and the internet chatter was intensifying. Everyone could feel it. Like something bigger was brewing. It was coming, Williams effectively kept telling everyone, but no one really knew what, when or where. The country was being whipped into a state of perpetual anxiety.

'Australia will not be held hostage by evil.' Brian Williams was braying on in that simplistic tone that he specialised in.

'Many of those who now wish to do us harm have been given a helping hand by this nation's open heart. We have given them safety and we have given them our trust. In return they have abused our generosity. It has to stop.'

To be fair, it wasn't just Williams – a lot of them spoke like that.

Sid turned it off.

'What does that mean?' Haifa scowled. 'Are we not going to give people the benefit of the doubt anymore?'

She knew the answer. They both did. There was a fine line between suspicion and guilt, and curtailing freedoms to protect freedoms, but exceptions were now being made. And more were coming. Tougher rhetoric was being backed by tougher laws and greater surveillance powers. Sid had spent the past two years working in the counter terrorism unit, and the past twelve months with K block. The unit's job was to track, find and disrupt potential terrorists and terror cells with a view to locking them away, using whatever methods and means it could. Sid still found the work morally challenging but increasingly harder to argue against. He knew most of his colleagues had no such moral equivocation. It was difficult and complicated to take someone off the street, even if you knew they were planning an attack. And it took time. Time in these cases was valuable. They'd already had a couple of close calls. But he was still uncomfortable about it; he couldn't help thinking something was being lost along the way. Maybe there was no other choice now but he hated how politicians loved ramping it up. Fear was so easy to tap into. Too easy.

'You hungry?' Haifa said, finally putting down her phone. She didn't wait for an answer. 'I'm starving. I'll show you the best Lebanese restaurant in Sydney.'

'Sure, we've got time.' After the scene at the barber shop, the last thing Sid felt like was food but he was happy to go along for the ride.

'Do you like Lebanese food?' she asked.

'What's not to like? Hummus, falafel, baba ganoush.'

Haifa laughed. 'Is that it? We need to get you educated. You're in for a treat.'

Sid smiled. He'd been pleased when Haifa had joined K block. She had a determined energy and a sense of humour – a rare quality in the squad. With the exception of Chip Walker, who'd come on loan from the FBI, most of the team tended to be either technology geeks on the autism spectrum or dour introverts.

Haifa's phone pinged with an incoming text alert.

'Damo's logged on. He'll start looking at the dead boy's online profile.'

'Where am I going?' Sid asked.

'Punchbowl – head for the station. But it's a secret, okay? Promise me you won't tell any of your Skippy mates.' Haifa laughed again. Sid could feel his mood lightening.

The traffic thinned out as they drove down Rookwood Road past the light industrial sites and the warehouses, then it banked up a bit when they hit all the new apartment complexes around Bankstown, but they made pretty good time. It was two-thirty when they pulled up on The Boulevarde just across from Punchbowl station. The Boulevarde was an ironically cruel name for the street, Sid always thought. This end of it at least was just five-dollar bargain shops, a bulk-billing medical centre and a couple of halal butchers. The Zahra Lebanese restaurant was next to Hoong Cheong Vietnamese seafood, which in turn banged up against a charcoal grill kebab joint. This time of the day there weren't too many people on the street: a few young mums pushing prams, a small group of old men smoking and a few older women in hijabs and chadors.

The look on the face of the young girl clearing the last of the lunch plates from the tables as they walked in said it all. A wide beam of delight spread across her face. She had the same striking features and poise as Haifa. She came running towards them, squealing, and wrapped Haifa in a joyful embrace.

'Mumma, Mumma, come. Look who it is!'

'Shoosh, Dana. You'd think I hadn't been here in months.' Haifa returned the hug with just as much enthusiasm.

An older, smaller, weathered woman came through the kitchen door – her arms raised.

'Hey baby!' she shrieked. 'Where you been? Sit down. Sit down. Who's your friend?'

Sid realised he was probably looking a bit startled. Haifa hadn't warned him of what to expect.

'This is my colleague, Sid Allen. Sid, this is my aunt Lamitta and my cousin Dana. It's true I haven't been here in weeks.' Haifa laughed.

'Sit down. Sit down. You must be hungry. Oh it's so good to see you.'

And then they were off, talking animatedly in Arabic, and occasionally breaking into English for emphasis. Within minutes the food started arriving. Baskets of bread, hummus, baba ganoush, falafel, a salad made of cauliflower, mint and dates. Some lamb kebabs, fresh tomatoes cut and drizzled with oil and salt. A plate of broad beans with lemon juice and garlic. Another with chickpeas, pine nuts and yoghurt.

Once the family news had been delivered, Lamitta and Dana returned to the post-lunch chores. Sid followed Haifa's lead as she tore off hunks of the flat bread and dipped it into the creamy hummus. The salads were incredible – flavoured simply with lemon, olive oil and garlic – and the meat was tender and grilled medium rare. He had his appetite back.

'Isn't this the best food you've ever had?'

Sid had to agree it probably was close to it.

'We didn't get a lot of eggplant in my family,' he said, 'and the only thing special my mum knew to do with a cauliflower was cover it with white sauce and cheese. But we had a lot of oranges.'

'Oh yeah?' Haifa seemed delighted at the turn of the conversation. 'Tell me more.'

'About what?'

'Oranges. Where did you grow up?'

'Griffith. Out west. My family were irrigation farmers. Oranges.'

'Were?'

'Yeah, they're long gone. Back when I was a kid you'd open up the channels and flood the place. All that beautiful Murray irrigation water sluicing around. You could grow anything. Can't do that now. Even if you do still have a water licence the water's too expensive and there's no point trying to compete with imports. Better off growing the other crop Griffith is famous for – although that would be something of a conflict of interest in my case. Me being with the law and all.' Sid shrugged.

Haifa nodded. Sid was sure she'd be well versed in the history of the Calabrian Mafia and their activities in Griffith. They'd been a big deal for decades in Australia and they were still in control of much of the trade in drugs and guns.

'Compared to all this shit we're dealing with now the Calabrians seem almost polite,' Sid said.

'Why do you say that?'

He shrugged. 'The mob had a sort of unspoken rule. You don't leave your bodies in the street. It just attracts the cops, the media and the politicians. Bad for business. Now –' He paused, looked across the table, unsure if he should continue with his theory.

'What?' Haifa stopped eating, lifted her gaze from the plate.

'Well, things are different now. The Middle Eastern gangs have a totally different approach to violence. You know the drive-by shootings. The guns. There're so many guns out here now. It's changed everything. Certainly changed Sydney crime.'

Sid knew he wasn't telling Haifa anything she didn't already know. He knew about her brothers. The one a few years older than her, Hakim, was a well-respected scientist and community leader. But she had two much older brothers who had both been in gangs. Drugs, extortion, rackets. They were both doing time and probably wouldn't taste a good falafel for a few more years yet. Sid stopped talking, took a big gulp of tea and stared over at the wall. A huge gold-framed poster of a brilliant, shining Sydney Harbour beamed back at him.

'Is it difficult for you?' he asked. 'You know, caught between the two cultures? Not just with the gangs either. This stuff – the jihadis. It can't be easy.'

Was this too much? Maybe. He pushed his empty cup into the middle of the table, not able to bring himself to look at Haifa directly. They'd only worked together on and off for a few months and they'd only ever really skirted around this stuff. Obviously it affected her. It must.

She looked across at him – her smoky, fiery stare drilling into his – a look of determination rather than anger.

'What you really mean,' she said, 'is how did my brothers and I take such different paths?' She went on before Sid could try and backtrack. 'That's just the way some Lebanese families are. When the family first comes out they have nothing and often can't take advantage of all that's offered in the new country. They have to fight for everything and they need money. It's even sort of expected that the older children will help make that happen. Crime is just part of the suburban immigrant experience.' She shrugged like it was no big deal. 'Then they draw a line in the sand. They devote themselves to ensuring the younger ones get an education and cement the family into the new society. In that sense, my family is no different from many others.' She sipped her tea, thinking.

'You know what? I don't usually talk about this much. I do my job and I keep my thoughts to myself. Sometimes I find it hard, yes. But I try to understand why. That's often more than I get in return.'

'Meaning?'

'You all see this as black and white. Good versus bad. "The vortex of evil", as Williams calls it. For me it's more nuanced.'

She waved her hand in the air as if to dismiss the discussion. 'I don't think we need to go there right now. It's a big topic.'

'What's not black and white about a bullet to the head and a severed hand?'

'You see that's just it. Who knows who killed that guy? Or why? All we know is he was on "the list".' Haifa leant forward and gave him a you-asked-for-it look. 'There are more than half a million Muslims in Australia. Less than fifty have been arrested on terror charges and there's a couple of hundred more we're watching. Now I'm not saying there isn't a problem. There is. But a wedge is being driven between a disenfranchised and marginalised community and the wider Australian society who are being encouraged to fear. Personally, I hate just about every religion. I hate all this preaching of mercy while you cut off someone's head. For fuck's sake. But this is about more than that. The blowback that's occurring now is a consequence of the carve-up of the Middle East over a hundred years ago by European colonial powers. The people who live here – my family – are living with the historical consequences of actions that took place over a hundred years ago.'

'Yeah,' Sid leant in too, excited by the turn of the conversation, 'but you don't have to blow people up to make a political point. You don't have to kill innocents. That's what we're fighting against here. That's why we do what we do, isn't it?'

Haifa pushed a piece of bread into the baba ganoush with no intention of eating it. There was no one left in the dining room now. Dana and her mother had retreated to the kitchen.

'You know a lot of Muslims do have a sort of siege mentality,' she said slowly. 'They believe they're being dominated culturally and religiously. And they get frustrated by what they see as the contradictions in Western foreign policy.'

Sid looked at her; at the intensity on her face. She's something else, he thought. Impressive. Smart. So why was she working for the Feds? She could've been secretary-general of the UN.

'In every Muslim household in this country there's anger when they switch on the news and see what's happening in the Middle East, in Palestine, Syria, Iraq, Guantanamo. Why did the West club together to get rid of Saddam Hussein in Iraq but do nothing to stop Assad killing thousands of innocent people in Syria? That's what they ask. And I think it's a fair question.'

Haifa paused. She looked across the restaurant to the brown Formica-covered counter, coffee pots placed in a careful row from large to small on the shelves behind it, faded posters of Beirut and Tripoli alongside pictures of Bondi. A small Lebanese cedar tree painted on the wall – the swinging doors into the kitchen worn from years of busy traffic.

'You know, my family has an easier time understanding why my brothers are in Goulburn jail than they do understanding why I'm doing this. That's the truth.'

Sid was about to ask her why she did it then. But his vibrating phone got there first. It was K block's project leader.

'Hey, AJ? What's up?'

3.

Sid pointed the Hyundai east along The Boulevarde and through the quiet suburban streets of Wiley Park. They turned right into Haldon Street. The bookshop was directly across the road from the Lakemba Hotel – an old-school boozer that probably didn't do as much business as it used to. Sid had a low threshold for irony but he did think that was sweet. The al-Ma-ana was on the ground floor of a relatively new block of blonde brick shops and units and whoever worked there would have had to look across at the pub all day.

Over the past few years, the bookshop and the Islamic centre attached to it had become an important meeting place for the extremist set and a platform for radical preaching.

A local preacher had just reported two dead bodies in an apartment above the bookstore. Turned out the two bodies were also from 'the list', but Sid's guess was that just about everyone who came and went from the centre would have been on it.

The most radical of the al-Ma-ana preachers had been a figure of some interest for years. Wissam Shalomar liked to keep out of the public eye but he was always happy enough to talk to the spooks provided his photo never appeared anywhere. He'd even briefed journos on a few occasions and just a couple of months ago conducted a sensational radio interview defending IS. It was with Stan Anderton, one of those frothing at the mouth, bloviating commercial radio shock jocks Sydney specialised in. Needless to say, the interview made a bit of news.

But then Shalomar could bloviate with the best of them. When Sid and Haifa arrived at the bookshop he was in full flight, ranting at the uniforms busy securing the site. Armed officers had been stationed at the entrance to the building. Others had taken up positions outside. Neighbourhood door knocks were already underway and checks were being run on every car parked nearby. The entrance to the upstairs apartments where the bodies were found had been taped off and a crime scene log established. Everyone going in or out of the building would be logged.

'What are you doing to protect us?' Shalomar was shouting at anyone within earshot, stabbing his finger in the air. 'You call this democracy? You call this freedom? Where's the protection for our people? We are peaceful, we are quiet and what do you do? You harass us. You watch us. You take our photographs. You bug our phones. And then you can't even keep us safe.'

The two dead were in a small bedsit apartment on the top floor. Two more officers were stationed just outside the door as a further level of security to preserve the sterility of the scene inside. The windows were closed and the air-con was off. Even out in the hall, the air was humid and thick with the smell of death.

Inside the apartment, a two-man forensics team was photographing the scene from every angle and establishing a grid that would allow them to cross-reference the floor space in precise thirty-centimetre segments.

One of the bodies was on the floor – facedown in a dark pool of coagulated blood that had seeped from a head wound remarkably similar to the one that had hit the barber shop body. The other was tied to a chair. Even from this side of the doorway it was impossible not to notice that neither of the bodies had their right hands.

Sid's stomach turned. He had no interest in getting any closer. He'd already seen enough for one day. The photos would be in soon, forensics would go over it, and they'd have plenty of time to sort through it all. Haifa, on the other hand, was keen.

One of the forensics came over. He pulled up his mask as he walked. Sid recognised him. Simon Arnold. Young guy, one of the best forensic crime scene managers around.

'They told me you guys would be coming.' He looked first at Sid then to Haifa.

'Found anything?' she said.

'Certainly looks like the same shooter as the one in Auburn but these two have been here a while now. Three days easy. We've got something for ballistics, not much, but enough to make a match and identify the weapon. You want a closer look?'

Haifa nodded.

'Suit up over there.' He pointed to a large blue carry bag further down the hall.

Sid stood a little distance away as Haifa followed the procedure carefully, tucking all of her hair up under a hairnet, putting on the overshoes and double sleeving the gloves as required.

Foot pads had been laid out on the floor like stepping stones marking a trail from the doorway to the bodies. Sid watched her step carefully past the body on the ground and stop at the stiff tied to the chair.

'Shot through the head. Left temple,' she said, dictating into her phone. 'Significant exit wound. Badly disfigured face. Looks like it's been hacked with a blunt instrument of some kind. Right hand has been removed.'

She walked back the way she'd gone, stopping at the body on the floor to record a few more observations. Only when she'd left the room did she pull up her mask and start taking off the gloves. She looked pale and shaken.

'Whoever did this was after something,' she said, looking past him, back into the room. 'It wasn't quick. This was torture.'

4.

K block was just a collection of desks and electronic equipment tucked into the far end of the open-plan investigations room on the fifth floor of the Australian Federal Police's Goulburn Street headquarters. A few slightly higher partitions were the only sign that it was separate from the rest of the office. Few people in the AFP really understood what K block was or what it did. Sid knew most people thought the unit was just a bunch of misfits involved in cloak and dagger work, who came and went at all hours and kept to themselves. There was some truth to it – more than half of the team didn't even have a police or an intelligence background. They were hired for their ability to think creatively. The unit had originally been called 'Operation Kandahar'. It was an eclectic group of investigators and researchers thrown together at the request of a commissioner under pressure from a government desperate for results. It was also in large part an effort to overcome the suspicion and sometimes outright hostility that coursed between the two Federal agencies that had to work so closely on counter terrorism. Every effort to get ASIO and the AFP to fully cooperate before had failed. They had their own units, they had their own specialists but mostly they hadn't worked effectively together. K block had been AJ's vision. It worked because of her, because it was different, because she was different and because she hired people who were different.

There was some low-level resentment about the way they worked, but no one probed too much. It helped that they had already delivered some big results – including the recent arrest of a cell of young second-generation Afghanis with crude but well-advanced plans to carry out public beheadings.

Sid and Haifa made their way down the empty walkway that separated the neat rows of desks – all the same except for the occasional snapshots of girlfriends, wives, kids, cars and dogs tacked up on the shoulder-high partitions.

Haifa picked up a notepad from her desk and took off almost immediately. She had a date, she said. They hadn't talked much on the way into town. She'd seemed distracted and withdrawn since she'd seen the bodies. Sid hadn't been feeling too good himself. It had been a tough day. Too many dead bodies. That familiar tickle of anxiety had begun to creep up on him and he knew it would get worse before it got any better.

Chip and Damien Murphy were the only two K block inmates left. That wasn't unusual for Murphy. Sid usually only saw him in the office when the sun went down.

Damo was a maths genius who had drifted into the dark side of hacking, pulling down credit information and breaching the cyber walls of some of the biggest tech companies, like PayPal and Google, while he was 'bug hunting' for them. He'd find vulnerabilities in their databases, steal their customer information and then tell them for a price how to fix it. Cyber blackmail effectively. The AFP stepped in and gave him a choice: put on the white hat or face a conviction. Since then he'd proved to be a loyal, trustworthy and very effective member of the team.

He was down in the far corner he'd made his own. The view from the fifth floor was spectacular but it was obviously of no consequence to the tech head because he'd shoved two desks together and covered the windows behind with black cardboard. He'd assembled four computer monitors side by side. Two TV monitors were sitting above them. It looked a little like a TV studio control room. The talking heads and pundits babbled on silently on Sky news and the ABC – consumed as ever with the ins and outs of what passed for politics for the insiders in Canberra. The four other monitors were alight with websites. Chip had the next desk along the wall.

'Much happening yet?' Sid asked.

Neither of the two men looked up.

'Hey buddy. How ya doin'?' Chip was clicking through the crime scene photos that had already made it into the system. 'Not much here yet but we won't be able to keep this quiet for long.'

Everyone in K block knew that the media – the national security reporters – would be trawling the online chatter for news, just like the K block investigators did. It was often only through Facebook or Twitter that you found out about foreign jihadis killed in battle. A post would go up and a video celebrating the holy sacrifice of the martyr. Sometimes the hacks learnt about it before K block did, but generally Murphy was ahead of them.

Right now Damo was scrolling down a couple of pages looking for any sign that the killings in Auburn and Lakemba had hit the jihadi Facebook sites or the Twitter feed. They hadn't.

'Here look,' he said in his slow Maroubra surfer drawl. 'This is the al-Ma-ana site. Nothin' up yet. Just the usual.'

The al-Ma-ana page featured the expected stream of invective and general support for the global jihad movement in both Arabic and English. One image had two AK-47s, a Qur'an and an IS banner with a slogan above it that read – 'The book guides and the sword triumphs'.

'No one's talking about any dead brothers,' Murphy said. 'Bit of a surprise really. Usually these things hit pretty fast.'

'We did ask the preacher, Shalomar, to keep it to himself for now. Seems he's sticking to his word. That's unusual too,' Sid said.

'Sure is.' Chip looked up. 'Doesn't matter if they're jihadis or chess nerds, this generation take a photo of every fucking thing and post it online almost immediately. They make a salad, they take a photo of it. What's with that? It's a salad, for fuck's sake. Not a fuckin' Picasso.'

'What's with the hands?' Sid asked. 'Maybe that has something to do with Shalomar's unusual bout of shyness.'

'Not sure yet. Could be a sharia punishment.'

'Fun-loving crowd, aren't they?' Sid said.

'How long's it going to take for the CCTV stuff to get here?' Murphy asked. 'We've got cameras all over the outside of al-Ma-ana and we've surely got some on Auburn Road.'

'We should get it tomorrow.' Sid didn't really know if that was true or not. Sometimes they had to shake a few branches to get a priority on the camera footage. 'We'll definitely get their phones tomorrow too. One of them had two on him. You never know, they may have been sloppy.' They all knew that was unlikely. It'd been a long time since any of the jihadis had used the phone network to communicate anything serious. They knew the spooks were all over them and often they didn't even carry a phone, let alone two, knowing their movements and their meetings were always logged and tracked.

'Fuck this. Time for a drink.' Chip stood up. He'd obviously decided to mark the end of the day in his usual definitive way. 'Let's see if there's anywhere we can get a good martini in this town. On the other hand – no, let's not even try.'

The Sydney martini was a long-standing sore point for Chip. Sid described him as a real American drinker, which wasn't as rare as many Americans might like people to believe. Chip was a devotee of small New York bars. The sort of places where the drinks were strong and the service was professional and discreet, as long as you tipped well. But despite the Manhattanisation of some parts of Sydney in recent years, particularly the Surry Hills neighbourhood where both he and Sid lived, Chip hadn't been able to find anything that filled the gap and he complained about it incessantly. In fact, most of the new bars that had sprung up just annoyed him.

They were either wine bars populated by pretentious hipsters with tight pants and bad facial hygiene, or they were try-hard cocktail bars and faux 'speakeasys'. But, as he pointed out loudly whenever they ventured into them, even if they offered pulled pork sandwiches and sliders you still couldn't run a tab at the bar and the bar staff never remembered what you were drinking.

Chip also had a weakness for what he called 'girly bars'. Cheap strip joints where twenty dollars got you a close-up of a bare arse and fifty dollars would get you considerably more. The cheaper the better. There weren't any of those left in Surry Hills either as far as Sid could tell. Well, not the cheap ones anyway. Even in the old days, fifty dollars wouldn't have got much at 'A Touch of Class'. Boy bars were more the thing round here now and Chip definitely didn't bat for that team.

For all that, Sid was more than just tolerant of Chip's enthusiasms. He owed the guy a lot. Chip was the one who had dragged him out of the self-indulgent misery he was swimming in after Rosie. He came all the way from New York to Griffith. Griffith, for fuck's sake. That strange country town where everyone knew everyone but no one asked any questions. Chip found him in the front bar of the Royal Hotel drunk and sorry for himself. Offered him another chance. A secondment to the US. It saved him.

So when Chip came calling with problems of his own a few months ago Sid returned the favour. He got him an attachment to K block and found him a small place just off Crown Street on a short-term rental.

It wasn't exactly the Lower East Side but it was about as close as it got in Sydney and it was just a few blocks from the little Arthur Street terrace house that Sid had been living in – off and on now – for the best part of the last ten years. Arthur Street had been a new beginning for him and Rosie after the first Iraq tour.

A lot had changed since then, including the neighbourhood. Some of the streets had been closed off. A lot of the traffic had been diverted from Crown and Bourke streets, cafes and restaurants had sprung up and the local pubs that had been either bloodhouses or Indie music venues had become gastro pubs serving twice-cooked pork belly and confit duck to bankers, advertising types and media people.

But a bit of the old Surry Hills lived on. Sid often walked home through Central Station and up Devonshire Street so he could drop in to the Shakespeare. Here they still served Reschs draught in old-school schooner glasses and you could buy a steak, salad and chips for $12.50. Chip seemed to find it an easier fit too. No one even pretended they could make martinis at the Shakespeare. They had trivia competitions every Thursday night and if there was music being played it was most likely Cold Chisel or The Clash. The inhabitants from the housing commission flats across the road were always well represented among the punters and they didn't seem to know or even care if the two blokes sitting at the far side of the bar were coppers.

It was still early when Chip and Sid entered, but it was busy enough. A group of older women were playing cards at one of the few low tables. A smattering of crusty old punters sat at the high benches on the far wall checking the races on the TV against the *Daily Telegraph* form guide and a few main roads workers with their high-vis vests were nursing beers at the bar, drinking them slowly like men who had no one to go home to.

A few younger drinkers in suits and short skirts stood outside smoking and laughing. Sid and Chip put their beers down on the old wooden drinks ledge that ran along the wall near the side doors.

'So we're either dealing with a serial killer, an internal jihadi fight for turf or – what I think is more likely – someone who really knows what they're doing,' Chip said, breaking the first drink reverence.

'Why do you say that?' Sid looked around to see if anyone was showing any interest in their conversation at all. No one was.

'I'll need to have a closer look and get the ballistics evidence but just looking at those wounds I'd say the killer used small calibre rounds and probably fired from something light. Difficult, sophisticated weapons choice. Anyway, just sayin'.'

'And the hands?'

'Yeah. Don't know what the fuck that's about. Could be done to throw us off. Maybe he – or they – want us to think it's some sick sharia payback exercise. I just don't know. It's a new one for me, that's for sure.'

Sid had no doubt that if anyone was going to know about that stuff, Chip would be the man. He was one of the best counter terrorism investigators around – Sid had seen him in action when they'd worked together in Afghanistan; Sid was with the AFP and Chip was with the FBI, both attached to their respective military units, but they'd worked on a number of cases together and developed a friendship. Chip had moved on to 'The Program' – the terrorism surveillance unit set up within the US National Security Agency by George W Bush after September 11 – and had spent most of his career working on extremist groups. Not just Muslim extremists either. As he told it, most of the dangerous nutjobs in the US were whiter than the Partridge family.

They had a few more drinks but they were finally driven out by a swarm of young hipsters. The 'trivia night' crowd. Chip went off to find himself a feed. After the big Lebanese lunch, the last thing Sid felt like was food. He walked up Devonshire Street and across Crown Street then turned down Arthur Street past what had been a Portuguese delicatessen when he first moved here that had sold fantastic salami and dried cod. Now it was a wine bar. He walked on past the well-heeled revellers, hoping they wouldn't be keeping him awake tonight. Getting to sleep was going to be hard enough as it was.

His place – his and Rosie's place – was halfway down the hill. A little single-storey terrace house. 'The Tunnel' Rosie had called it. When they'd bought it, it was just three rooms inside with a lean-to bathroom tacked on to the rear. In the first year they did what everyone did – tore the back off and rebuilt it. Inside now was a sleek modern space – one bedroom, a bathroom and a large kitchen and living area that spilled out into the courtyard at the rear. Rosie had been determined to do nothing to disturb the Victorian façade so no one ever suspected anything had changed internally. The old cast-iron gate still creaked and groaned, and old worn sandstone steps led up to the small verandah, but tonight there was something out of place.

The woman sitting on the edge of the verandah was wearing a purple pants suit and a bright red scarf. The legs stretched out in front of her finished with a pair of fatally high heels. She was smoking. As Sid pushed open the gate, she flicked a wayward strand of an expensive haircut off her face and blew a stream of smoke up into the night air.

'Sid,' she said by way of greeting.

'AJ. What's up?' Sid tried to remain casual, but he knew AJ wouldn't turn up unannounced unless something really was up.

'You got anything to drink?' she asked, tossing her butt over the fence onto the street.

Sid led her into the house, opened a bottle of red and put out two glasses on the dining table. He slid open the glass doors at the back and a rush of warm jasmine-scented night air wafted through from the small courtyard garden.

'You look tired.' He poured AJ a generous slug of shiraz.

'Yeah. I am.' She took a big drink. AJ had been a relatively senior journalist for a while, then she was a private investigator for a time and then, somehow, she'd made the switch to ASIO. Maybe she'd been ASIO all along. Some thought of her as hard and Sid had to admit she looked a little older than she was. She wore her experience in the lines around her mouth, her eyes and the solid crease between her brow that could be mistaken for lines of cynicism. The wear and tear of anguish. But it wasn't. She was just smart.

She put her glass down. 'I've just spent the last four hours being grilled by Gray.'

'Really? Hasn't he got help for that?' It seemed unusual the head of ASIO would spend four hours questioning AJ. He was usually too busy holding press conferences or giving lengthy prime-time TV interviews warning of the increasing dangers of terrorism and the need for greater powers. Putting the fear on the record but also offering a reassuring guiding hand. Sid always thought it was too orchestrated. Part of softening up the public for tougher laws.

'There's another body,' AJ said. 'Or there was. Same thing – small calibre bullet to the head.'

'Was?'

'Yeah, was. The spooks haven't let that one sit around – don't want any attention. It was Mohamed Jilal. He was one of ours – ASIO. Deep cover.'

Sid grimaced.

'Shot at his mother's place up in Beecroft,' AJ continued. 'Hadn't been home for ages. Whoever did it knew what they were doing and what they were looking for. The spooks think whoever is doing this got the list off Jilal. Too much of a coincidence.'

'So this one went first?'

AJ nodded. 'Jilal copped it last week. Three days before the rest of the killings started.'

'Whoever's doing it isn't wasting any time then.'

'Left Jilal with both hands though.'

'That's nice,' Sid said. 'Just one shooter or more?'

'Just one. At least, only one shooting. And the spooks are pretty convinced it's someone with serious weapons exposure. Someone who really knows his shit.'

'That's what Chip said too. But he's only seen the photos.' He topped up AJ's glass.

'Thanks.' She took another drink before continuing. 'The spooks confirmed tonight that the same bullet and weapon were used on all four bodies. The west is swimming in Glocks from Marrickville to Cabramatta. The Lebs love 'em, the Vietnamese use them – all the gangs. But this guy's using an H&K MP5 variant. Lightweight, designed for use in close personal protection and hostage recovery.'

Sid lifted his glass. He stared into it and swirled it around. Even before AJ showed up it had been quite a day and then the beers with Chip, the wine. He was tired, but his hopes that it would end with a long comfortable, uninterrupted sleep were fading. Why would anyone go to the trouble of using a weapon like that? He took a sip of his wine, felt the warmth of it linger in his throat.

'Special forces?'

'Exactly.' AJ took a cigarette out of a packet and flicked open an old Zippo lighter. 'The only group using that stuff here is Tactical Assault Group – East, the 2 Commando counter terrorism unit. Even the New South Wales Tactical Operations Unit doesn't have access to those weapons. Not that someone else couldn't have got their hands on an MP5 from somewhere, but whoever's using this one knows how to do it properly.'

Sid had seen the special forces guys in the field in Afghanistan. How fast they could strip a gun down and put it back together. How intimately they knew their weapons and exactly what they could do. Sid wasn't an expert but he knew that having the right hardware and using it properly were two different things. This shooter clearly knew what he was doing. But why was he targeting the watchlist?

'So it's some commando with a grudge?'

AJ nodded.

'It's a theory anyway – the only one we've got.'

She stood up from the table and walked out through the back doors.

'I need a smoke,' she said.

5.

THE CLOCK READ 4.12 WHEN HARRISON JOLTED OUT OF HIS usual light sleep. How long had it been? Half an hour? His sleeping these days was fitful at best. An hour here, twenty minutes there. The nightmares and the flashbacks never stopped long enough and it'd been months since he'd slept on anything resembling a real bed. The Commodore had been home now for more than a year. It was comfortable enough. There was space in the back of the wagon to stretch out and he never had to worry what he might say or do to anyone else. He just had himself and his own idiosyncrasies to live with. That was the way he preferred it these days.

His was a 'classic' case of PTSD the shrinks had said. Post-traumatic stress disorder. Two long tours of Iraq backed up with four in Afghanistan. That'll do it to you. The IEDs; the attacks that came out of the blue like the one that killed Robbie, probably his closest mate; the night-time operation that ended with his patrol grenading the compound where an insurgent was firing from. When they went in, the insurgent was dead enough, but there were others in there with him. A teenage girl and four little kids. All dead. Afterwards that fucking big dust storm blew up out of nowhere and all Harrison could think was 'We've destroyed the only good in this dust-driven hell. We've upset the natural order of things and now the payback is coming.'

And there was worse to come after that. He should have stayed home but he couldn't settle, couldn't sit still. He took another deployment. One more tour, he thought. That's when the school went up. Not long after that he had his meeting with the Scorpion.

He'd told the shrinks everything, or nearly everything. He hadn't told them about how he grew up in a fucking shithole. He hadn't told them how his 'father' would beat him and come in to his room at night when he was just a little kid and put his hand down his pants. He didn't tell them how, when he reached sixteen, all he wanted to do was become a gangster so he could kill people, only he couldn't find a gang that would have him so he thought the army would be a better option. At least then he could kill people legitimately. He didn't tell them how that made him feel alive for the first time in his life. Or that he eventually worked through the just being angry stage and that he came to see the military as a calling. A path to positive redemption. A way to give back to society rather than to take. A way to serve. But that was then. Another world – another life. The army had abandoned him. He was no use to them or to anyone now – after Scorpion. What good was a broken soldier with one hand and a busted mind?

But now he had purpose again. Just a few hours earlier he'd driven into Belmore and parked on Leylands Parade. Lying flat in the back of the car, he had a good view of the small block of red brick flats. He parked the car so it was pointing west, having concluded that would be the direction his target would head once he pulled out of the driveway. It was the shortest route to the Croydon Street mosque.

It wouldn't be long now. Friday prayers were about to start.

This one called himself Jake even though his real name – his list name – was Jihad Rifi. Hard to knock around unnoticed with a name like that, he supposed. It had piqued his interest as he was going through the list – but generally, deciding who was next was a mixture of the random and the pragmatic. Of the 364 names, only 216 were listed as living in Sydney, the vast majority of them lived in and around the southwest – Lakemba, Belmore and beyond. It was just a matter of working through them. Some of the addresses were out of date but they were proving easy enough to track. Harrison didn't own a phone or a laptop but a Facebook search on a public computer was usually all it took to identify family, girlfriends, regular habits and the like. And Mum and Dad were usually in the White Pages. They always came home to Mum.

It was ten past five when Jake Rifi came swaggering down the concrete steps at the front of the block and headed over to a small white early nineties model Corolla. He was wearing fashionable white sneakers, tight black jeans and a hooded sweatshirt that mocked the already oppressive heat and humidity. Harrison noted the licence plate number and the bad ding in the rear of the car. He let it drive off and out of sight before he started up the Commodore and drove slowly towards Croydon Street. He knew he'd have about half an hour to get set once the dawn prayer got underway.

The little Corolla was easy enough to find. It was parked just a few blocks down from the mosque towards the quieter end of the street. The mosque itself was a small white weatherboard building with a flat roof and no distinguishing markings. To drive past it you'd have no indication that it was one of the most productive radicalisation factories in Sydney. Friday prayers here were a small affair.

Harrison parked his Commodore around the corner, well away from the mosque. He put the H&K in his backpack along with the various other bits and pieces he always packed for these jobs – a piece of heavy plastic packing tape, rope, a knife, the little tomahawk and the heavy granite pestle from one of those cheap Asian mortar and pestles used for crushing spices. Then he walked back to the Corolla. A faint dawn light was starting to break but there was still no one about. The street was quiet. The worshippers had all drifted inside. He used the packing tape to lift the lock on the little car's door and slid into the back seat to wait. The floor was covered in old Maccas' meals – half-eaten boxes of fries and burger wrappings. It didn't smell too good. Not for the first time he wondered how someone like this would get on in a place like Raqqa. No wi-fi. No McDonald's. Just rice and falafels to eat and a few beheadings and public hangings for entertainment. Did they know what they were getting into?

The prayers broke just after six. Harrison watched the faithful go through their departure routine – shaking hands, the three-cheek kiss. As Rifi and others started moving to their cars, Harrison wedged himself down as far as he could behind the front seats. The back seats of Corollas weren't made for six foot special forces soldiers, even ones who'd wasted away a bit from their prime fighting weight. He'd almost certainly be seen if Rifi looked in the back before he got into the car. Most people never look.

6.

Salt Pan Reserve was a largely forgotten bit of reclaimed wasteland up one of the fingers of the Georges River at the back of Roselands. There wasn't much to it. A football oval and some scrubby park dissected by the M5. Obviously no use to developers and no good for soliciting council kickbacks. They'd cleaned up a lot of the river in the last decade or so but this bit was still a windswept tidal sand belt that looked okay when the tide was in, but for at least a few hours a day revealed itself to be a stinking mess of shopping trolleys, car tyres and other skeletons from its long suburban and semi-industrial heritage.

The Bankstown station had received a call at about 7.30 am from a distressed elderly Chinese lady who had arrived with her tai chi group for their regular morning workout. They met every day, she said, but there was nothing peaceful or meditative about what they'd found this morning.

Once again, Sid noticed that the uniform boys had the scene well established by the time he and Haifa arrived. The uniforms had taped off a corner of the car park next to the oval. A small white Corolla was the main focus of the evidence-gathering activity. Two of the uniform boys were standing at the car park entrance turning the public away and checking police and emergency services workers through. Sid parked the Hyundai on Wiggs Road. The young constables watched them approach – or rather, Sid noted, they watched Haifa approach. Not that he could blame them.

Sid showed them his ID. Itchy and Scratchy were more interested in hers.

'Away you go,' one of the uniforms said, motioning them into the car park without taking his eyes off Haifa. She didn't seem to notice. She was focused on the job.

Cavan Maskey was there again. He had his notebook out jotting things down like an old-school copper then occasionally stuffing it in his back pocket to free himself up to take photos with his phone as well.

'Well, fuck me. Seems we can't have a quiet Middle Eastern murder anymore without the Feds and the spooks getting involved.' He was smiling at them, already sweaty and red-faced from the heat.

'Cav,' Sid tossed out a greeting. They shook hands.

'We wouldn't keep troubling you lot if you could do your job and keep the past century of Middle Eastern injustice, disenfranchisement and payback off our quiet suburban streets.'

Haifa didn't bite but she nodded an acknowledgement towards Maskey and walked straight over to the scene.

'Hello there, and very nice to see you too,' Maskey said as his eyes followed her path towards the car.

'Put it away, Cav,' Sid said under his breath. 'Just thinking about it could give you a heart attack in your condition.'

The body was slumped against the driver's side window and the front half of the car was a bloody mess. This one had been shot through the back of the head but not before he'd been subjected to some rough treatment. Once again, Haifa was getting in as close as she could.

'He's really been worked over,' she said. 'Looks like he's been tied down somehow and then had his face smashed with something heavy.'

Like the others, the man's right hand had been removed.

'It's not easy to do that,' Haifa said. 'He's not just killing them for the sake of killing, is he? He wants something from them. He could just shoot them but he doesn't. He works them over first. Then he shoots them. Then he takes the hand. Or does he? Does he take their hands first while they're alive?' She was talking to herself.

'We don't know yet,' Maskey said. 'But forensics are working on it. The way the blood spreads it seems he could be chopping them off while they're still alive. Gotta hand it to him, he seems to know what he's doing.'

Haifa laughed.

'Sorry, poor joke.' Maskey looked surprised that Haifa had a sense of humour.

'So this is number four,' Sid said, testing whether Maskey knew about Mohamed Jilal, the dead deep cover.

'Yeah, four of them. S'pose this one's on your list as well?'

'It would seem so.' Sid took another step towards the car, looked in at the bloody mess then turned back to face Maskey. 'Jihad "Jake" Rifi. You must have known about him. He was a bit of a celebrity around here I gather.'

'Yeah, the locals have had an eye on him for years. He's been a bad boy but, despite the cute name, he hadn't been into the black flag for long. He was into everything else, for sure. Speed, meth, whores, you name it. Started out small. He was nicked for putting a few shots through the front door of the Lakemba station when he was fifteen. His brother was one of the ringleaders down at Cronulla in '05. He drifted into gangs, into B4L – then seemed to make a quick and permanent progression to zealot. And they say Islam's a peaceful religion. Religion's got a lot to answer for, I reckon.'

'Yeah, well, you'd know all about that,' Sid said.

'True that. True. But we didn't want to take over the world, we just wanted to kick those Provo cunts out of Ireland.'

'And if that meant blowing up office workers and tourists in London then that was okay, was it?'

'I'm not defending it. That's why my family got the fuck out of there, for sure. But, like I say, this seems to be on a different scale. What do they call it – the politicians? An existential threat?'

'Yeah, whatever the fuck that means.'

Haifa had walked off towards the river and was talking to two officers in forensic suits who'd obviously been working their way through the long grass and the undergrowth.

'The threat to these guys would seem to be that they're on that watchlist,' Maskey said.

'It doesn't look like a coincidence, does it?' Sid replied. 'I just hope we can keep it quiet for a bit.'

'Yeah, good luck, that little cunt Jenson Burton from the *Daily Telegraph* has been ringing around. I reckon he's on to it.'

Sid knew keeping anything quiet for long in this city was all but impossible. And Jenson Burton was one of the more well-connected hacks around. Sid wouldn't have been surprised if Maskey himself had been trading information for a bit of a return. He and Burton went way back. Mind you, Burton went way back with a lot of the NSW boys. That was just the way it was here. A few years ago – back before ICAC at least – you couldn't get to the bar at pubs like the Cauliflower Hotel in Waterloo or the White Horse in Surry Hills without tripping over criminals, cops and journos all buying each other drinks. It wasn't so public these days but old habits died hard and old contacts had long memories.

Sid's phone buzzed in his pocket.

'Hey there, AJ. No more bodies, I hope?'

'No more yet,' she said. 'But the ballistics guys have confirmed it's the work of the same person and the same weapon. And that fat fucker Jenson Burton seems to be on to it too.'

'Funny you should say that. Maskey's just told me the same thing and used almost the same colourful description.'

'Yeah, wonder why. We need to keep him quiet – at least for as long as we can.'

'How do you propose to do that? He hasn't built his reputation on a record of sensitivity, has he?'

'No, but he does like being a player. Gray wants to see if we can do him a trade. Eyeball him and make him feel important. Offer him something bigger later if he holds off on this one. Gray wants to try to bring him into the tent and he wants you to hold his hand and take him down for a face to face at Russell tomorrow.'

It had been a while since Sid had been to Canberra. Unlike a lot of people, he actually liked the place but chaperoning that fat prick Burton around wasn't something he was looking forward to. Jenson Burton had a cockiness about him that translated all too often in print as petulant and bullying. Sid didn't like him. Never had. For all his confected concern for personal freedom and liberty, Burton had a reputation for prosecuting agendas in return for scoops. He aligned himself with factions. He did people favours, wrote up rumour and gossip, and backed up people's agendas with a few hundred words of thunderous opinion. He didn't like Brian Williams, that was well known, but he was close to others in the party – the anti-Williams crowd.

It was going to be a tough few days. No cocktails at the Hyatt or long lunches at Ottoman, just suffocating grey offices, half-dead bureaucrats and angry, frustrated security chiefs all of whom, Sid knew, felt exactly the same way about Jenson Burton as he did.

7.

Jenson Burton was already waiting at the security gate as the taxi pulled into the driveway of the Ben Chifley building. ASIO HQ. For the life of him, Sid couldn't understand why so many referred to Burton as 'little' before whatever pejorative of choice came next. The guy was short, sure, but it'd been a long time since he'd been 'little'. In fact, he was almost impossible to miss. He was wearing a suit two sizes and twenty kilos too small. He had his jacket off and sweat stains were already spreading in wide pools across his blue business shirt.

Sid paid the driver and walked over.

'Hi Jenson. Long time no see.'

They shared a sweaty handshake.

'Welcome to Canberra,' Burton said. 'Freezing cold in winter. Baking hot in summer. Don't know why anyone would live here.'

'Oh I don't know.' Sid looked up at the building in front of them. The newest addition to the collection of impressive modernist brutalism housing the nation's security. 'Spooks have to live somewhere. Might as well be here.'

'There's a lot of them, that's for sure. Can't send a text, make a phone call, or talk to a contact without someone knowing who you're with and what you're doing. A fucking danger to democracy, that's what it is.'

'Got to keep the community safe,' Sid said. A few years ago he might have shared Burton's concerns but the longer he was in counter terrorism the more convinced he was that the evil intent that was out there had to be tackled with the best tools available.

'There are worse things to lose than a little personal freedom. A little more surveillance isn't going to hurt anyone who hasn't got anything to hide.'

Burton gestured with his thumb towards the other side of the lake. 'The politicians are over there, but the real power is here.'

'Two different pillars, Jenson. There are still checks and balances. There's a real and a metaphorical lake separating the two.'

'Very philosophical for a cop, aren't you? I'm glad you still have such faith. With political leaders like Brian Williams – well, what could possibly go wrong?'

Once past the perimeter security, they were directed to the front entrance where they had to surrender all electronic devices. Burton was allowed to take his notepad and pen in with him but nothing else. Next they were put through biosecurity screening booths, just to make sure they weren't trying to sneak anything in. The tubular screening capsules whirled and whooshed for fifteen seconds or so then eased them out the other side. Drummond Gray himself was there to greet them.

Gray was almost as round and unfit as Jenson Burton, although taller and more well pressed. He was wearing his trademark three-piece suit and his best and most reassuring public bedside manner. He looked like someone's aristocratic uncle from the 1930s – three chins and a face that was deeply creased with jowls of concern. A haircut that was extremely short on the sides and longer at the top. The sort of cut that needed hair cream to stay in place. It was such an old-fashioned look that Sid thought he'd seen it starting to come back in the streets of Surry Hills.

Despite the picture of benign reassurance, Sid and everyone else who'd ever worked closely with Gray knew that underneath the fresh dry-cleaning was a tough, decisive and, at times, ruthless security chief. In security circles, Drummond Gray was a respected and celebrated Cold War warrior – Sukarno's Indonesia in the 1960s, Vietnam, China. Gray was an Asian specialist. He'd worked in the field and led operations that would have broken weaker men.

And now here he was, all smiles, hand outstretched, working the public relations with Jenson Burton.

'Welcome, Jenson, welcome. Nice to finally have you here in our new home. I know you were very critical about how long it was taking for us all to move in here but, as you no doubt appreciate, this is a very sophisticated building and we had to make sure it was all ticking over as it should before we shifted the bookcases and filing cabinets in.'

He turned and placed both hands on Sid's – a more intimate greeting. 'Sidney. Good to see you.' He held Sid's gaze as if to say 'stick with me here'.

'Follow me, gentlemen.'

Gray led them down a long corridor past three big glass display cases. One of them held the three recently completed volumes of the official history of ASIO – an uncharacteristic and for some uncomfortable attempt to at last appear partly accountable to the public. The books had generated some excitement in the media but really only confirmed a few long-held suspicions and raised a few more questions about the security agency's role in some of the more politically charged moments of the nation's history. There was still plenty of unofficial history that would never be told. The other two cases housed a collection of spyware and surveillance equipment from the archives. Books and transistor radios with cameras in them, recording devices hidden in briefcases. Quaint and crude as it all seemed now they would have been the cutting edge of technology in their day.

At the end of the corridor they turned right onto a walkway that looked down into a large open expanse filled with monitors and banks of technology lined up in front of a huge screen that covered the two-storey wall at the far end. Not a bookcase or filing cabinet to be seen, Sid noticed. Above the screen was a digital map of Australia and a row of clocks dividing up the time zones.

Burton was clearly impressed. He started scribbling into his notebook. Gray continued with the small talk.

'This is the heart of the building. A 24-hour multi-agency nerve centre. We call it SCIF – the Sensitive Compartmented Information Facility. If there's a crisis or an attack of any sort then all the security agencies – defence, defence intelligence, ASIS, the AFP and ASIO – will all convene here. There's a direct, secure line to the prime minister's situation room as well. We can run off the grid for up to three days. We have our own water supply, our own sewerage system and it's all fuelled by a 600,000-litre underground diesel tank. That's all already on the public record, by the way, so I'm not really giving away any secrets.'

A look of mild irritation and disappointment surfaced in Burton's flushing pink face.

Gray led them down another corridor and into a large boardroom with windows that looked out across the lake towards Parliament House and the Brindabella Mountains in the background. It was a view Sid knew well. In winter, the mountains were sometimes capped with snow. Even on this hot summer day, they framed and softened the harsh modernism of the institutions – the national gallery, the national library and the high court – that lined the foreshore on the other side.

No one would spend much time admiring the view today, he thought. The stretch of glittering lake and mountains was interrupted by the hulking presence of General Hurlstone Darwin. Known as 'Hurls' by his friends and enemies alike, the chief of the defence force was a formidable figure. Six foot five and 120 kilos of bench-pressed muscle. Hurls had a neck hidden in there somewhere but at first glance you couldn't tell. His hulking physique was topped off by a short diamond-sharp buzz cut and narrow bull terrier eyes.

'General Darwin,' Gray began the introductions as if it was a cocktail party they were all attending, 'Sidney Allen you know, of course – and this is Jenson Burton from the *Telegraph*.'

'Pleased to meet you, Mr Burton. Please sit down.'

The general gestured towards a black leather and chrome couch in the centre of the room. Burton sat on the couch. Darwin and Gray sat in a pair of armchairs opposite. The light from the big picture window behind them meant they were slightly silhouetted and Burton had to squint a little to see them properly. Another piece of careful orchestration, thought Sid. He took a seat on an office chair off to one side.

'It seems your sources have been telling you a bit more than we'd have liked,' the general said, barrelling past any further formalities.

'Let me start this conversation by stating that everything said here is off the record and if published will be immediately denied. It'll be your word against ours and I hasten to guess we'd win that one.' Burton shifted uncomfortably in his seat and placed his spirex notepad on his lap in full view.

'I would also like to put what you know into a bit of a broader perspective,' Hurley continued. 'When I heard that you had this story I was having afternoon tea with the parents of corporal David Little. You know who I'm talking about, don't you?'

'The special forces guy who was killed in Iraq last week.'

'Exactly. He was the first casualty of our latest deployment. Those soldiers are on an extremely dangerous mission as I'm sure you'd appreciate. Now we know we won't be able to keep these murders quiet for too long. We're not naïve about that. But right now we're at a delicate stage in the fight against these insurgents and we have soldiers in – how can I say this –'

The bull-necked general squinted across the table.

'They're working very closely with their Iraqi counterparts, let's just leave it at that. So what we don't want is a headline story about someone not only killing the jihadis on the ASIO watchlist but also taking off their right hands. A move certain to be seen by some Muslims as desecration of the body. You understand me?'

Darwin looked across to Gray.

'Drummond here tells me that you are also aware there is some suspicion that the killer might have benefited from some of our own training. We don't yet know who the killer is but we would like that kept between us for the moment. I know it's highly unusual but –' Now Darwin played his trump card, 'Mr Burton, you wouldn't want to have blood on your hands now, would you?'

Burton seemed genuinely shocked. 'Surely the public has a right to know about this and the possible impact on our operations?'

Sid knew Burton was trying to look confident but he seemed uneasy.

Darwin and Gray exchanged glances.

'Well, Jenson,' Gray took his cue. He spoke calmly, slowly and deliberately. 'As much as we admire your work, and believe me we do, you make a valuable contribution to the national debate, I think what General Darwin is trying to say is that while we don't have any problem with the story coming out eventually, we would prefer it if we could just buy a little more time and, in fact, help you make it a better and more informed story. For the benefit of the public of course, but also to prevent an already dangerous situation becoming more dangerous for our brave troops than it already is.'

'Look let me be straight with you.' Darwin leant in now, assuming the role of bad cop again. The veins on the side of his forehead were pulsing. 'You know how it is. Whatever horseshit you might spout about the public's right to know, the fact is that anything you write is propaganda for IS and likely to have blowback on our troops and inflame the situation we're facing. All we're asking is that you hold off on the detail for a while. The murders will get out, but we don't want it known that they are all on that list or that their bodies have been mutilated. We'll give you something in return and if – or when – we hear of anyone else with even a sniff of the story we'll make sure you run with it first. And we'll give you something else to make it worth your while.'

'Sounds like you want me to pull the story because it's an embarrassment for you, not because you're worried about the national interest,' Burton said, showing some unexpected spine.

'Not at all.' Gray's voice was soothing. 'Not at all. But let me just say this, there's a lot more to this story.'

'There is?' Burton raised a pudgy eyebrow.

'There always is,' Darwin growled.

'And what do I get out of this?'

'The knowledge that you're doing something for your country. And when the time comes, we'll make sure you understand just how much we value your cooperation.'

Darwin's patience was clearly running out. Like most in the military he didn't have much time for journalists.

Sid could see Burton's mind sifting through the information. The prospect of having some leverage at the upper levels of intelligence was clearly attractive – as unreal and unlikely as it was. Sid reckoned Burton's first instincts were right. Darwin and Gray didn't give anything away – ever. They were doing this to avoid any potential embarrassment. Something else was driving this intervention.

'Okay,' Burton said eventually. Greed and self-importance clearly got the better of his instincts. 'I'll hold off for now. I haven't even told my editor yet. I must say all this has taken me a little by surprise.' He threw up his arms, chuckling at the situation he now found himself in. Sid could imagine the hard-on it must be giving him, talking face to face with the two most powerful security figures in the country.

'Mr Allen here is in charge of the investigation – or at least our side of it,' Gray said. 'As soon as there are any developments we want in the public domain, he'll let you know.'

Jenson Burton's fat face beamed back at them.

The thought of having anything further to do with the mound of obsequious blubber sitting across from him sent Sid's stomach churning.

'Mr Gray will show you out,' Darwin said. 'Sidney, can I have a word?'

The general waited for the door to close.

'Rosie Marcello, you were close to her, weren't you?'

Sid flinched. He certainly hadn't been expecting this. There wasn't a day went by that he didn't think about Rosie. 'Yes, I was. Very close.' The conversation was unsettling. 'We didn't tell anyone but we were planning to get married. Why?'

He tried to remain matter of fact. It had been nearly six years now. They'd both been working at Tarin Kowt in Afghanistan as AFP investigators attached to Special Operations Task Group. He was supposed to be in the patrol that went out that day looking for 'Sabre'. They were following a lead that he may have been knocked off by one of the local Taliban commanders. One of their informers had told them there was a body. An exchange had been offered. Who knows what exactly – money, positions of influence, trucking routes. Matuilah Kahn, the local warlord who was apparently on their side, was doing the bidding for the ADF and with him anything was possible. It was a long way from Australia to Afghanistan but Sid returned there in his head way too often.

'I'm sorry,' Darwin said. 'It was a dangerous mission. It could have been anyone.'

'It should have been me.'

'You can't beat yourself up about war. "Shit happens" as someone once said.'

Shit happened that day all right, Sid thought. He was heading out with the patrol to help identify the body, to make sure they really had got Sabre, in the unlikely event that it came to that. But at the last minute he'd been hauled off to write a report into the 'Wandering Body' incident – a stupid stunt that had seen a group of special forces return from an operation with an Afghan elder who had been shot. They failed to report the shooting and then left him with the Dutch who ran the base hospital. The old man died a few hours later, but not before his son came to the front gate of the base looking for him. He just wanted to know what had happened to his father. The body was taken to the morgue but, because there was no identification, they refused to take it. In the end, the body was returned to the man's family in a taxi.

The sad thing was that the man's son was captured in a fierce firefight a year later. He'd become an insurgent fighter with a deep hatred of the Australians.

But on that day Sid chose to stay on base and Rosie was sent with the patrol. None of them ever came back.

'We know how hard it was for you,' Darwin said, jolting Sid back to the air-conditioned comfort and the Canberra view.

'Still is,' Sid said. He was trying to contain his emotions but he was failing. 'I don't think I'll ever get over it to be honest.'

'Indeed.' Darwin turned and walked towards the window. The big general started pacing back and forth. It was an imposing and almost intimidating move. Sid really wasn't sure where this was heading. What the fuck was the general expecting him to say?

'You remember Harrison?' Darwin asked. 'The 2 commando who survived?'

'Yep, I remember him. You don't forget people you spent time with at TK. He never came back to base though. He was medevaced out of there.'

'Sent to Germany for emergency surgery,' the general said. 'You know he lost his hand? His right hand? The towelheads were sending us a message.'

Sid looked up.

'You think . . . ?'

'No one's seen him for months. Not even his family. We know he hasn't been well. He has some serious psych issues. He's not using his bank accounts or his phone, we can't see him online anywhere. He's disappeared.'

'And you think he's the one out there knocking off the jihadis?'

'Makes sense.'

One of the two phones on the desk rang.

'Excuse me.' The general picked it up and barked, 'Darwin here.'

There was a long pause as whoever it was on the other end spoke.

'What the fuck have we been doing here then?' the general said eventually, clearly furious.

His face was turning bright red.

'What, everything? Not that . . . Just the list . . . Yep. Okay.'

Darwin put the phone down gently.

'Shit,' he said, quiet now. 'We'd better get that cunt Burton back in here. The prime minister's office has just leaked the story to *The Australian*.'

'What?' Sid almost barked out his obvious frustration.

'You heard me right. They've only gone and fuckin' given it away for free. Well, not all of it. They've left the uncomfortable bit about the fact that it's one of ours doing it out.'

'Why would they do that?' Sid said, but he knew the answer.

'I suspect Williams' political problems may have triumphed over any security concerns.' The general walked over to the big picture window and looked across to Parliament House. 'But, fuck, what would I know?'

Sid thought he could almost see the lake slowly draining away.

8.

'Isn't that your brother?'

'What?'

'There on the television.'

It was 9.30 pm. Sid and Haifa were still in K block trawling through the CCTV footage for anything that might give them something to string together. A thread of commonality in the murders – the same cars, a motorbike; anything. Murphy was in place as usual 'driftnetting' – sifting through the internet and every now and then calling Haifa over to translate some Arabic or decipher some jihadi chatter. Now he was looking at the site for the jihadi magazine *Inspire*, which had been one of IS's big drivers of recruitment, and the glossy IS periodical *Dabiq*, a slickly produced magazine that spun the idea of terrorism and holy war into a fantasy of honour and duty.

The wall of screens above Murphy's desk was alight. The 24-hour news channels, the free-to-air channels, a replay of an AFL semi-final game from last year on Foxtel, and the *Crossroads* program on the ABC.

'Yep. That's him,' Haifa said, looking up at the screens.

'Hey, Damo. Get your head out of that sick terror manual and turn up the telly,' Sid called across the room.

Murphy looked up from his laptop, picked up a remote and pointed it at the screen.

'In tonight's program,' Father Ryan Kelly was saying, 'we'll focus on the recent brutal murders of four young Muslim men in Sydney's western suburbs. It's understood all four were on ASIO's terror watchlist. Who is doing it? What does it say about what's happening in our Muslim communities, and are we as a nation doing enough to combat the threat and attraction of violent extremism?'

Ryan Kelly was as dour as ever. The program had run its day, Sid reckoned. It had been going now for what must be nearly thirty years. Hosted the whole time by a failed priest who'd come to journalism for his salvation. As Ryan often said, 'I tried celibacy but had been found wanting.' The nation had watched Ryan Kelly turn from a dark-haired Ken doll with a crucifix to a wise old silver fox who'd known every prime minister from Menzies.

Yet despite the internet and the fact attention spans were said to have decreased due to the time it took to read a tweet and order a cafe latte, *Crossroads*' audience defied all fashion. Sid wasn't one of them regularly.

'Tonight we're joined on the panel by the Minister for Immigration David Sullivan; Wissam Shalomar, a Muslim cleric from the al-Ma-ana centre in Lakemba in Sydney's western suburbs; and the prominent and much respected

Muslim community leader and spokesman, Dr Hakim Hourani. Gentlemen, welcome to you all.'

'Jesus,' Sid said. 'Shalomar must be fired up to come on the telly. He's obviously getting over his media phobia. This might even be fun. Turn it up louder, Damo.'

Sid noticed Haifa was looking a little uncomfortable. On the screen her brother looked cool and confident, dressed in a sharp, finely tailored suit and a neat collar and tie. Shalomar was on his left and wore a taqiyah over his bald head. His long beard spilled down across a blue business shirt that remained crumpled, even though it was stretched across his barrel chest. His dark suit coat looked as if it had been thrown on as an afterthought. The minister, David Sullivan, sat on the other side of Hourani. Sullivan was a bullish-looking man too, like a rugby forward gone to seed. He had a reputation as one of his party's toughest operators with a 'whatever it takes' political philosophy. He was togged out in the conventional manner – an expensive ill-fitting suit. He looked like his neck had been squeezed reluctantly into his shirt collar and his attempts to tame a shock of prematurely grey hair with product had failed. In appearance at least, he reminded Sid of the flamboyant British politician Boris Johnson but he had none of Johnson's likeable eccentricities.

Kelly addressed his first question to Hakim Hourani.

'Dr Hourani. What's happening in your community? Why are some young men turning to extremism and why do you think that's now playing out on our streets? Four young Muslim men dead in less than a week? What impact has that had on your community and what can anyone do to reassure them?' Kelly asked in his velvet broadcaster voice.

Hakim Hourani shuffled in his seat, put his hands on the panel desk in front of him and turned to address the camera and the audience. For such a relatively young man, he carried an air of considerable authority. Hourani was reassuring and articulate without being aloof.

'Well thank you, Ryan. The problem we have at the moment is very real. Out in western Sydney my community is being torn apart by this barbaric so-called Islamic State. They are targeting our youth with their propaganda and hijacking our peaceful religion as a tool for their political campaign. We need to understand that there is some disquiet in the community; there's some who feel left out of this wonderful multicultural society we've created here but we all have to accept that this is Australia. We have a responsibility to abide by the laws and to keep the population safe. We community leaders support any action that preserves the safety and security of Australia.'

'Of course, not everyone in the Muslim community feels that way do they, Wissam Shalomar?' Ryan turned to the cleric and the cameras cut away to Shalomar who was scowling angrily.

'With great respect to Dr Hourani,' he said showing no respect at all, 'the fact is the entire response shouldn't be what Muslims are doing or not doing about extremism. No one is discussing what Western governments are doing to the Muslim world. Radical groups don't come out of nowhere. They exist because of the unjust occupation of Islamic land and the violence meted out to our people. It's not Muslims who are flying the bombers that are dropping bombs on innocent civilians. What did the West do? What did your government do or say about the slaughter of a million innocent Iraqis?'

Shalomar was addressing his anger at the minister now, leaning across in front of Hourani, alternately stabbing at Sullivan with his finger then lifting it to the sky in preacher mode.

'Shit, this is good,' Murphy said. 'The fucking producers will be loving this.'

Haifa said nothing.

'So are you saying it's right to join the extremist groups? Are you really?' Sullivan said, answering the aggression with his own. He was always an aggressive defender of the government's position and loved nothing better than an on-air stoush with interviewers or interlocutors like Shalomar.

'C'mon. Why can't you condemn them like Dr Hourani?' he continued, baiting the preacher. 'What your community needs is more sensible, honourable leaders like him; people with spine and courage. Don't ask what the government is doing, ask what you can do for your community. How can you as Muslims protect and nurture your own community?'

Ryan Kelly was about to open his mouth to try and bring some order back to the debate but Shalomar didn't give him a chance.

'Oh yes,' the cleric said. He was red-faced and shouting now. 'The public will see through your dog whistling. That's just what you and Prime Minister Williams want, isn't it? You are famous for it. You marginalise us then divide us because you don't want to confront the truth. The truth is it's not Muslims who are occupying foreign lands and killing innocent civilians and shaking hands with tyrants –'

'But, sir, while there is some truth to all you've said, why not just condemn groups like Islamic State outright?' Ryan Kelly finally got a word in.

'I'm not here to play to your prejudice,' Shalomar said, ignoring him. He kept stabbing in Sullivan's direction. 'We know you just want to make out all Muslims are evil.'

By now the audience was beginning to grow restless. A few had started heckling from the floor. Occasional camera cutaways showed some people getting up from their seats and leaving, others were looking uncomfortable as unrest began to rise in the crowd.

'Please, Mr Shalomar. We're here to have a reasoned discussion if we can.' Kelly tried desperately to get the show back on track. But Sid knew Kelly would be loving this. This was Kelly's thing – robust, challenging, confronting television.

'No, you're not. I don't think that's what you want at all.' The cleric raised his voice even higher and rose up out of his seat. 'Let's not forget that a million people lost their lives based on a lie.' He was almost screaming now, leaning even more menacingly towards the minister. 'Let's not forget, Minister Sullivan, the whole charade around the weapons of mass destruction. This conversation is absurd. Why is this discussion about what Muslims are doing or not doing?'

He was pointing at Hourani now.

'What are *you* doing about it? That's what they are asking, Dr Hourani. It's *your* fault. It's *our* fault. Is it? No, I say. This is the absurdity of this so-called discussion.'

'Why don't you condemn it?' Sullivan fired back. 'Why don't you condemn the pictures of the little children holding up the severed heads, of the rapes and the sexual slavery?' Sullivan was shouting and pointing now too. Some people in the audience were threatening to push forward and join in. Sid watched as the floor managers and security did what they could to keep the audience back. People were shouting, pushing, screaming at each other and at the stage. Then Shalomar turned and spat at Sullivan, a great gleaming glob of phlegm hung off the lapel of the minister's fine Zegna jacket. Father Ryan tried to intervene but Shalomar had already stormed off the stage.

Throughout it all, Hakim Hourani had remained almost completely impassive. The cameras showed him simply looking straight ahead. His fine features set, revealing nothing.

'Jeez, your brother's unflappable, isn't he?' Murphy said, clearly impressed. 'What a show.'

Sid spun around looking for Haifa's reaction but her seat had been pushed under her desk – empty. Her bag was gone.

9.

Haifa joined the usual commuter crowd waiting on the train still sitting at Cronulla station. It was the first stop on the line so there was always a seat but she usually tried to get on a few minutes early so she could choose a spot where she'd feel comfortable. She liked being in the last seat of the carriage upstairs so there'd be no one behind her and she'd have a good view of her fellow passengers.

Every day she took the train, she marvelled at how the journey gradually revealed the ethnic layers of the city as it moved through the ghettos and enclaves that defined the different parts of the line.

On a week day, Cronulla was white bread and Vegemite. Old-school suburban Anglo Australia. As Aussie as a Meadow Lea margarine commercial. On the weekends, of course, it was different. Then the migrant families descended on the beach. The Chinese, the Lebs, the Somalis. They turned up with their picnic rugs and their portable barbecues to invade 'our beach' as the locals called it. But today, like most weekdays, Haifa was the exception. A few seats in front of her two men were talking at the top of their voices. The conversation moved fluently from the cricket to real estate – and in particular 'the fuckin' Chinese' who were apparently 'buying up everything round here'.

'They put up a block in Hurstville last week. Three thousand units . . . they all sold off the plan in twenty-four hours. The Chinese bought 'em all.'

'Yeah, why don't they just buy their own real estate?' the other one said. 'Haven't they got enough flats in China? Why do they have to buy ours?'

A copy of the day's *Telegraph* was wedged into the space between the seat and the window. Haifa pulled it out. 'Terror Tantrum' the bold front-page splash read above a photo of Shalomar and Sullivan shouting at each other on the TV the night before. The shot was taken from below – obviously the photographer had been in the crowd. Haifa's brother Hakim sat expressionless between the two raging protagonists.

The article focused on the growing divisions within the Muslim community itself. 'It was up to the community to deal with the radicals.' 'Why wasn't it doing more – stepping up and taking responsibility to stop the violence.' The prime minister Brian Williams commented that Islam was often described as a religion of peace but he wished more Muslim leaders would say that more often and mean it. 'Why weren't there more community leaders like Hakim Hourani?'

Hakim was quoted too.

'I am the first one to acknowledge that we have some extremist elements within our community,' he said. 'But at the same time, there are some racist elements in the broader Australian society and if we let them use something like this to further their hatred and their racist agenda then we will all be losers. The country – this beautiful country Australia – will be the loser.'

Haifa put the paper down. The train was rolling across the bridge over the Georges River. Boats bobbed up and down, tugging at their moorings. Further out a few big power boats were leaving extravagant wakes behind them as they surged east towards the more expensive waterfront real estate.

Once you roll out of 'the shire', as the locals called it, the demographics took a significant shift. Within a few minutes the train was pulling into Hurstville station. The platform was lined with school kids – almost all of them Asian. They scrambled on in a noisy crush. A bit further on into Rockdale, the Serbs and the Russians would get on, then by the time they'd picked up the hipsters and the pensioners around Sydenham, and the mix of artists, young bankers and managers who now called Erskineville and Newtown home, the transformation would be complete – from the 1950s to the twenty-first century in just fifty-five minutes.

The move to Cronulla had been Haifa's idea of a personal statement – her response to the riots that erupted there between the 'Aussies' and the 'Lebs'; riots whipped up by the hysteria of shock jocks and local anger at what was described as 'harassment' by young Lebanese men. According to some, the Leb boys had been making unwarranted advances towards white girls on the beach and had thrown things into the pools of the big houses that lined Gunnamatta Bay. All probably true, she reckoned. But one day it all boiled over. Text messages started circulating calling on 'every fucking Aussie in the shire to get down to North Cronulla to help support wog bashing day. Let's show them this is our beach and they're never welcome back.'

Five thousand mostly angry young men turned up for the fight. Many of them had Australian flags tied round their necks – 'the Cronulla cape' they called it. Some sported Southern Cross tattoos and slogans scrawled across their tanned chests: 'You flew here – we grew here'. The Lebanese boys responded to the taunts and the whole thing went down in infamy, forever known as 'the Cronulla Riots'. At the height of the fracas a seventeen-year-old Lebanese boy climbed the flagpole at the RSL in Brighton-Le-Sands, stole the flag and burnt it. He was convicted of malicious damage and even went on a 'walk of repentance' along the Kokoda Track in Papua New Guinea, apparently so he might better understand the connection between Australian military 'sacrifice' and the flag – especially a flag flown outside an RSL club. Jenson Burton from the *Telegraph* had written at the time that the boy had 'committed the ultimate insult' and had become 'public enemy number one'.

So Haifa had decided to live in Cronulla. Not to build bridges – she didn't tell anyone she was Lebanese. Most people probably thought she was Italian. It was her 'fuck you' statement to the racists and the haters, but it came with some pretty good benefits. No one knew her there. No one asked much. The beach was beautiful. She had a nice apartment. And it was culturally as far away from Lakemba, her past and her family as she could get.

•

At Central station she took the escalator up out of the subway and walked, against the flow of people streaming into the city, over to platform eighteen. Twenty-five minutes later she got off at Auburn station and hailed a cab to take her over to Carnarvon Street in Silverwater.

A group of boys had set up a slalom course of bins and ramps on the footpath on the corner of Carnarvon and Suttor streets. They were practising their moves with skateboards and trick bikes.

Haifa stopped the cab in front of number seventy-eight. She told the driver to wait – she didn't think she'd be long and she knew from past experience getting another cab to come back and get her here wouldn't be easy.

The Syaada family lived across the road from the Harvey Norman warehouse in an unassuming fibro cottage with faded and flaking blue paint – two rusting cars on blocks in the front yard and a lawn that needed attention from more than just a mower. Carnarvon Street was the last frontier before suburbia gave way to the huge Shell oil refinery – for a time it was the biggest refinery in the southern hemisphere. It operated all day and night. The petrol stench was overwhelming – particularly when a westerly wind was blowing like it was today. Haifa had heard people say that sometimes it was so bad it was hard to sleep. If there was a breeze from the north then the residents of Carnarvon Street also had to put up with the burn-off from the medical incinerator a few blocks away in Wiblin Street. Like most Federal coppers, Haifa knew that it wasn't just medical waste that went into the furnace either. The AFP and Customs regularly used the Wiblin facility to dispose of the take from big drug busts. The residents of Carnarvon Street didn't know it but, from time to time, they were also living under clouds of cocaine and meth.

The front steps of the Syaadas' house had been replaced years ago with a concrete ramp to accommodate the patriarch of the family, Khaled Syaada. Haifa remembered him and his wheelchair well. He'd been a fixture around here for many years – a cheery man who despite his disability got about a lot and seemed to enjoy his life. He was often up on Auburn Road holding court in the Turkish cafes and kebab shops.

Maha Syaada had been happy once too.

Haifa pressed the bell on the door.

'*As-salaam alaikum*,' Mrs Syaada said when she saw Haifa. Peace, mercy and the blessing of Allah be upon you.

'*Wa-alaikum salaam*,' Haifa returned the greeting. They shook hands and embraced.

'*Ta – fadaaliki*. Please come in.'

Mrs Syaada was a tiny woman – barely five feet tall. She was wearing a dark hijab and she looked exhausted. The last few months had been tough. She'd lost her husband and then a daughter.

She closed the door quickly.

'It's very bad today. I'm sorry. The smell. Worse on hot summer days like today.'

If anything the air seemed even thicker inside the house.

Maha Syaada was one of a network of Muslim women that Haifa and others had been working with. Concerned mothers mostly who'd agreed to be 'guardians' in the community. They didn't like to use the word 'informers', rather they hoped they were doing what they could to counter the radicalisation of their young and to prevent them being groomed for jihad. They were particularly useful in identifying the sweet talkers – the recruiters – often men in their twenties who took younger boys under their wing, brought them into the radical circles and introduced them to the temptations of jihad.

But it was girls now too. Groomed online with appeals to a higher calling and promises of marriage and adventure.

Haifa followed Maha into the kitchen. The radio was tuned to the Lakemba community radio station 'the voice of Islam'. They were talking about the war in Iraq and the latest battles. There seemed to have been so many. Maha turned it off.

'They're always on about that,' she said.

She'd already laid out coffee and some small squares of baklava on the table. She sat down but could barely look at her guest. Then she started to cry, softly. Small tears rolled down her cheeks.

'I'm sorry,' she said, still not looking at Haifa. 'But I have nothing now. I have nothing more to give. Not to you. Not to this country that was so good to me. Not to my family. I'm sorry.'

'I . . . You know I am sorry too. If we could have done anything . . . If we'd only known –' Haifa felt totally impotent in front of this mother's grief.

Maha's daughter, Lola, had worked at a childcare centre in Lakemba. A few months ago, she hadn't come home one day. For weeks, Maha had no idea what had happened to her – Lola's Facebook page was quiet – it was as if she'd jumped off the world. Then Lola finally sent a message that she was in Syria. She started a blog detailing her journey from the suburbs of western Sydney to Raqqa. It was full of hatred for the complacency of Western countries like Australia and what she called the 'corruption of democracy'. She condemned the 'dirty kafir' – the infidels and the non-believers – and swore allegiance to the fight for a caliphate.

Maha had watched her daughter transform with growing alarm in the months before Lola disappeared. It had started after her father died, when Lola had become withdrawn. She spent hour after hour in her room on the internet, reading jihadi websites and watching videos posted by the radical preacher Feiz Mohammad. Maha now knew Lola had also been talking to radicals who were already in Syria and Iraq on Skype and Viber. Lola changed from a girl who liked going to the beach and to nightclubs with her friends to one who stayed indoors and wore the hijab. She started reciting passages from the Qur'an and railing against the immorality of Australian society, even berating her mother for leaving the house and shopping alone.

'They knew,' Maha said now across the table. 'People knew. I'm sure. They just did nothing.'

Haifa's eyebrows raised, her antenna up.

'What do you mean people knew?'

'I went to see your brother, Hakim. I told him.'

Haifa was a little disappointed at the anticlimactic revelation. 'He is a very busy man,' she said.

She knew Hakim held community appointments on Wednesday afternoons at his home. There was always a queue of people who came to him with their grievances and complaints. Sometimes they were just lonely elderly folk but often they needed someone to translate bureaucratic documents, write letters on their behalf or point them to a trustworthy and understanding lawyer. Some had children in trouble with the police or the courts. But Hakim couldn't help everyone and he couldn't solve everything.

'I told Sheikh Shalomar at the mosque too, of course. I asked him to look out for her. To please do something.' Maha reached across the table, finally lifting her eyes to meet Haifa's. 'Nobody did. And now? Look where I am. I have no one left.'

'Have you heard anything from her? Anything at all?' Haifa asked.

'She has sent me only two messages. One about two weeks ago telling me she was getting married and asking for my blessing. My blessing? What could I do about it anyway? Then last week she sent this –'

Maha picked up her phone and scrolled through her Facebook posts. She pushed the phone across the table.

'They will bring doubt upon your values and upbringing but, my mother, you must stay strong,' it read. *'You must ignore them. Know that you have raised a lioness among*

a land of cowards. Know it in your heart. Forgive me, my mother, for leaving without warning – forgive me for I am never coming back.'

'I know she has been in touch with some of her friends as well. She's trying to get them to go to Syria too. People are worried. Very frightened. She paints the picture of sacrifice and honour that some of the young girls find attractive. What can we do?'

Haifa knew Lola had been active on Twitter. Murphy had given her the brief. He followed all the jihadis' Twitter feeds and Lola had quickly become one of the chief facilitators coordinating travel and security arrangements for other young women heading to Syria. She posted regular tips and advice for young girls looking to leave. In one she wrote:

'Sisters, your day will include cooking, cleaning and looking after children. That is the reality. We have been created to be mothers and wives as much as the Western society has warped your views with a hidden feminist mentality.'

'Who else is she talking to, Maha? Who are her friends?' Haifa pushed a notepad across the table.

Maha scribbled down a few names and addresses.

'Here, these are some I know of – or at least I think I know. The parents are very worried.'

'If you hear she's talking to anyone else, anytime, tell me. Okay? We can do something to stop others going. If you hear anything at the women's groups let me know about that too, okay?' Haifa squeezed the older woman's hands softly.

'She was a good girl. She wanted to be a doctor.'

The two women embraced. There was nothing Haifa could say that would ease the pain. She got back in the cab, and noted the fare had run up to sixty-three dollars.

•

Soon after the taxi driver pulled away one of the skateboard boys took out his phone. He pressed one of the apps on the screen. Instantly the same app came to life on another phone in another place. The message had been sent.

10.

'Here's what we know.'

AJ was carving up a whiteboard into three columns with a black pen. At the top of the board she'd written 'The List'.

'We know there are 364 mostly young men on the watch-list. Of those, 216 live in Sydney. Well, that was a week ago – now there're only 212 in Sydney.'

She scribbled the 212 figure in the left-hand column and wrote the names of the four dead underneath.

'Is there any other connection between these four? Anyone?' She looked around the room.

It had just gone twelve o'clock. Still early by K block standards. Murphy looked like he'd just got out of bed and Shandy Wilson looked like she shouldn't have. Shandy was often a bit rough around the edges but today she had big dark rings under her eyes and her dreadlocks were even more unkempt than usual. The look was set off by a crumpled and worn-through Western suburbs football jersey from the days when Tommy Raudonikis was king of the paddock.

Sid wasn't at his best either. He had been at his desk since eight that morning after a late one the night before. He noticed Haifa looked pretty good, as usual, turned out in a skirt and a designer jacket. Madelaine Alston, dressed in one of her many lilac-coloured outfits, was flicking through a notebook looking for something. She always looked like a suburban librarian, but she was a tough former legal investigator with great contacts and an ability to see things that those who'd spent a life in police investigations might miss.

Chip was missing – but then midday was never going to work for him and AJ had finally given up waiting.

'Do they go to the same mosque? Do they eat at the same kebab shop? Do they go to the same knock shops? Which knock shops do they go to?' AJ asked rhetorically, her impatience beginning to show.

'Shandy? Anything?'

'The community's clammed up. After all the media attention, no one wants to talk. Not that they were saying anything much about it before then.' Shandy wasn't Muslim but she had an uncanny ability to reach out to the Muslim communities and she worked hard to build trust. She scoured the community websites, worked contacts and kept her ear to the ground. If she didn't have anything then there was nothing there to be had. 'People hadn't even really connected the dots,' she continued, 'until the papers started talking about the list. And now – well, there's plenty of shit on the internet and lots of conspiracy theories but none that stack up. As usual, the people who talk about it know nothing and the people who know aren't talking.'

'Damo?'

'There's a bit of blowback on some of the websites and on Twitter, a bit of chat about targeting Muslims – the usual stuff – but there's no martyr declarations or threats of retaliation. And no connections mentioned. There's no talk about it yet from the Middle East either. All quiet. Someone's keeping a good lid on it for sure.'

'And the phones?' AJ asked.

'There were only two. We're going through the data now. Haven't found anything yet. We've gone through the CCTV footage. Nothing. The camera on Auburn Road didn't have a fix on the barber shop and there's nothing unusual on the Lakemba job either. They weren't big fish in the scheme of things but we're going back through the data – who they met in the last few days, when they met, where they went. Maybe that'll lead us somewhere but the big guys don't take their phones anywhere anymore so even if they hooked up with some of them we wouldn't necessarily know. We did have the Stingray up though so we're having a sift through all that. All it takes is one mistake.'

'Stingray' was what they called the International Mobile Subscriber Identity catcher – a controversial cellular phone surveillance device that had been in widespread use in the United States for some time but had only recently been adopted by Australian agencies. The device effectively overrode a wireless carrier cell tower and forced all the phones and any other cellular devices within its radius to connect to it. It still functioned as a normal cell tower – calls came and went – but the data and the calls were captured. Stingray was particularly good for tracking who was active in a given zone at any point in time. Thousands of phones could be monitored at the same time. Individuals of interest could then be tracked and calls could be monitored.

For all the freedom it gave everyone the mobile phone had become the greatest boon to surveillance ever. Even if a phone was never used to communicate with it could easily be infected with malware and the microphone and camera could be turned on at will. If you were in any way a person of interest and you had your phone with you then you were potentially leaving a transcript of every conversation you had, and even video evidence. The big dicks in organised crime and terrorist groups were smart enough to know that and to play a careful game.

'Right.' AJ sighed. 'What about Shalomar and some of the others not on the list? I assume we've been combing through them too?'

Silence.

'Sid? Haifa?'

Chip Walker ambled in, took a seat at his desk and began the process of turning on his computer.

'What the fuck? Welcome to the coalface, Chip,' AJ said. Chip grunted.

Sid could feel AJ's exasperation but like everyone else he had nothing more to offer. Haifa explained she'd been out to Auburn. Maybe the mothers' network would turn up something in the next day or two.

AJ turned back to the whiteboard. At the top of the second column she'd put two photographs of the same man. One in military uniform, the other a head and shoulders close-up. Underneath it she'd scrawled his name – Mick Harrison.

Madelaine spoke up. She'd found what she'd been looking for in her notes.

'We know that he takes the cards from the wallets of the dead kids and he uses them immediately after – Paywave point of sale. Food, bread, water, even booze,' she said, ticking them off. 'We've got itemised lists of everything he's bought. Petrol too, but only in plastic twenty-five-litre containers. No car to be seen anywhere in any of the footage. And he's careful. He only ever buys stuff in the immediate neighbourhood. Never uses the cards again.'

'So where is he?' AJ asked. 'We need to bring this guy in. In fact, I don't really care why he's doing it we just need it to stop. Because these guys . . .' and here she scribbled in the third column 'Prime Minister Williams, CDF Hurlstone Darwin, Drummond Gray'. She put the pen down. 'These guys are really getting the shits and we're here specifically to get results for *them*.'

'Ahh. You might want to have a look at this.' Chip hadn't looked too good when he'd arrived but now what colour there had been in his face had completely drained away. 'Mrs Syaada. She's one of yours, right, Haifa?'

11.

Mehmet Celik arrived every morning at 3.30 am. He took out his keys and unlocked the two padlocks on the bottom of the roller door. He slid the door up then unlocked the metal grille that concertinaed across the entrance to Auburn Mall. As always, he was careful to pull the roller door down behind him and to lock the grille again. It was still dark at 3.30, no matter what time of year, and Auburn wasn't as safe as it once was.

This little pocket of Sydney was his first stop as a newly approved migrant out of Villawood immigration centre nearly forty years ago. He'd opened a bakery the next week. In Ankara, he had been a tailor and had inherited his father's shop, but when he arrived in Australia he noticed people were a lot more informal. Not too many suits. And, anyway, there was already a tailor in Auburn, so he opened a bakery and he'd been churning out bread, pide and pastries ever since. He did a nice line in Turkish delight and other sweets too. When the Lebanese came, he started making baklava as well.

Auburn had been good to him. Australia had been very good to him. He had two grown boys and a happy wife.

It was a visit from Turkey's foreign minister in 1968 that changed the course of Mehmet's life. The minister had heard Mehmet was going to follow his brother and move to Germany.

He said he wanted three suits made before his favourite tailor 'followed almost everyone else and left the country'.

'Please, Mehmet, don't leave. We need good people like you to stay.' But he knew Mehmet's mind had already been made up. Life was hard in Turkey then, even for successful tailors.

'If you must leave, don't go to Germany. Take my advice. Go to Australia. That is a country with open arms. A country of vast space and opportunity. They want good people like you. They will treat you well. Seriously. Beaches like you have never seen. Everyone has a motor car. Everyone lives in a big house, swimming pools, sunshine. Not like Europe.'

And so it had proved to be. It was a decision Mehmet had never regretted. His life had settled into a comfortable routine. He had many friends. Loyal customers.

Today was just like any other. He'd turn the ovens on, begin cutting yesterday's rise into loaves, lay out the meat, cheese and other fillings for the pide, and load up the bread-mixing machines to begin the cycle again. He would flour the benches and clap his hands together. The flour would rise and fall in a familiar and promising cloud. His day would begin. That was all he was thinking as he walked towards the end of the mall, past all the other small businesses towards the roller door across his little shop. But this morning something felt different. Was it a different smell? Or perhaps just a different atmosphere. Both. Something wasn't right, and the unease seemed to be being carried on a slight breeze wafting through the back of the mall – down by the alleyway leading to the toilets. Had someone left the back door open? Unlikely. It had never happened before. It was dark at the back of the mall, but – yes – he could see the door leading to the car park was open. He looked around. Was someone here? Had there been a break-in? There was no sign anyone had tried to prise open any of the roller doors to any of the shops. If they had broken into the mall, they had come no further. He stopped –

'Anyone there?' he said quietly. Too quiet.

'Anyone there?' he said again. Louder this time.

No reply. He walked on further, stepped down into the gloomy concrete corridor towards the toilets. The floor was wet. He nearly slipped. He could feel the damp ooze through his sandals and socks. His eyes weren't what they once were, but perhaps there'd been a leak? A broken toilet or washbasin. But the liquid underfoot felt thick and sticky. He reached across to the wall and began to feel for the light switch. He fumbled – found it. The strange blue-coloured fluoros that had only been installed a few months ago began to flicker, then they held.

He turned to look into the first cubicle. Nothing. The liquid, black-looking and syrupy, was coming from under the door of the second cubicle. The one closest to the exit.

'Anyone there?' he said.

No answer. He tentatively pushed the door. It wasn't locked. He swung it open – his knees buckled underneath him, a pain ripped across his chest.

12.

On any other Friday afternoon the bottom half of Auburn Road would be thick with the sweet charcoal smoke of cooking kebabs, all the tables would be full at the cafes, children would be chasing each other through the crowds, and groups of men and women would be clustered here and there passing on the news of the week. Today the footpath tables were empty and the traffic had almost come to a standstill in the block after Queen Street.

Frustrated drivers were hitting their horns.

As Sid finally steered the Hyundai past the Queen Street corner they could see why. A tall, thin, bearded man was standing in the path of the traffic. He was in the middle of the road talking on his mobile, totally ignoring the chaos he was creating. Cars were slowly manoeuvring around him but no one stopped to say anything. No one got out of their cars to suggest he move on.

'What's he doing?' Sid put the handbrake on and went for the door.

'Don't,' Haifa said. 'That's exactly what he wants you to do.'

'Who does he think he is? He can't just stand there like that.'

'Yes he can. That's Bilal Al Hamzi. You know? The *Al Hamzis*,' she said. 'He can do whatever he wants around here. And he's doing this to make a point. Just ignore him. Seriously. It's not worth it.'

Al Hamzi was standing in the road just fifty metres or so before the Auburn Arcade. Police tape had sealed off the entrance to the old-fashioned mall and a crowd of mostly older people had begun to gather.

Sid manoeuvred past Al Hamzi and resisted the urge to wind down the window and give him a free character assessment. He pulled the car into an empty driveway.

Outside it was bedlam. The crowd were all yelling something he couldn't understand and it wasn't clear who they were yelling at. Car horns were still blaring in the background.

'Jesus. They're pretty enthusiastic, aren't they?'

'They're angry,' Haifa said. 'They want to know who's killing their children. Just wait for the response when they find out this body is someone their own age.'

They showed their ID to the constable manning the entrance to the mall and walked towards the detectives and the uniforms gathered at the far end. A few of the shopkeepers were there too, giving statements. Cavan Maskey wasn't on the ground this time but Sid recognised the detective in charge, a bloke called Clarrie Stewart, an old-fashioned copper who went all the way back before ICAC, almost certainly bent, but a survivor none the less.

'They told me you were coming.' Stewart's welcome was hardly warm. 'That fella over there – he's the owner of the little bakery in the corner. He's the one who found her.'

The old baker was slumped in a chair, looking distressed. A young female police officer sitting next to him was taking notes as he spoke.

'Can we have a look?' Haifa asked.

'Sure. It's not pretty. She's in the ladies – down there.' Stewart pointed to an alleyway off to the side at the rear of the mall.

They walked into a damp concrete passage. More tape marked out a square of ground outside the toilet door and two forensics had begun sectioning off the area. The body was still lying across the toilet basin. At first, in the gloom, it was hard to see what had happened. The cubicles had been fitted with blue fluorescent lights in an attempt to stop addicts using them to shoot up in. The blue lights made it almost impossible to find a vein but they also made it harder initially to see the mess that had been made of Maha Syaada. Someone had tried to take off her head.

'Fuck. Maha.' Haifa almost fell into Sid. He felt her weight press against his shoulder and reached out to steady her.

'It was only a few hours ago. I –' she stumbled.

Then the anger surfaced. She turned on Stewart.

'So no one saw anything? Nothing? Not a fucking thing?' Her voice rose in pitch and volume. 'No wonder they're screaming out there.' She pointed back out to the street. 'I'm going to start fucking screaming too. Who the fuck did this? How can we let this happen? An old woman. If we can't protect them then they'll all turn to the fucking jihad. And why the fuck not?'

'Hey, don't get angry with me, lady,' Stewart growled back. 'We're just here doing our job. Why don't you do yours? Aren't you supposed to be on the front line? To me this looks just like one of those sick jihadi videos. Someone's trying to send these people a message.'

'Yeah, well, whatever the message is they've got it and we don't seem to be able to help.' Haifa turned to address the body. 'I'll find these people, Maha. I'll find them if it's the last thing I do.'

She said something in Arabic as well, almost under her breath. Sid couldn't catch it but assumed it was along the same lines. He only got the last bit.

'*Inshallah.*'

Clarrie Stewart heard it too.

'Yeah. Peace be with you too, sister.' The old detective spat on the floor. 'But maybe you should be more careful about how you do business. They all know she was talking. The old fella over there – the baker – that was the first thing he said.'

'What about the cameras? Anything?' Sid said, searching for some way to calm things down.

'Nothing. There's one out the front but nothing out here.' They were all still standing in the concrete corridor next to the toilets. 'This leads out to an alley at the rear of the building,' Stewart said pointing to a door at the end of the passageway. 'There's a small car park out there. The body was brought in through the back.'

Haifa pushed her way past, heaving in gulps of fresh air but she couldn't seem to get enough. Sid could see she was beginning to tremble and then she heaved the contents of her stomach into the dirt.

Stewart spat again.

'Get her out of here, Allen. For Christ's sake.'

•

They didn't talk on the drive to Cronulla. Haifa just stared out the window – sullen. Sid was happy enough not to go there just yet.

She finally spoke up as they got to the end of the Kingsway and it became clear he'd need directions. Sid hadn't been to Cronulla in years and he had no idea where Haifa lived.

'Turn right,' she said. 'Then left into Ozone Street.'

'Ozone Street? Cute.'

'Yeah, go figure. A certain lack of imagination on council's part.'

He turned in. A row of smart modern-looking apartment blocks with Italian-inspired surfside names like 'Bella Vista' and 'Il mare'.

'Over there, number twenty-two.' Haifa pointed towards the end of the street.

'Tiana? What sort of name is that for a beach pad?' Sid was still trying to lighten the mood. He pulled into the kerb.

'You can park here. Want to come for a swim?' she asked.

He laughed at the unexpected invitation.

'Umm. With what? I've got nothing to swim in.'

'You can watch then.' That was unexpected too. She got out of the car and waited for him to follow.

The apartment was on the fourth floor and the view was stunning – right up against the water. Sid sat on the balcony and watched Haifa stroke up and down the ocean pool that had been cut into the rocks just below the apartment block. The swell was low and the water in the pool was flat and glassy. Despite the warm evening, Haifa was the only one swimming. She swam well. An effortless stroke. Not fast but efficient.

By the time she finished the light was starting to fade. The sky had turned a deep purple and the ocean a soft grey. Haifa changed into a bathrobe and came out onto the balcony with a bottle of scotch, two glasses and a small box with an intricate mother-of-pearl inlay on the lid. She poured the scotch over the ice in the glasses.

'Open it,' she said. 'Let's get wasted.'

Inside the box there was a handful of leaf and head, cigarette papers and a lighter. Good quality, obviously. It had been a long time since Sid had seen weed like that and even longer since he'd smoked any himself.

'Really?' he said, unsure.

'Yep. Really. It's a cultural thing.' Haifa laughed.

'What? Lebanese gold? Is getting stoned part of the Lebanese culture now?'

'No. The Brothers for Life culture. I blame my brothers.'

Sid rolled up a joint. Even he had to admit it didn't look too bad for someone so out of practice.

The scotch he was more familiar with. They smoked and drank and sat there silently watching the light fade. It was an easy silence. Like they'd known each other for years. The dope and the whiskey began to take the edge off the day. So much so that Sid felt he'd be happy sitting there like that for hours, watching the light fade and the moon come out. Silent. Still, he was the first to break.

'What about your other brother – Hakim? You don't talk about him much.'

'We don't really get on. I see him every now and then but he's working on becoming a pillar of Muslim society. I'm not interested and he knows it. He's – how should I say it? – he's critical.'

'Critical?'

'Yeah. This –' She gestured around the apartment. 'My life. He doesn't get it. He's not prepared to get it.'

'So why do you live here?' Sid asked. He felt the conversation was getting into new territory. This was more personal than they'd ever been. He sensed Haifa was weighing it up. How much to tell. How close did she want him to get?

She didn't answer immediately. When she eventually did she spoke slowly and deliberately.

'I need space,' she said. 'I need to be away from my family. From Hakim, from my cousins, my aunties and uncles. I need to be away from the suffocating expectations. The constant questions. "Why are you working in intelligence?" "Why don't you get married?" "What are you going to do with your life?" It's easier here to ignore it – and to forget sometimes. It's a dark place, all that.'

'We all have our dark places,' Sid said.

The dope was really kicking in now. He was feeling numb.

Haifa lit some candles and put on some music. A haunting Middle Eastern melody that seemed to Sid to come from the same strange well of grief as all those dark places. A sound steeped in tradition, ritual and expectation. All that stuff Haifa said she was running away from. A lilting female singer was underpinned by a driving acoustic guitar riff and an insistent, almost jazz-like, acoustic bass line.

'It's Tara Tiba. It's beautiful, isn't it?'

Sid nodded. 'Another Lebanese cultural experience?'

'Hah, no – Iranian.' Haifa smiled.

She reached out for his hand and led him through the dark apartment. The dope was much stronger than anything he remembered having had in the past. They lay on the bed. Haifa took off her robe and curled into his body. Spooning against him. She was smooth and golden. She placed his hand across her flat hard stomach and lay the other on her breast.

This is complicated, Sid thought. Complicated but good. It had been a long time.

13.

The magazine had been delivered as promised. Hakim found it pushed under the front door. He pulled off the plastic wrapping.

He had resisted their efforts to dress him more fashionably for the cover photo. They had wanted to photograph him in a tight-fitting blue suit, a coloured shirt and a more 'modern' tie but he was glad he had followed his instinct. It was a good photo. He looked strong and serious.

A thank you letter was attached. Pro forma. Nothing personal – an inked-in signature from the editor at the end. He put that to one side, opened the magazine and turned to the article on page thirty-seven.

Dr Hakim Hourani has an outward calm that belies his perpetual motion. His is the most important face of modern Islam in Australia today. He is trusted by politicians, business leaders, ordinary workers and grandmothers. He is a world-renowned scholar, a respected community leader and a confidant to both the powerful and the weak. And as GQ *found, a day with Hakim Hourani will cover all that terrain and more.*

This is the man who Brian Williams has hand-picked to be his link to the community and he's the man the Muslim community in western Sydney, and increasingly around the nation, has picked to be their advocate in a turbulent time.

It's 3 pm and Dr Hourani is in the thick of his regular Wednesday afternoon community consultations. He's been up and running now since 6 am – a telephone hook-up with the prime minister and his chief of staff, a few hours spent checking in with his team at the Lucas Heights reactor where he is one of the leading researchers in nuclear medicine, a speaking engagement at a lunch for the local Lakemba chamber of commerce, and now he's helping an elderly man translate a legal paper. While this reporter is certainly beginning to fade, the elegant forty-one year old is showing no signs of tiring. He's wearing a fine tailored suit and a conservative blue tie. He greets everyone who comes to his office the same way – a traditional Arabic greeting, 'As-salaam alaikum.' He is, he says, 'a traditional type of guy'.

For some, though, he's not traditional enough – or perhaps he's just not radical enough. There is a difference, as we found. It's just a few days since the now infamous Crossroads *fracas on ABC television that disintegrated into an uncontrollable melee and saw the cleric Sheikh Wissam Shalomar spit on the Minister for Immigration David Sullivan. Throughout it all, Hakim Hourani remained the calm voice of reason.*

> 'It's my duty to minimise the backlash caused by this extremism. It's my duty, it's your duty, it's the duty of politicians, police, everyone in the community to do this,' he says with that now familiar steely determination, 'but we are not a homogeneous community. We have different views, we have different opinions and we are all entitled to our views. Hizbuht Tahrir are entitled to their views too,' he says, citing the radical extremist group that the prime minister has decided to ban – against Hourani's advice. 'We are all Australian citizens. We all have the right to speak our mind. It is my job to educate and influence as much as possible to show that Muslims remain a trusted and valued part of this society – but, yes, this is a difficult time for us.'
>
> GQ *conducts this interview in between Dr Hourani's seemingly never-ending meetings. The doctor is treated like the local member by his 'constituents' although he has so far resisted all attempts to formally draft him into politics.*
>
> 'I don't rule it out in the future,' he says, 'but I think at the moment it's important that I am not identified with one side of politics or the other – I am not a creature of the left or the right. I am a creature of justice.'
>
> *This is a man with important work to do. He is committed not just to his community but to science and medicine.*

And that was just the first page of a four-page spread. Hakim was pleased with the result. He had been a little nervous about it. You just never knew what would appear and he hated not having control. He had had to overcome his long-held suspicion of journalists but he had to admit the result wasn't too bad.

When the prime minister's office first suggested he subject himself to an entire day with a reporter for the 'feature' article, he had taken some convincing but he could see now that it had, indeed, been the right thing to do. Brian Williams had rung him personally to urge him to do it and it was amazing how many doors had opened for the reporter. They had even agreed to giving the magazine access to at least part of the Lucas Heights workplace.

The reporter himself was a nice enough young man – perhaps a little impressionable – but that was no bad thing. Obviously he wasn't considered a security risk in any way, although Hakim had to admit the security regime at Lucas Heights, Australia's only nuclear reactor, had become increasingly lax.

To Hakim, it simply confirmed his view that, on this issue, the government was more interested in posturing than reality. Even as they talked tough and demanded more laws and powers, they had been consistently shaving money and personnel from the security area of Lucas Heights over recent years.

Many older scientists had also been forced into early retirement. Science was not the priority it once was. Hakim knew if something big happened – if there was a crisis of any sort – there would be few people who would know how to deal with it. Even unusual weather incidents were causing problems. What if someone really wanted to cause trouble? Lucas Heights was not a big facility, it was a research reactor so it ran at much lower temperatures than a power reactor and used considerably less radioactive material. It also ran on uranium that was purposefully enriched to just below the twenty percent required to make a bomb of any kind. Not many people knew that though and the reactor was a target because of what it was, not what it couldn't do. Nuclear frightened the public.

He said nothing of this to the reporter of course. Angus was his name, Angus Graves. A young man from good Anglo stock, in his late twenties Hakim would have guessed. Angus had wanted personal details, and asked about motivation with annoying questions like 'What really drives you?' He asked, of course, about Islam and terror and taking a leadership role in the community. It was, thought Hakim when it was over, both predictable and almost insensitive – rude. But if that was what it took to build trust with the public, well that was what it took.

There were so many assumptions made by those who wrote and talked about Muslims in this country, he thought as he reread the piece. Australians want a story. They want to know where you come from, why you're here and, above all, they want to hear that this is the best country on earth. Hakim was more than happy to give them a story.

Hakim Hourani has made the most of whatever life has thrown at him. When he says he has always been a 'rich man', what he means is he has always had an inner wealth to draw on. 'I don't need money, I need strength, and I have had plenty of that. In that way I am a rich man.'

If he has material wealth then – apart from his well-tailored wardrobe – he doesn't show it. He drives a fifteen-year-old Toyota Camry, and his office is in the front room of his house in suburban western Sydney. But it is true he has a rich life. In the last few years he has achieved national prominence and he now sits at the table with some of the country's most powerful people. But out here, in Sydney's Muslim heartland, he is unremarkable and that, he says, is the way he likes it.

His story is a familiar one. The family's early years in a new country were difficult. His father worked as a factory labourer back when the industrial heartland of south-western Sydney still made things. By his second week in Australia, he was hired as a boilermaker with a company called International Construction Pty Ltd.

'They made steel girders mostly for bridges and he worked alongside a United Nations of migrants – Ukrainians, Turks, Greeks.'

Hourani says his father worked there until the early 1990s when the company started its long slow decline.

By that stage Hourani senior was well into his late fifties. There were no more jobs.

'It was hard for him. He was a hard-working man. Very disciplined; a quiet man. I learnt everything from my father. He put his family first at all times and he never let his disappointments or hardships rule his life. He remained eternally grateful to this country until the day he died. This is the country that saved him and his family.'

But there have been many hardships and disappointments along the way. Hourani's brothers, for instance, are a well-known part of his story. They 'drifted' to the wrong side of the immigrant experience, became two of the most feared local crime leaders and were convicted almost ten years ago for murder and trafficking of both drugs and people. They're now locked deep inside the maximum security wing of Goulburn jail – home to the nation's most dangerous criminals. Hakim Hourani's eyes narrow only slightly when the subject comes up.

'They are not good people. It's true. But circumstances led them down a different path. They have made some bad decisions and now they are paying for them. My family has been badly affected but we are not the only family to have suffered in this way.'

Hakim Hourani is a remarkable story of triumph and perseverance. But his brothers are nearly fifteen years older than him and his younger sister – 'almost a different generation,' he says.

He says he was a 'determined' child and his parents put everything into his education. His future was their future and it remains a responsibility he takes very seriously. His family's journey from war-torn Lebanon to Lakemba has taken him through Sydney University, years of extra study in Geneva, a prestigious post with CERN (the European organisation for nuclear research), and important years after that spent reconnecting with his faith. It has all made the man who many believe is set for even bigger things. Asked again about a potential political role he remains firm.

'Politics is something I am learning. I can see that there could be a more formal role for me in the future in the political realm but my place for the moment is here. These are difficult

times we are going through now but we will overcome them. I am working on that.'

'The difficulties.' We talk about that too, of course.

'There is a search for meaning in our community, particularly among the young,' he says. 'There is fear too. We are losing a generation of Muslim youth, either to crime or to jihad. We need to ask ourselves why this is happening. What is it that we can do to bring these young people back into society? If anyone is to blame for the radicalisation it is the barbaric false prophets who have targeted our young people and brainwashed them. They have used our peaceful religion as a tool for their political campaign. But we are to blame for letting them go, we – and I mean all of us Australians – must do more.'

It is this passionate and heartfelt response that so many people want to hear. When Prime Minister Brian Williams urged Muslim leaders to speak out more against terrorism and to mean it, he was really saying he wished there were more leaders who would follow the example set by Hakim Hourani.

'Everyone needs to speak out about terrorism. And that includes Muslim religious and community leaders. They need to bring it home to their own community that these people, these terrorists, are anti religion. They are preachers of hate and they must be stopped,' Williams has said.

'I agree' is the simple and direct response from Hakim Hourani.

Hakim put down the magazine. He felt slightly uncomfortable about appearing as a feature article for what they'd called 'the Power Edition'. He shared the magazine with articles on others deemed to be powerful in some way or other – Barack Obama, Richard Branson and the broadcaster Stan Anderton.

He was even more uncomfortable about appearing on the cover of a magazine that also boasted articles about sex toys and Victoria's Secret models.

Still some things were worth sullying yourself for. Building a path to the truly powerful was more important than any of his own personal moral concerns, no matter how unclean. It wasn't the first compromise he'd had to make and it wouldn't be the last. He was now, finally, getting to the point where he'd become that trusted figure, someone able to straddle the two cultures and make a difference. A man with access to the highest office in the land. He knew his parents would be proud, even his brothers – particularly his brothers. It had been a long time now since he'd spoken to them but he had taken the right path and they would be celebrating his success, he was sure of it. And Haifa? What would she think? She had taken her own path too. Different again. Who knew what she really thought. She had lost her way was his view. She hadn't married. She showed no signs of wanting to either. He was ashamed of the gulf that had grown between them but he didn't know how to bridge it. She had been seduced, he thought, seduced by the septic path of secularism.

14.

AJ HAD TAKEN UP HER FAVOURITE POSITION BESIDE THE WHITEboard again. She'd taped up a photo of a young man in his late twenties – head and shoulders only. He was wearing a blue and white Bulldogs cap and looking straight into the camera.

'Overnight, we've had another one. This is – was, Tone Bringa, also known as Abu Khalid al-Bosni. Most of you would know him. He was found this morning in the warehouse owned by our friends from the al-Ma-ana centre. Same drill. Shot in the head, no right hand, a bit messy given all the blood but on the whole a very professional job.'

Sid thought he could detect almost a touch of admiration in her voice.

'Now we've had cameras and surveillance all over the centre since the last two copped it but the warehouse is a couple of blocks away and isn't used for much – storage, books that sort of thing. Anyway, I'm still not totally convinced it's Harrison, it could be and all roads do seem to lead in his direction but we just can't find the clever bastard.'

Was it really Harrison doing this? Sid still couldn't quite believe it either. He hadn't ever been that close to Mick Harrison, but you got to know people on base and what he did know didn't suggest Harrison was a sadistic serial killer. War fucks people up, for sure. That war fucked a lot of people up, he knew that – but this was *really* fucked up.

AJ continued, 'He doesn't drive to the spot – he either disables cameras or chooses entrances where there are none. Like I said, he's good. But this time we do have something.' She turned to Murphy. 'Damo?'

Murphy stood up and pointed to one of the monitors hanging above his desk. The screen was filled with a series of numbers and connecting lines. It meant nothing to most of the people in the room.

'As you all know,' Murphy said, 'we've been using Stingray to track who comes and goes from the al-Ma-ana centre, and in the general area, for a fair while now – and well, to cut a long story short, if Stingray finds someone of interest it tells this little fucker here.'

Murphy pointed to an animated little green box marked FRED in the corner of the screen, lines attached it to numbers.

'This is FRED. Short for – Fucking Really Excellent Decoder. Fred's my baby. A malware bug that we've developed and put in a few phones here and there and – well, we've had Bringa under watch for some time now and, without him knowing it, his phone has been carrying FRED around for a while.

'Now at 10.15 pm last night he gets a call from Shalomar, but Bringa never gets a chance to answer. Anyway, Stingray picks it up and whether Bringa answers or not FRED clicks in and the mic on Bringa's phone turns on. So FRED hits record – and eventually we get this.'

He reached back to his desk and clicked a computer mouse over an icon on another screen.

A slightly muffled recording came through the big speaker sitting at the back of the desk.

'Hey ... what the ... ?' A male voice – barely audible followed by a soft click and a thud.

Murphy stretched across his desk and turned up the volume.

'Hey brother, brother ... what's goin' on. Shit. Shit.'

'Sit. Shut up. And do as you're told.'

He stopped the recording.

'The first voice you heard is Bringa. The second one – that's Harrison.' He hit the space bar and the recording continued.

'Sit in the fucking chair.' Sid recognised Harrison's voice again. He was calm. Speaking with menace but softly.

'Okay, okay.'

There was nothing but noise for a minute or so. Occasionally an unrecognisable exclamation. Harrison told Bringa to 'shut up' again.

'This is him taping him to the chair,' Murphy said.

'What do you want, man?' It was Bringa's voice now, still sounding defiant.

'Who's ...' It was clearly Harrison again but inaudible. Sid leant in closer to try and pick up the words.

'What?'

'Tell me. Who is ...'

'What's he saying?' Sid said, struggling to understand what Harrison was asking.

Murphy stopped the recording. 'It's a bit hard to hear exactly but listen closely. He's asking him "Who is Scorpion?"' He took the cursor back a few centimetres, hit the space bar and that bit of the recording ran again.

'What?'

'Tell me. Who is Scorpion?' Sid heard it this time.

'I don't know no fuckin' Scorpion. I don't know what you're talkin' about.'

'I don't believe you. And here's what I'm going to do.'

The sound of more shuffling, rustling and banging went on for about a minute.

'We can do this slowly if you like, I don't mind.'

'What? Oh fuck. Fuuuuck. My finger. Fuck. You've taken my fucking finger off. Fuck. Fuck. What are you doing? Fuck. Cunt.'

There were more indeterminate scuffling sounds. A thud.

'Shut up.' Harrison again. Louder. Angry and determined now. 'Who's Scorpion?'

'I don't know. I told you – I don't know.'

'You sure? One last chance. Who is Scorpion?'

'I tell you I don't know . . . Oh fuck. Don't. No! *Allahu akbar* – ahhhhh . . .'

The scream was cut short by a silenced bullet.

'That's it . . . pretty much.' Murphy hit the space bar again.

'Jesus,' Sid said.

'Well, no, Allah actually, but close,' Chip chimed in from the other side of the room.

'Smart-arse. So who – or what – is Scorpion?'

'Maybe Harrison could clear that up for us?' AJ said. 'He's still out there knocking these young guys off. It seems he's working harder than we are at finding him. We need to start asking the same question. Shandy get on to it. Any mention of a Scorpion on any of the websites. Any mention in the community. See if anyone knows anything. Anything at all. What's the Arabic name for scorpion?' AJ said, scanning the room. 'Where's Haifa?'

Her gaze came to rest on Sid. In fact, Sid felt like the whole room was looking at him.

'Dunno. She hasn't turned up yet,' he said a little too forcefully.

It was normal that everyone would look at him, he reminded himself, he usually partnered Haifa on jobs and no one suspected anything more had happened between them. He was just being overly sensitive. They had agreed to put that night at her apartment down as a one-night stand – a moment of comfort at a time of high stress. A mistake. A nice mistake but a mistake none the less. Yet here he was a few weeks later, still finding it hard to compartmentalise it. He remained professional most of the time but then she'd do something – an expression, a laugh, or she'd brush past him – and his excitement levels would soar.

Sid recognised this was dangerous territory. He hadn't felt these emotions for a long time. It could potentially compromise everything they were doing with K block. He'd just have to put it behind him. Move on.

15.

Haifa was swimming. She'd been in the water for about half an hour and was starting to get into that zone where the pain and fatigue gave way to endorphins – if that's what they were. The zone where exercise became transcendental – that moment she loved – when breathing and timing took over completely and pushed everything else out of the way. She'd woken up late, slept through her alarm and decided to turn everything off and try and forget about the world for a while. She had nothing set up for the morning and K block wouldn't miss her for a few hours.

She was worried about how to deal with Sid. He was fragile in so many ways. The night he'd stayed at her apartment, they'd talked until dawn. He'd told her about Rosie, about the guilt he still felt, about the plans they'd had for the future. He was a man carrying pain but he'd been a gentle considerate lover, tentative at first but then strong and in control. The sex had been good. So unlike the urgent fumblings of the others she'd taken to bed in the last year or so. They were too eager, too full of themselves and almost unable to talk once it was over.

She'd met one of them on the beach – he said he'd been watching her try to bodysurf and offered to help her learn properly. They'd had a fun afternoon then dinner and on it went. The other had been staying in one of the apartments in her block that had for a time been on the Airbnb circuit. He was nice enough – younger than her, small but fit. They ran into each other on the stairs, at the entrance to the apartment, in the pool. Eventually he worked up the courage to ask her out for a drink. Why not? she thought. After the sex he'd showed almost no interest in her other than as a conquest. What was she expecting? Respect? She wanted more than she'd been able to find anyway. When they asked her what she did, she told them she was a cop – which was sort of only half true these days really – but that just spooked them. On the whole they had been deeply shallow and disappointing experiences. But she wasn't looking for commitment. She wasn't looking for anyone to change her world. No one could do that. She had to do that for herself.

She stopped – looked at her watch – she'd been swimming for almost an hour. She was breathing hard. She felt the warmth of the full sunshine on her face and the cool of the rock on her back. She noticed the traffic on the coastal walk was fairly heavy – pedestrians, bikes, young mothers with prams, older people sitting on the park benches taking in the view. The full length of North Cronulla and beyond to Wanda Beach and all the way to the Kurnell refinery in the distance stretched out before her. It was a glorious summer day – a big, bright, blue, cloudless sky. There was so much going on she didn't notice the man standing at the top of the path just before it curled left beside the cafes and disappeared from view. But he was looking at her.

16.

MICK HARRISON USED TO LIKE THE HEAT AND THE BEACH. HE'D been a good surfer himself once – before. Not now, of course. Hard to surf with a stump. The sun was shrieking off the water – even with his sunglasses on the bright light was boring into him, tearing at his concentration. He was trying to resolve a dilemma. Would he take the girl?

He'd been watching her pound out the laps – one after another – without stopping. She was a strong, confident swimmer. Fit, obviously, and determined – not a quitter. He liked that in a girl. She swam for nearly an hour and had now finally stopped, resting against the far wall, looking straight up the beach towards him. She wouldn't notice him, he was confident of that. There were too many others around taking in the morning.

She was breathing hard, but she seemed pleased – and why shouldn't she be? Young, beautiful – the world could offer her so much – unless, of course, circumstance and luck changed. That could happen to anyone.

He popped another two painkillers. He'd been throwing handfuls of them down lately, but no matter how many he took they no longer seemed to work for long. The pain throbbed in the stump of his arm and snaked all the way up to his shoulder and across his chest. It had become worse over time, not better. He hadn't slept for a long time. Not really. How long? Who knows? The days tended to meld into one another. Maybe he'd close his eyes soon and rest. Maybe the dreams won't be there this time. Maybe he could get his old life back. But his old life was another world. A world before the war – before the six tours of duty, the broken, bloodied bodies, the car bombs, the limbless torsos, the dead children.

The first nightmares came between tours in 2006. He came home after his second rotation jumpy. Any loud or unexpected noise – or a big storm – would see him bracing for an artillery strike and expecting an explosion of dust and mortar, even in the safe and comfortable confines of his own bedroom next to Cate. He tried to tell himself to stay calm but sometimes he'd wake up in the middle of the night shaking by the bed or in another room entirely – cowering from dreams he couldn't even remember. Other times, the dreams would be so vivid he'd wrap his arms around Cate to try and protect her. Or worse, he'd lash out at her, unable to sort fact from fantasy. They were coming for him – they were coming for her – they were coming for them all – he was sure of it.

Cate tried hard. 'We'll work through this together, darling. We will,' she'd said, but he just felt angry, confused and irrational. He couldn't talk to her about the well of darkness. He couldn't talk to her about the corpses, the fear and the stink of war. He wanted to protect her, for God's sake, not drag her into his abyss. He felt himself slipping away from her and from everyone. No one understood – they had no idea what the soldiers had been doing in a country so far removed from them. And if they did ever think about it, they only wondered why we were there in the first place. He would try and tell his friends – they'd feign interest for a while but then he could see their eyes shift away and, within minutes, they were keen to get on to another topic. The conversations never lasted long.

That's when he saw the first of the psychiatrists. The doc went through the motions but showed no real interest either. He asked what it was like, 'What was your job there?', 'What did you see?' Insipid, ill-informed small talk. It was hard – no, impossible – to put it into words, to describe the constant intensity of knowing you're going outside the wire day after day, sometimes for days on end. The dull times, the boredom and the routine, shattered by unpredictable moments of terror and adrenalin. Somehow he managed to push the pain deeper and deeper inside, but the only real solution seemed to be to go back – the only salve for the pain was more pain – and even he knew that could never end well. But he pulled himself upright. Pretended everything was going to be okay. And outwardly it was, or it seemed to be. More tours followed until even back in the battle zone sleep didn't come easily. The soldiering was unremitting; the constant fatigue ate away at his core. Then Robbie Reid got hit. They were on patrol together. Robbie was in the turret of the armoured vehicle – he shouted 'Over there' and swivelled to point his machine gun towards the target. As he did, a single sniper's bullet hit him just under his helmet and his head disappeared in a spray of blood, brain and bone. That was bad. Very bad. Hard to shake off. Although Harrison tried. He tried to drown it in drink.

But Robbie was nothing compared to the day at the school.

The school was the biggest of half-a-dozen the Australians had built in the region. It took a hundred kids from ages six to sixteen, many girls among them. It was a first for an area that had never had formal schools, and certainly a first for the girls who had never even had informal schooling before. The school was in the centre of the village, an open-air market on one side and the local municipal building on the other. Behind the building was a small walled play area that was only big enough for thirty kids. The teachers would stagger the lunch break over two hours so all the kids got to play at some point.

That day he was with a small delegation that had come to see the local mayor, a cousin of the local warlord – a tall, thin angular man who had a liking for wearing paramilitary-style uniforms. The mayor was a sleazy personification of the corruption that ate away at the core of Afghanistan. He wore a peaked cap over his greasy hair, a thin moustache and dull eyes that never held a gaze. They were taking tea in his office when the first explosion hit. The dull, deep thud of a military-grade explosive. A plume of dust and smoke and the smell of burning metal blew through the open window. Then another blast – this one even closer and louder – everyone in the room hit the floor thinking it was an attack on the council building. The explosions were followed by silence – a few long seconds – then the screaming began. It was coming from the school. Harrison and the other Australians raced out of the mayor's building and into the street. They could see immediately that the school had been the target. A large truck had been driven through the market and into the side wall of the play area. The front of the truck had been blown off completely. Large chunks of it had sprayed across the playground. Now a more pungent visceral smell of blood and oil cut through the fog of dust, a thick soupy vapour that smacked you in the face as if to beat you into retreat.

Out the front of the school, it was chaos. Children and adults began spilling out everywhere, screaming, many with serious wounds and burns. A young man – a teacher Harrison recognised – came running out of the building holding a child with no legs. There was blood pumping from the little girl's stumps. Harrison and the others rushed to the playground, pushing against the mob of people running and screaming the other way. Inside the compound almost everyone was dead. There were small bodies and bigger ones. Half limbs hanging off them. Heads blown off. Clothing, hijabs and identities torn to shreds. One was a middle-aged woman Harrison assumed was the principal although he had never really seen her face before. Closer to the epicentre of the blast, the bodies became harder and harder to identify. Many were burnt beyond recognition. The smell was overpowering. Near the crater left by the force of the bomb there was nothing but pools of blood and shreds of clothing – as if the bodies themselves had been vaporised. Cloth and plastic was all that was left – floating in the mess. A few plastic bags drifted in the air currents created by the lingering heat.

Amid the carnage, Harrison's eye caught something in the centre of the playing field. A cricket bat – a 'Kookaburra' brand. The one he'd given Karim – a twelve-year-old boy he'd befriended. A special kid. Always smiling. He and his mates had been playing cricket with a fence post for a bat when he'd first met them. When he presented Karim with the real bat it was as if he had showered him with gold. Every time he had come back since they had insisted he join in the never-ending game. Now they were gone – all of them. Only they weren't. They came back night after night in his dreams.

Then the final mission, the one that went so wrong. The hunt for Scorpion, or 'Sabre' as they had known him then. And Harrison was the only one who survived. Why? Luck? Design? Did Scorpion deliberately single him out and kill everyone but him or was it just a case of the last man left? And then the line – 'This is for all the brothers in Lakemba'. Did he want Harrison to come back and find him? Did he want the fight to continue here? Of course he did. Harrison could only conclude he'd left him alive for a reason.

When he came through the treatment – six months in Germany – and eventually returned home, then the war really got bad. His head couldn't leave Afghanistan behind. The dreams haunted him. Nothing seemed right. He hated himself. He hated the world and he held a special reserve of hatred for the politicians who continued to preach their justifications for the conflict. Their ability to make political capital out of the war abroad and their attempts to co-opt the war at home for their own ends – the 'War on Terror' as it had become.

He tried so hard to be normal but it was a constant struggle that he lost over and over again. He became swamped in a tsunami of sadness. He was part of what he'd heard one general describe as a lost generation. But he just felt alone. Alone and angry. So angry. His fuse was so short it had vanished. He couldn't stand in queues; he couldn't go to supermarkets without feeling trapped or barely able to control his anger and fear. A woman slipped in front of him in the queue for the self-service cash register at Coles one day and he lost it. He began shouting at her to 'get back in the line'. Then a young bloke told him to calm down and he backed him up against a rack of baked beans and threatened to kill him. Another time he was sitting outside at a cafe when a truck backfired – he overturned the table before collapsing onto the pavement in a flood of tears. Some people laughed; others tried to help – he pushed them away. Eventually he pushed Cate away too. He couldn't blame her. She tried to stay with him. She tried to help. She got him appointments with more psychs. But in the war between his rational and irrational self – the crazy won. He had become the sort of person he used to look down on as weak. And still the dreams wouldn't leave him. That place, that war, had taken his heart and his humanity. Now he was fighting to get them back.

This was his 'War on Terror' – his own suicide mission. He had strapped on the metaphorical explosive jacket and he would find Scorpion – Scorpion was here, he had no doubt about that now. He could see it in the eyes of the young jihadis when he asked them. Soldiers of Allah or pathetic opportunistic criminals – they liked to think of themselves as tough, committed, terrorists but he could read the fear. If there was one thing he knew it was fear and he could see it in them.

He could only hope one of them would give eventually. One of them would spill it – give up the Scorpion. But he could do with some help. He had been surprised when he saw it was Sid Allen on the case. Sid needed to know. If anyone needed to know it was Sid. Harrison had never had the chance to tell him. Above all else, Sid needed to know how and why he – Harrison – was still alive when all the others were gone.

Harrison had thought the swimmer girl might be the best way to get at Sid. He'd followed them and watched them. He'd seen them at work and at play and it was obvious that they had gone well beyond the professional. He was jealous of Sid's carefree and inevitable transition; he was, of course, also angry. How could Sid move on from Rosie if Harrison himself couldn't?

But he wasn't sure Allen would want to see him. He was a stubborn bastard if he remembered right. So should he take the girl as bait? But now – looking at her – he couldn't do it. Beautiful. Precious. Why damage her? There had been so much damage already. But there was something else about her too. What was it? It troubled him, scratched at something in him. He couldn't pin it down. The drugs. They fogged up his head.

17.

BRIAN WILLIAMS LIKED TO GET IN TO THE OFFICE EARLY – JUST before 5 am if he could. It was quiet then and he could spread the papers out on his desk. He'd done it every day of his working life. He loved turning the pages of the real papers and clipping and ripping those bits that struck a chord. He was old school, he knew that, but he was fucking effective.

As expected, the latest jihadi death was the day's big news. Like all the others, this one had had his right hand removed and a clean shot to the head. Gruesome way to do business – targeting thugs who wanted to blow people up and cut off their heads – but not all bad. It certainly kept the issue alive – people were worried, scared. There was political mileage in that and Brian Williams was ready to take it. Or thought he was.

It was a matter of national security. This evil was a threat that required strong national leadership and tough new laws – laws that with any luck would also divide his political opponents, or at least they would have in the old days. But even the left had been supportive up to now, which really hadn't been part of the plan at all. They'd wised up. And the danger was – politically at least – it might all be starting to become counterproductive. The longer it went on now the more it began to look like the government was unable to provide the security the nation needed at this time of crisis. Even if these young men were bad guys, someone was out there killing them and no one seemed to be able to stop it.

Christ, they even knew who was doing it. A rogue former special forces soldier who no one seemed to be able to find – even with all the new laws and powers. What good were the laws if they didn't even work? And that useless pompous cunt, Gray, didn't have any answers. All that extra money – millions – a brand-new building, a public profile and nothing, nothing to show for it. What use was a fucking intelligence service if there was no one intelligent in it? No one capable of even bringing in a broken-down, psychotic soldier.

Williams had created a monster by allowing Drummond Gray to put his mug on the telly. Gray was supposed to be a tough operator – one of the best spooks of his generation – but these days he devoted his entire life to preening and self-promotion. And for what? In a few years' time he'd be slipping off to retirement in Umbria or some-fucking-where, and probably spilling all his secrets, writing crappy spy thrillers just like Stella Rimington. A career sucking on the public tit, a big pension and a million-dollar book deal. At least Stella Rimington was good looking.

And Gray and AJ and the spooks were telling him there was someone in the mix who called himself 'the Scorpion'.

For fuck's sake, you couldn't make it up. Well, that wasn't going to get out. That's just what they needed in the public domain. A madman called Scorpion. Jesus. What would the papers make of that? What would the dickheads on Twitter make of it?

Williams knew he'd have to find a way to stop Gray. But the bigger and more immediate problem he was facing was the image of his government and the perception that he was a leader who was unable to guarantee security and control. How the fuck did it get to this?

He yearned for the good old days when the issues were easier to manage. Back when he was just a ministerial minder or even later when he became an MP and then a junior minister. Back then, it was as easy as a drop to a favoured hack. The story got a push along. The blowhards got hold of it and then the 'serious' radio coverage in the morning. After that the tellies followed at night. And if he didn't like the way it was done he'd get on the phone and give the journo a fucking earful. You didn't get along in this business by being shy.

But these days, you didn't know where to look there was so much white noise out there. There were still some pointy heads who could be relied on – part of the club. The think tankers and pseudo intellectuals who would follow the line as long as they were well fed with exclusives. They'd even prosecute it with a venom that no politician could. They were easy enough to keep onside. A special dinner at Kirribilli House. A handwritten thank you note. Make them feel important. Then there was the ABC – public broadcasting. Fuck. Not much even he could do about that. He'd tried – Christ, he'd tried. And worse than all of them, now there was Twitter, a nonstop rolling commentary run by left-wing undergraduates with short attention spans – truly vacuous know-it-alls; and then there were the boutique left-wing subscription sites. And the fucking *Guardian* – which was free for God's sake. How did that work? They didn't even seem to care if they were frozen out. In fact, they liked it better that way. They weren't after any special leverage, they weren't even after favours.

And to top it all, he still had to deal with fuckers like Jenson Burton. Fuckers who if it wasn't for his office – if it wasn't for Brian Williams – would be lucky to still have a job. In a few years' time even his benevolence wouldn't save the likes of dinosaurs like Burton. The papers were dying. Soon, Williams thought, all we'll be left with are the tweeters and blowhards.

Disruption was what they called it. But it wasn't just the papers that had been disrupted. The whole model of society was fucking broken. Nothing was reliable anymore. The internet had disrupted the fundamentals that had kept things stable for more than a hundred years. In a world where anyone could say any-fucking-thing at any time and have it published to millions of people, politics itself had become disrupted. What was the use of so called 'opinion makers' like the old newspaper mastheads? Did anyone care anymore? It was like there were two parallel realities – one populated by an ever-diminishing number of people who still got their information from the usual sources – the papers, the TV bulletins and the like – and the other populated by people who lived online in a world of self-reference and self-confirmation where they only ever read or watched information that mirrored their own beliefs. That was the real disruption. Controlling the information was the key to power. Once you lost that the only other thing that worked was fear.

Jenson Burton for fuck's sake – he'd have to do something about him. Maybe a sit-down one on one with the prime minister. Make him feel important. They fucking loved that. Or maybe even better, a story with Hakim Hourani – 'working together with the community to beat the terror'. What a find Hourani was proving to be. They'd have to find him a seat. But, no, maybe not a puff piece – not yet. That would look too soft. And fair enough, Hourani was a solid mainstream Australian, but he was still a Muslim. Bring him inside the tent but don't let him stay overnight just yet. The public's not quite ready for that. Hell, he wasn't sure he was quite ready for it either.

Brian Williams needed to get on the front foot. The polls were still shit and not shifting. They'd been stuck there for months – it was a bad look. Some were even talking about a spill against him if things didn't improve. The jackals were queuing up. Backgrounding the media behind his back with stories about focus group responses to his weight and his generally untelegenic style. Schmoozing the back bench. Busting their arses to get on the radio and the morning television to talk about anything. That weirdo Terry Cardinal was injecting himself into every issue going. He was the fucking foreign minister for fuck's sake, but get him on the radio talking about a cyclone in the Pacific and before you know it he's offering up budget solutions and suggesting it might be a good idea to wind back negative gearing. For fuck's sake! No, Williams knew he had to get things turned around. Perhaps the PM in the counter terrorism nerve centre, planning and coordinating raids with the counter terrorism squads. There's an idea. Sleeves rolled up – getting to grips with the crisis. Yes, there's an idea. But not an exclusive for that cunt Burton. They'd do an all-in picfac instead. No questions. Just get the TV cameras in there. Get on the front foot.

He eased himself up out of the chair. Told himself again that it really was about time he got serious about the weight problem and walked over to the new Nespresso coffee machine he'd just had delivered. He put in one of the dark blue 'intenso' pods and hit the espresso button. The day was looking better already and it was still only 5.30.

18.

On the walk home up Devonshire Street, Sid could see flashes of the news bulletins running on televisions in the front rooms of some of the terrace houses he passed.

The news was leading with the images of a prime minister in charge. The 24-hour channels had been running the pictures on rotation all day.

What a lot of horseshit.

He was tempted to stop at the Shakespeare for a beer but, even there, they'd turned the sport off and almost everyone was watching the news. It was too much. He walked on. The footage was so completely and utterly staged. A trumped-up situation room with people looking serious and determined, the prime minister looking over their shoulders at computer screens, uniforms hovering in the background – even a few pixelated faces because 'the identity of the agents engaged on this important case can't be revealed'. Jesus, it was hard not to be cynical. It was more than he could cope with after a day spent buried in the jihadi websites trying to find any reference to a 'Scorpion'. He was given the job of combing through back issues of *Inspire* – the magazine that gave the Boston bombers the blueprint for their homemade pressure cooker explosives. There were all the usual searing exhortations for jihad on America and helpful pointers on how to hijack aircraft and blow up public figures, but no mention of a 'Scorpion'. Sid was exhausted and irritable.

He walked on up Crown Street. It was a warm night, the restaurants were all busy, the tables outside were full. The city was enjoying itself. Wouldn't it be nice to be there, drinking, eating, not a care in the world. What sort of a job would give you that sort of life? Sid wondered as he turned into the quiet of Arthur Street. Not the one he had. Maybe once this job was out of the way he'd try and find something else. Maybe that something else would include Haifa too. Not tonight, though. Tonight all he wanted was a glass or two of red and a good sleep. That was where his mind was wandering when it happened.

The hit came from behind. The full force of a big weight slammed into him. His knees crumpled. He hit the pavement. A few stunned shouts was all he could get out before a foul rag smelling of old engine oil was shoved into his mouth and gaffer tape wound around his head to keep it in there. The cuffs went on fast too. How many attackers were there? He had no idea. One or two? Then a sharp pain in the neck. A jab. A needle. Where was everyone? Why wasn't anyone helping him? A weight came crashing down on his back pinning him to the ground. He tried to buck it – to fight back, but he felt his strength leaching out of him as the drugs began to take hold. The ground started to roll, his vision began to blur, then the long slow and inevitable fade to black. He could see it coming. He knew what was happening. Even as he drifted away, his rational mind was still putting the pieces together. Then he was gone.

•

He woke in a soup of hot, thick, cloying darkness. His eyes fluttered open but for a while he could barely tell the difference if they were open or closed. The air was damp and smelled of salt water. It was so quiet he could hear his own breath – in and out, a bronchial gurgle, slow and painful. His ribs ached and his hands were still cuffed but the only trace of the rag and gaffer tape that had been wrapped around his head was the pain of the torn skin around his mouth and an aftertaste like a dirty garage floor. He coughed. Then shouted –

'Hey!'

Nothing. No response.

'Fuck.'

Gradually his eyes adjusted to the gloom and the room began to reveal itself. A cement floor – covered in dirt or perhaps fine sand. He kicked out hard at the concrete walls but they were thick enough not to budge or give out any sound. His head was still heavy but his thoughts were coming together now and the fear was beginning to rise within him as well. His mouth was so dry, and his neck hurt but other than his equilibrium nothing seemed to be broken. He told himself to stay calm. He'd trained for a kidnapping. He'd studied the psychology of captivity and how to behave in a hostage situation. What to say; what not to say. What to give up; what not to give up. But all the theory and training drills couldn't prepare anyone for the real thing. Details. Remember details. That's what they always said. What did it smell like? What could you hear? Try and pinpoint some identifying features. How long have you been here? He couldn't answer that one. Was it night or day? He had no idea. He drifted in and out of consciousness – or he thought he did. He had no reference for time. The light never changed but his thirst grew to become a torture. Every now and then he'd shout out but nothing ever came of it. Then bang. A blinding light so bright it was painful – and before he could adjust to it the lights were off again. A door opened. A breath of fresh air rushed in – the door closed again.

'Hey. Fucker. Come and show yourself. Come on, you coward,' he yelled.

Nothing. Not a whisper. His feet kicked out, hitting something heavy and plastic. It crumpled like a plastic water bottle. Was it? He scampered across the floor trying to find whatever it was he'd hit. Feeling for it with his feet. Yes, there it was. A large bottle of water. His hands were still clamped behind his back. He crawled nose to the floor and managed to get his mouth around the top. He placed the bottle between his knees and began tearing at the cap – eventually twisting it off. He sucked in a huge, wet, torrent of relief. Drank the lot in greedy, desperate gulps then struggled to keep the water in his stomach. He lay on his back, spent with the exertion, and again drifted in and out. Time became meaningless. It was hot as a fever. Maybe that was it. Maybe he was running a fever. Maybe this was all a delusionary hallucination. His mind playing tricks on him. But no – it was just hot.

He'd been hot before. He knew hot. Afghanistan was hot – forty-five in the shade some days. It was hot like that the day when news of the patrol disaster had filtered back to base. He'd felt like this then too. When they told him about Rosie. Hot, weak and nauseous. The terror of helplessness. The inability to change anything – the lack of control. The finality of it. He'd never forget it.

They sent three people to tell him, one to talk, the others to restrain him if needed. But the news paralysed him completely. He couldn't speak. He had nothing to say. It should have been him. They knew it and he knew it. When they told him he just sucked in the hot desert air and tried to keep from throwing up.

It was Colonel Jim Malone who broke the news. He was the deputy commander of the international mentoring force Sid was attached to. Jim wasn't a bad guy but he wasn't what you'd call a people person. He was a man who liked process but was afraid of emotion. Plenty of soldiers were like that. Sid was like that. They came – they broke the news – then left. They were 'sorry'. He could 'see the psych whenever he wanted' and he should start 'preparing to withdraw'. Then the silence, the heat, the pain. He cried, he wailed until he was empty. Empty of everything. Emotionless.

They brought the bodies back to the base. He went to see her but it wasn't the laughing, spirited, determined Rosie he'd loved. It was a corpse that didn't even look like her. It meant nothing to him and that surprised him, compounded the guilt. There didn't seem to be anything he could do to overcome it. It was all he could do to just concentrate on one step after another. His packing was methodical. He cleaned out every trace of their life. He didn't want to leave any trace of her – of them – there in that place.

It seemed like a long time ago and like it was only yesterday. In the semi-consciousness of the hot little concrete bunker he was in now he couldn't stop his thoughts drifting back to Afghanistan, back to Rosie, back to certainty. Back to a time when the future seemed sure and predictable.

His confused thoughts began to surge and whirl, Rosie one minute, Haifa the next. The time he'd been with Haifa, the curve of her body, the sound of the sea and the hypnotic music. Haifa's face, Rosie's face – the two began to blur. He drifted in and out of the delirious fantasy. It was a nice place to be even if he wasn't exactly clear what it was. But the heat and the pain coursing up his neck kept dragging him back to the hot dark little room in – fuck knows where he was. And where was Haifa now? Even though they'd tried to limit the contact, he was falling for her fast. So fast. More guilt. God, what was with the guilt? Get over it. Move on. Rosie would have approved. He knew that.

And then the light. Another blinding flash of light. He put his head between his knees, desperately trying to protect his eyes from the pain. A heavy door slid open. Someone walked in. They were followed by a rush of damp fresh air. The door clearly opened to the outside. He still couldn't see but the air rushing in was sweet and laced with salt, like it'd just been scooped off the water. He could hear the faint sound of a train in the distance, nothing else, no cars. The door closed with a heavy bang. This time the light stayed on.

19.

'Come on. Sid just wouldn't disappear. Not now. Not in the middle of all this.'

Haifa and Chip were standing on the street outside the office about to head in their separate directions. It was 6 pm, the second day with no sign of Sid. For the first day, no one seemed particularly concerned. It wasn't unusual for him – or for anyone in K block for that matter – to go AWOL for a while. It was the nature of the job. But two days was pushing it. And since the night at her place, Sid and Haifa had been in slightly more regular and slightly less professional contact. Not hearing from him at all was already unusual. She didn't want to appear too close but there was something wrong. She knew it. A text, a phone call – there had always been something.

'Something's happened. I know it,' Haifa said.

'Maybe he's just gone for a drive,' Chip replied, but he looked like he could barely believe that himself. 'Maybe he had to get away. Maybe he's gone on a bender. You don't know him that well.' He was staring at Haifa, looking for a reaction, she thought. 'Let me tell you, he's not some innocent altar boy, and it has only been two days.'

'Or maybe he's lying in a gutter somewhere bleeding to death. Or maybe, just maybe, one of these crazy jihadis we've been spooking has decided they've had enough and it's time to do something about it.'

'Let's go past his place then,' Chip said. 'Knock on the door. If there's no answer we can bust in and have a look for ourselves.'

'I've already done that.'

'You what?'

'I found his spare key. Not hard. Lift a few paving stones, a few pot plants. You'll find it eventually. You know how it is.' Haifa shrugged as if it was just routine.

'You obviously know him better than I thought. Must be a story there,' Chip said meaningfully.

'Yep. There is. But you don't need to hear it yet.'

Chip nodded. 'I'm happy to live on in ignorance. Let's go past his place anyway. You can let me in and I'll have a poke around. Let's just hope we don't find him at the bottom of a bottle or even worse in mid spank with some happy hooker.'

'Not everyone's an immoral deviant, Chip.'

'Dream on, darlin'.'

They hailed a cab and got the driver to drop them off at the Clock Hotel rather than negotiate the maze of closed-off streets that had helped push up the real estate prices in Surry Hills. Sid called it his 'renovated bankers' ghetto'.

The lights were on in most of the houses they passed on the way down Arthur Street. Sid's house was dark. They knocked on the door and called out a few times. No answer. Haifa pulled the key out from under one of the old flower pots on the verandah. Chip turned on the flashlight function on his iPhone so he could get the key into the door. Inside, nothing looked out of place. An empty wineglass, a plate. No sign of any disturbance or rushed packing.

Haifa noticed a phone charger still in the socket on the kitchen bench.

'What about his phone?' she said. 'That'd be easy enough to track, wouldn't it?'

'Sure it would. What do you guys say? A piece of piss. We'd need to go back to the office though. Tomorrow, if he hasn't shown up by then. Come on. There's nothing to see here now anyway.'

Haifa took out her own phone and hit the redial button. Sid's had been the only number she'd called all day. She jumped as the ridiculous 'Bad to the Bone' ringtone broke through the silence. It was coming from out the front. Outside.

'Sid?' Haifa called out, hopeful. 'Sid?'

But the phone kept ringing. They followed the faint bluesy notes out the front door. Sid's phone was lying on the ground blinking, just inside the iron railing fence at the front of the house.

'That's not good,' Chip said, stating the bleeding obvious, as he bent down to pick it up. 'Eight missed calls. Most from "H".' He looked across at Haifa. 'One from AJ and one from "No Caller ID".'

'What do we do?' Haifa asked.

'Is it the jihadis?' Chip didn't wait for an answer. 'We ask a few people a few tough questions. And I say we start with Shalomar.'

'So, what? We just turn up and say, "Hey, where's Sid?" Sure, that'll work.'

'No, we bring him in and we shake him up. There are a few other things we can ask him about while we're at it.'

'Bring him in? On what grounds? We can't just pluck him off the street.'

'Yes, we can.'

'We have no proof or even suspicion he might be about to commit a terrorist act. This will just play right into the fears everyone has in the community about how these laws work. We can't do that.'

'Okay. We'll go and pay him a visit, have a cup of tea and come out with nothing. Or we'll use the new preventative detention orders. We can hold him for up to two weeks if we need to but, of course, we can't ask him any questions. What use is that? Or – we just do it the old way.'

'Shit.' Haifa shook her head. She knew if it wasn't about Sid she would never agree to go along with Chip's plan. She'd always taken a stand against this sort of policing. Cops taking liberties because they could. Because it got results. For a while now she'd been thinking that K block was taking too many shortcuts. There were so many conflicts. So many contradictions. She was finding it increasingly hard to be a Muslim, even a secular one, and to be part of the state apparatus that was watching Muslims. To always feel her community was the topic of everyone's focus all the time. So many pressures and so many questions. She had been thinking of asking AJ if she could be reassigned to another unit. That would have to wait a while now. Things had suddenly become even more personal.

'Believe me,' Chip said, 'the old ways are best. Too much process otherwise and you know how I feel about process. Court orders, paperwork, publicity, media. No way.' Chip took out his phone. 'I'll call AJ. We'll have Shalomar in for a private chat by the morning.'

•

The two commandos from the counter terrorism unit pulled the preacher out of bed at 3 am. They blindfolded him, cuffed him and dumped him in a small concrete cell out at Clyde.

This sort of information gathering wasn't something the Feds liked to see happening in the cells at HQ in the city, so Wissam Shalomar had been taken to the unmarked warehouse – just one building among a cluster of warehouses, smash repair joints and brothels.

Chip got there around seven. The two lads who'd delivered Shalomar were still there, sitting in a small office with little in it other than a few chairs, a table and monitor. The table was covered in empty sports drink bottles and burger wrappers, a half-finished crossword from an old newspaper, and takeaway coffee cups. They were dressed in black t-shirts and track pants, young but tough looking. One was big and gym-conditioned the other small and wiry in that special forces way.

'What's he been doing?' Chip said. No formalities. He didn't ask their names. They wouldn't have told him anyway.

'Pacing. Ranting. Praying. He's not happy. He's like a cornered bull,' the wiry one answered looking over at the monitor.

Shalomar was sitting in the corner, his arms wrapped around his knees, head up looking straight into the camera. He looked like you'd expect someone to look who'd been dragged out of bed at three in the morning. His hair was sticking up at odd angles, he was wearing tracksuit pants and sandals and the bottom of his stomach was poking out of a torn, too small t-shirt.

The only other thing in the room was a concrete bench.

'Okay, let's go and have a chat.'

The commandos both put on black balaclavas and the big guy handed a spare to Chip.

Shalomar didn't move when they walked in, just kept looking straight up at the camera sitting above the door.

'Are you recording this?' he said, spitting out the words. He was already behaving like a caged animal. Angry. Defensive. Wild. And they hadn't even started.

'No, I'm afraid not. Too bad if you want it for your show reel,' Chip replied.

'You can't do this. This is against the law,' Shalomar spat back, indignant.

'Do what? There's nothing to see here. We just need to ask you a few questions. But, as far as any records go – this never happened.'

'That's how your democracy works is it?'

'Only when we're faced with an existential threat.'

'What do you want from me?' Shalomar asked, turning finally to face Chip.

'We've lost someone. We were hoping you might be able to help us locate him?'

'Oh yes. What would I know about that? I'm a humble preacher. You should go to the police.' His mood shifted momentarily and he allowed himself a self-satisfied chuckle.

'The sort of humble preacher who likes dressing up in military fatigues in video clips calling for jihad against the infidels,' Chip said. 'The sort of humble preacher who schools impressionable young men in hatred. The sort of humble preacher who encourages young men to attack innocent people, to behead even people from their own community. The sort of humble preacher who sets up travel routes through Turkey to Syria and Iraq so those same brainwashed souls can line up as cannon fodder for your so-called holy war. Humble. Sure.'

'If you're so convinced of that, why don't you just arrest me instead of this farce?'

'Because we're a democracy. We believe in free speech.'

Shalomar laughed again.

'I don't know anything about anyone you might have lost. No one new has turned up at the mosque for weeks. But we are a brotherhood of love and everyone is welcome.' He put his hands out in front of him, palms up, as if to show he had nothing to hide.

'What about the old lady? Maha Syaada. How much love was there for her?'

The preacher dropped his arms and leant forward, almost lifting himself up off the floor.

'I don't know anything about that,' he said. His voice was quiet now but he was choosing his words carefully. 'But yes, it's terrible. Maybe it was the same monster who's been killing all the young innocent Muslims. Why don't you do something about that?' he asked. 'You don't seem to be working too hard to find him.'

Chip's patience was running out. He gave the nod and the two enforcers picked Shalomar off the ground, sat him up on the concrete bench, cuffed his hands behind his back and tied his ankles together with plastic packing tape.

'Are you thirsty?' Chip said. He was holding a heavy, dark-coloured cotton bag.

'Why? You going to waterboard me now?'

'You think I'm stupid? We don't do that.'

'Oh yeah. Come on. You're an American. I can tell by the accent if not by the attitude. Man up. Give me the full treatment. You know you're good at it.' Shalomar scowled.

Chip pushed his own face close to Shalomar. Enough to get a good look into his inky black eyes but not close enough to give him the chance to try to headbutt a response. The preacher's breath stank. He was sweating and a musky smell was starting to come off him. The smell of fear.

'They say Khalid Sheikh Mohammed lasted more than two minutes before he cracked. But then I've also heard from my own more reliable sources that they only had to wash his face before the man who had no qualms about organising the jets to fly into the World Trade Center and kill thousands of people actually spilled everything.'

'Go on. Tell me something else. Tell me how you tied them up at Abu Ghraib. Tell me how you put them on stools and tied nooses around their necks and left them there – worried any slight movement might see them hang themselves. You Americans, you never learn.' Shalomar spat at his interrogator.

'Water is cleaner. You're right,' Chip said, moving back – out of range.

The cleric pulled his wrists and ankles – testing the resistance. He looked up and spat again. A long steaming arc of saliva.

'And unlike pulling out fingernails or screwdriving a scrotum it doesn't leave any marks or bruises,' Shalomar said. His tone was mocking. 'Don't lecture me. Get on with it.'

'Really? You could save yourself a lot of trouble. Do you want to tell me who has our friend? Sidney Allen? He's missing and we're more than a little worried about him.'

'Who? Is that what this is all about?' Shalomar seemed genuinely surprised. 'I have no idea what you're talking about and if he's a friend of yours good riddance to him. I hope he rots in hell.'

Chip turned away and nodded to the bigger of the commandos. They left the room. The door closed heavily behind them.

'Just the two of us then?' Shalomar said. 'How cosy.'

Chip held the heavy bag and approached the cleric.

'What, no water? You haven't got the courage, have you? You're weak. Like all Americans you're all show and in this case no bottle.' Shalomar chuckled at his own joke.

'I wouldn't give you the satisfaction of confirming your pathetic prejudices. This isn't a game we're playing here. One more time. What's happened to Sidney Allen?'

Shalomar shook his head. 'I don't know what you're talking about.'

Chip put one hand on his captive's forehead to hold him still then forced the cloth over his head. He turned and walked towards the door.

'Have a think about it. I'll be back. In the meantime, I hope you like the music. Have you heard of Cannibal Corpse? They're very good.'

The door closed with a solid clunk behind him.

The two commandos were in the office outside. When they saw Chip coming the smaller of the two pushed a button on a touchpad screen on the wall.

'Turn it up,' Chip said.

Even outside the heavily padded and reinforced room the music was loud. It must have been almost making Shalomar's ears bleed on the other side of the door.

Chip knew from experience that it could take some time. Shalomar would hold out. But at some point he might just crack. Waterboarding. What a fiasco that was. It was effective, sure, but too effective really. Waterboarding broke everyone eventually. And they'd say whatever you wanted to hear just to stop it. The quality of the information wasn't always reliable. Chip preferred noise. It was clean too.

After two hours of pumping, thumping, grinding heavy metal into the interrogation room they turned the sound off and left it for another five minutes. Chip pushed the door open and turned on the lights. They came on with a fluorescent flickering and cast a pale bright light into every crevice of the room. Shalomar's bagged-up head was hanging down in front of him. It didn't move. Chip reached for it and pulled the bag off in one smooth motion. The preacher lifted his chin and tried to turn his eyes away from the burning light. There was nowhere to turn.

'I have nothing to say to you,' he growled.

Chip put the bag back on his head. Left the room again and the whole procedure was repeated. By the fourth round, Shalomar was barely able to sit up anymore. He slumped forward, his handcuffed arms the only thing stopping him from falling to the floor. He was semi-conscious now. Not answering questions at all. That was counterproductive. Chip fetched a bucket, filled it with water and tipped half of it over the cleric's head. It had an immediate impact – shook him upright, spluttering, retching and fighting for breath.

'If I could tell you what you wanted to know, I would,' he gasped finally. 'I just don't know.'

'What about the old lady? Who did that?'

'She deserved to die.'

'Fuck you. Who did it?'

Chip felt like hitting Shalomar in the face. But that would have left an ugly mark and wasted the entire day. So he threw the remaining half of the bucket of water at him.

Then he called the muscle in again and instructed them to unstrap him. They lifted the preacher off the bench and rolled him onto the floor. Shalomar lay there, gasping for breath, coughing and sobbing.

'One more thing,' Chip said. 'Do they call you the Scorpion?'

Shalomar, still on all fours, stopped retching and looked up from the floor. He scowled directly at his torturer – the hatred bringing him strength. And then he started laughing. An uncontrollable cackle that came from deep within his diaphragm.

'Fuck this. Get him out of here,' Chip said.

20.

Sid lifted his head and squinted into the light that was scalding his eyes, burning through to the back of his brain. Was this it? Was this the end? He'd survived Iraq and Afghanistan only to have it all brought to an end by a homegrown jihadi in a hot little soundproof concrete box somewhere in Sydney. Would they shoot him first? Or was he going to star in his own cult snuff movie – a slow beheading from some crazed seventeen year old coached by an internet warrior on how to bleed a kafir – an unbeliever – for the camera and how to get maximum impact from it. This is what people had been expecting. This is what they'd all been fearing. K block and ASIO had managed to intervene in time to stop something like this happening so far but it was inevitable one would slip through. Sid had just never thought it might be him who would become the public relations coup and the recruitment driver. A slow painful death in front of a black IS flag and a camera. Just like those they'd had to sit through as they surfed the deep cesspit of the web. At least, he thought, his death would be nicely produced. A slick video clip set to stirring Islamic music, intercut with triumphant images of advancing IS fighters brandishing AK-47s, flashes of exploding vehicles and the exhortations of some baby-faced jihadi dressed in a bomb vest and black battle fatigues.

Sid certainly expected to see a group of them right now bristling with weapons. But as his eyes began to adjust it was clear there was only one of them. He was big. A full beard but no black gear, no flags. Rather, he was wearing a flannel shirt. In one hand he had a handgun – pointing at Sid's head. In the other hand, also stretched out in front of him, he was holding a banana.

'G'day, Sid. Have this. You need it. You're weak.'

'For fuck's sake.' He knew that voice. 'Harrison? Is that you, Mick?' Sid said, confused but relieved. 'How am I supposed to take the banana? You've cuffed me.'

'Oh yeah – sorry, let me fix that.'

The cuffs came off. Sid took the banana, tore it open and stuffed it into his mouth.

'Got any water there?' he said.

Harrison handed him a plastic bottle. Sid drank half of it and tipped the other half over his head, the cool water washed away at least some of the fog of captivity.

'What the fuck is all this about?'

'Yeah. Sorry.'

'Sorry? Is that it? Sorry? What the fuck, Mick? What are you doing? This is what they do, you know? The fucking jihadis.'

'Yeah. I know. I needed to talk.'

'You needed to talk. Fuck. You talk with your mouth. I listen with my ears and we're done. You didn't need to bash me, lock me up, starve me and nearly kill me.'

'I don't know why I do half the things I do now, Sid. I'm fucked up. I hurt. That's what I know. That's what I do. I needed some time to think. Now I need to talk.'

'Yeah, well, I'm all ears.'

'I know you've been looking for me.' Harrison was pacing back and forth and rubbing his neck and shoulder with his good hand. Sid could see the guy was in some serious pain but he didn't have any sympathy for him.

'Well, you can't go around chopping people's hands off and killing them without getting a reaction.'

'I know but there's a reason.'

'Sure there is.'

'You don't know how much danger we're all in.' Harrison stopped pacing and looked directly at his old colleague.

'No? You might be surprised.' Here we go, thought Sid. The rant of another deluded and traumatised veteran. He'd seen enough of it to know what it looked like. 'Tell me,' he said.

Sid could see better now and he took in Harrison's appearance. He was recognisable but only just. He obviously hadn't shaved, cut his hair or washed for a very long time. He was wearing good Gore-Tex hiking boots and track pants. His red checked flannel shirt was hanging open over a stained white singlet.

'Ever heard of someone called Scorpion?' Harrison said.

Sid looked directly into Harrison's dull, milky blue eyes.

'Not until a few days ago,' he said. 'Not until we heard you talking about it.'

'You what?' Harrison had been standing on the other side of the room. Now he took a pace towards Sid.

'Bringa. It's a long story but we heard. Everything. We heard you cut off his finger. We heard you chop off his hand. We heard you kill him.'

Harrison took another step. He was close now. So close Sid could smell the sourness of his breath. Sid's back was up against the wall. He couldn't move.

'Nothing he didn't deserve,' Harrison seethed. Almost a whisper.

'Really? Come on, Mick. You can't believe that. Going around knocking these guys off isn't going to stop them. One goes down, another is motivated to step into his shoes. You know it.'

Harrison stepped back.

'Well, locking them up doesn't stop them either. You put those fuckin' Pendennis guys in the slammer and when they got out they headed straight to Syria and started posting Instagram shots of themselves holding severed heads.'

'But we stopped them doing anything here,' Sid said. 'And how did we stop them? We were tipped off by others in the community. You can't go around chopping people's hands off and expect that to continue. Anyway, Pendennis was a long time ago. They were amateurs compared to the guys we're dealing with now. Those guys just wanted to blow up the MCG. This generation wants to rule the world.'

'Yeah, but you know as well as I do others are still sitting in Supermax directing the traffic.' Harrison started moving again. Back and forth, back and forth.

'Jesus, Mick. Give us a break. You've nearly killed me and now you want to lecture me. Might surprise you but my head hurts. Got any more water?'

Harrison pulled another bottle out of a box just outside the door. He handed it over.

'What's all that got to do with Scorpion anyway?' Sid asked.

'Nothin'. Well not that I know of.'

'Shit. My head hurts, Mick. You're really fucking me up here. What is this all about?'

'It's about this.'

Harrison raised his right arm, revealing the hard black plastic sleeve that started just below the elbow and wrapped around the stump of his forearm and beyond to a gloved swivelling prosthetic hand.

'When this happened he looked me right in the eye and said, "You people call me many things but around here they call me Scorpion" ... it's also about you,' he said, lowering his voice now as if even here in the concrete box someone might overhear them.

Sid turned his gaze back to the face of the sick veteran in front of him.

'What's it got to do with me?' he said. Sharp. Angry. Uncertain.

'Fuck, Sid, think about it. Scorpion did this to me. On that mission.' He paused to let it sink in. 'Scorpion killed everyone else. Scorpion killed Rosie.'

Sid felt like he'd been hit in the stomach. He stopped breathing. A tiredness washed over him. A deep heavy fatigue that drilled into his bones. He knew Harrison was telling him the truth. Scorpion. This was the guy who'd killed Rosie. This was the man who'd drained his life of meaning, who took away the only thing that meant anything to him. Until – well until very recently.

He looked up at Harrison.

'And he's here? You're sure?' he said after a long pause.

'He's here. I just don't know who he is or where he is. Here.' Harrison handed him a USB thumb drive. 'There was more than one list I found in Jilal's bedroom.'

'You didn't win any friends killing him, mate.'

'Don't kid yourself. He'd turned. The cunt was praying when I found him and he wasn't saying his Hail Marys. He was down on all fours on a rug bending towards Mecca.'

'What did you expect? Jilal was pure hummus and falafel. Mohamed Jilal,' Sid said matter of fact.

'Well, maybe he wasn't what you all thought he was either. Or maybe he'd become something else. Have a look at that. It's a plan for terror attacks on a scale that we've never seen before. Coordinated – all at the same time. Designed to create maximum chaos and destruction. Have a look at it. It's incredible.'

Sid took the drive.

'There are plans for thirteen different attacks all to happen at the same time on the same day. Incredible detail. My Arabic's a bit rusty but I know enough. It talks about how "Allah will triumph", "the kafir will feel our sting" all the usual *Allahu akbar* shit. But then it gets to the detail. A truck full of fertiliser overturned in the M5 tunnel heading east. A chlorine attack in the Virgin arrivals terminal at the airport; something on a ferry; another truck in the Harbour Tunnel heading south; a bomber hits Martin Place train station. They're going to cripple the city and go for the big bang. The Opera House is one, George Street is another; the Shell oil refinery at Rydalmere. This is a big coordinated plan.'

'Fuck,' Sid said, hardly able to comprehend what he was hearing.

'Yeah. Fuck.'

'When?'

'Well we don't know, do we? At one point it talks about commemorating the "big defeat". Not sure what that's about. But at least one person does. They call it the Scorpion's list.'

'So why have you sat on it? Why didn't you take it to someone? Show someone?'

'What and give myself up? I know you've been looking for me. I needed time to think. The brain doesn't work the way it used to.' He tapped his head for emphasis. 'I'm giving it to you now. Because I realised we're after the same guy. I can help you but you also need to help me. We both need to find Scorpion. You can try it your way. You can pull people of interest in for a chat. You could even pull a few fingernails but you won't get there as fast as I can. And you know it.'

Sid had to admit he had a point. But could he sanction leaving a trained killer to continue killing in the hope that eventually it'd lead to finding the bigger danger? And the decision was now even more difficult. He was still reeling from the news that the man who killed Rosie was out there – *here* – somewhere. In the first few months after her death, he'd been desperate to get back to Afghanistan. As crazy as it was, he thought another tour of duty might lead him to those who killed Rosie. But after what had happened, and his state of mind, they were never going to send him back. He'd grown to accept that, but time hadn't healed the empty hole in his life and revenge remained an unexplored course of therapy.

Some people might think the greater imperative would be to protect the community from the current, real threat – Harrison, a killer on the loose – not the potential bigger threat. But, deep down, he wasn't sure he really believed that. What was the life of a few hotheads worth, who'd probably end up sacrificing themselves in Syria if they had the choice anyway, compared to the possibility of preventing a mass terrorism event? And seeing justice finally delivered for Rosie? What would Haifa think? What would AJ think?

'I don't really have a choice, do I? And neither do you,' Sid said eventually. 'You're going to let me go. I now have the information and I have to decide what to do with it and you have to take the chance that we won't come after you – at least until you've delivered Scorpion.'

'I don't care if you do – couldn't give a shit. I'd rather not even be here to be honest. This is the only thing that's keeping me going. When it's done, you can have me if you can find me before I do it myself.'

Sid could tell he wasn't joking. The guy was in a world of pain. A long way from the soldier he'd known in Afghanistan, the self-assured man who was always in control. But then how combat affected even the toughest of them was unpredictable. Some walked away from the horror without a scar, others carried their wounds inside them forever, forced to live with the torment and the humiliation. We all had to find ways to deal with it and to heal if possible, Sid thought. And if healing was too hard, distraction and diversion seemed the only way for most. Drink, work, revenge. Each to their own.

'Okay? You with me?' Harrison spoke up.

Sid studied him for a moment. A wreck of a man. Hollow and haunted. What path had he taken? We all have choices, Sid thought, until something snapped and for some people the rational became elusive. And what did Harrison think of Sid now? Did he look like someone who had it all together? Nothing was ever as it seemed on the surface.

'Yeah, I'm with you. I think I am anyway. What you're asking is – well it's . . . I don't know how we'll do it but I'll figure it out.'

'All right. If I need to contact you I'll find a way. No phones. If you need me for any reason do something different that I'll notice.'

'Like what?'

'Fuck, I don't know. Iron your shirt. Clean your shoes. Something different.'

'That's a bit rich coming from you.'

'Fair call.' Harrison ran his fingers through his shabby beard as if he'd only just realised it was there. 'You got a bike?'

'A bike?' Sid had no idea what he was talking about.

'Yeah, you know two wheels and a bell. I hear it's all the rage in your neighbourhood. The new golf or something, they say. Everyone's doing it. If I see one chained up on the fence outside your place, I'll know you need to see me. But don't fuck me up. You need me. Remember that.'

Harrison was sweating now. His pacing was getting more frantic. He pulled a blister pack of pills out of his pocket. Popped two of them out, threw them in his mouth and swallowed.

'Here,' he said. 'Three of these should do it. Takes away the pain.'

'What are they?'

'Oxys. Oxycontin – take 'em.'

Sid did as he was told. He placed his trust entirely in the hands of a deranged killer. Foolish? Maybe. But at that moment he felt he had little choice. He'd take relief from the pain and the confusion, in any form, from anyone.

21.

The two men came from either side of the car park, they stopped between two poplar trees and greeted each other with kisses. One was dressed in a suit, the other wore long robes. They stood facing the train line, their backs to the lines of parked cars and The Boulevarde of Punchbowl beyond that.

'Peace be upon you.'

'*Wa-alaikum salaam* – and upon you be peace.'

'Praise be to Allah, my brother.' The man in the robes spoke softly. He lit a cigarette.

'You should give them away you know,' the other man said, chuckling softly.

'Ha, yes. I have tried many times. It's good to see you.'

'You too. Have you recovered?'

'I'm getting there. They were tough but they didn't break me. The American. You know him?'

'I know of him. Yes. Our friends have kept me informed.'

The man in the suit motioned with his hand – patting the air between them. They stopped talking. The man in the suit took in the scene. He scoured the car park looking for anything unusual. Finally satisfied there was nothing out of order and that they were indeed alone he took up the conversation again.

'What do they know?'

'They know of Scorpion. They know there is talk. Beyond that, I think not much.'

'We must be patient.'

'Yes, but we must not let this indignity pass unnoticed, brother. Praise be to Allah. Many are watching us. They are looking for leadership and strength.'

'And they will get it. But yes, brother, we will serve justice in this case for you as well.'

The men embraced and left the same way they had come.

22.

Kamel heard the bell as usual. Except for his brief spells in solitary it had been the same for every day of the past fifteen years. They rang the bell and the day shift for the prison officers began. The bell itself was 200 years old they said. A relic of the colonial past when this country was built on the sweat and blood of criminals – shameless irony, he often thought. Today, like every other day, would begin to unfold as it always did but today he would have a special job to do. He would wait with the other occupants of his 'deck' to be called down to breakfast. They would be sectioned off into the yards as usual. Asians in yard six, Islanders in yard seven. He and his fellow Arabs and Lebanese would be given yard eight. The whites kept to themselves and the Aborigines came and went as they pleased. Most of the blackfellas liked to hang with the Arabs. Some had even converted, they were brothers. Kamel remembered what it was like before 'ethnic sectioning'. Goulburn had been an even more dangerous and unpredictable place than it was now. Gang wars erupted over the smallest things, usually small bits of territory and benefits: someone had taken too long on the basketball court or someone's food parcel had gone missing. The wars would go for days, weeks even. Deaths were inevitable as were the regular bashings from the officers. Membership of a gang was the only protection. But it required absolute loyalty, obedience and often, religious conversion. It helped to have a network of brothers at your back.

These days the prison hierarchy kept the gang wars at bay with clear ethnic delineation backed up with capsicum spray, closed circuit surveillance, chemicals and a crack squad of snipers known simply as 'the men in black'. They wore black jumpsuits and balaclavas to hide their identities and they were trained in close combat and hostage negotiations. They shot to kill.

It was quieter now as a result. It was a different sort of rule. In the old days, the gang leaders were the top dogs. If you were a big deal on the outside you were sure to be a big deal on the inside as well, and for the past decade or so Tariq and Taleb Hourani had been the big deal. Among the Arabs they had decided who had favours, who did what, how the justice was meted out. They still had some respect but they were in their fifties now. In prison that was old and in recent years the limelight, and subsequently the fear factor, had been stolen by the 'Double As' in the Supermax. The terrorists.

Some in the yard still thought the terrorists were at the bottom of the pecking order. But things were changing fast. Kamel saw it. The Houranis knew it too. The terrorists now had the quiet cred. Nothing escaped their attention. It was a different rhythm. Even though they played at being model prisoners they were forensic with their attention to detail. They knew everyone, they knew their families and they dished out the justice in their own way, through their own people. A word here, an order there. They had the fear with them but they weren't interested in showing acts of force or retribution. They did their enemies slowly. They were the masters of the long game and, as everyone in this place knew, long meant really, really long. These guys were playing for life. They were waiting for their moment, a time in the future when their purpose would be revealed. But in the present they had begun to dictate the unwritten code. They delivered their messages and orders through the 'sweepers' like Kamel.

The sweepers were the trusted few – usually older men who'd been in for years, long enough to build reputations with the officers as low risk and quiet. They were given the maintenance and food delivery jobs. And consequently, unlike others, they were free to roam through the various sections of the prison as they went about their routines.

Supermax had a fearsome reputation but Kamel reckoned it wasn't as bad as the politicians liked to portray it. When he read some of the stuff they said in the papers about the conditions – about how they'd 'thrown away the keys' for some of the worst of the worst – he couldn't help laughing. The terrorists had it better than those doing their time in the regular prison. Sure Supermax was high security but they had TVs, they had natural light. They didn't spend time in solitary because they all behaved so well. They had the patience of the righteous.

Their mail was checked but if the spooks didn't know what they were looking for – well. And they got to talk to their families. Even if they were no longer allowed to talk in Arabic they managed to get messages out, usually through the wives and, of course, through sweepers like Kamel.

As Kamel had said to his son Abdul many times: 'Supermax isn't really an isolation wing. Even the Double As have visitation rights.'

Abdul was a conduit – part of the message board. He was coming this afternoon and Kamel had been told he would have a message to give him.

23.

Sid was still feeling a bit ropey. He was back at work and the pain in his head was starting to fade but getting over the Oxycontin hangover was proving to be tough. He could hardly remember leaving the concrete room and being bundled into the car. Harrison had cuffed him again and blindfolded him first so he still had no idea where it was he'd been held, but the trip back to Surry Hills had taken a while. About an hour, he thought, but he'd drifted in and out and his memory of the journey wouldn't hold up under cross-examination.

He'd woken up on the front porch of his house totally disoriented. It was dark and he had no idea what time it was. He couldn't find his key, it wasn't under the old pot where he usually left it and he had no phone. He'd stumbled up to Crown Street but the restaurant strip was shut up and there were only a few stray partygoers and drunks on the street. He'd asked someone what the time was and was greeted with the sort of response mostly reserved for the mentally ill. The clock on the appropriately named Clock Hotel said it was about twenty to four but he couldn't remember if the clock actually worked or not. It was obviously sometime early in the pre-dawn morning. He must have looked a mess. The few people out were making a wide arc to avoid him. He staggered further up Crown Street looking for a phone but of course there was none for blocks and blocks and then finally there were two within a hundred metres of each other all the way up near Albion Street. The first didn't work. The second did – he dialled triple zero.

After a day in hospital for observation he was sent home. The doctors told him he was in pretty good shape physically, at least given what he'd been through. It was his mental state they were most worried about. Truth be told, he was a bit worried about it too but he wasn't about to admit that. Not now. Not having come so far. The last thing he wanted was to be grounded again and to be put back on the psych list. There was so much to do.

Haifa had come round once – late. But she hadn't stayed long. She seemed concerned, but distracted, and obviously wanted to keep her distance. Sid could understand but he'd been a bit surprised. She told him Chip knew about their thing – that's what she said: 'Chip knows about our thing. We should cool it for a bit,' she'd said. 'You need to rest.'

She was right. But what he also really needed now was to cry and to hug someone and hold someone – Haifa; to hold her close. He also needed to talk. He needed to talk to someone about the list. But he couldn't quite figure out who. AJ?

Chip? They could keep stumbling forward on their own but they needed Harrison. Would the chiefs really let Harrison carry on knocking people off and would they sanction the contact without actually bringing him in? Sid doubted it. But the stakes were high. Seriously high. He needed to take this right up the chain.

The debrief was the first thing he'd have to worry about though. And that was on this morning – here. He'd have to spill it all, wouldn't he? Otherwise what was it all about? Why did Harrison take him? Why did he let him go? What the fuck? His mind was still working at sixes and sevens. A hundred kilometres an hour in a fog. He couldn't think straight. Maybe he should keep it to himself for a day or two or at least for a while longer until he'd sorted out his thoughts. But he hadn't had a chance. As soon as he could get out of bed, they were calling him back to work, and before he could even get a one on one with anyone, he was in the briefing room – or the interrogation room, depending on who was answering the questions. He knew it was just the easiest place to do a full interview 'for the record', given that it was the only place permanently wired up for sound and vision, but it was still intimidating. It put Sid on the defensive straight up.

They'd been over the details a few times already. How it happened. When he was taken. Now they were getting to the 'What happened?' and 'Why?'.

AJ had been doing most of the talking, Chip was there too. No one else.

Sid looked across at the camera in the opposite wall and then at the door. 'Can we have a break for a bit?' His gaze swept from Chip to AJ and back to the camera.

'Sure. Let's have a break,' AJ agreed.

They walked out into the corridor. Sid cast an eye around to make sure they were alone.

'What's this about?' AJ asked.

'I need to talk. We need to talk. Just us. No camera.' He looked at each of them in turn.

'Oh yeah? Okay.'

'Can we get some air?'

'Uh huh.' AJ looked at Chip – eyebrows raised.

The three of them walked out of the office and up Commonwealth Street to Hyde Park. It was another warm, sticky February day. Hot already and only just gone 9 am. The drunks and the homeless had all been well and truly moved on by now and the park was pulsing with commuters heading in to the shops and their office jobs across the park's patchwork of paths. The benches were all but empty though, too early in the day for any contemplation in a city that seemed to have less and less time for that sort of thing.

Sid chose a bench under a tree with some shade. He sat down, opened the laptop he'd brought with him and doublechecked to make sure the wi-fi was turned off. He put the stick into the USB slot and clicked it open.

'Here.' The screen came to life. A revolving scorpion motif with animated Arabic script was running across the page. One click behind that and the detailed list of planned attacks came up.

'What is it?' AJ asked. She was turning her head, trying to read the swirling script and clearly struggling to understand any of it.

Chip saw it though – straight away. 'Holy shit.' He whistled.

Thirteen dot points with detailed descriptions and plans for each of them. Directions, maps. In the few that involved trucks and explosives there were instructions on detonating the load. The same for the plans for chlorine attacks to be used in both the Virgin terminal and a Manly ferry. Entry points for the Opera House were all marked clearly on a map with instructions for a number of suicide bombers to detonate themselves. An extraordinarily detailed map of the oil refinery at Rydalmere.

'Jesus. They're planning to fly a light plane from Bankstown airport into that one,' Chip said, reading through it. 'And what about this – number thirteen. It just says "The martyr's switch". Any ideas?'

Sid shook his head. 'Beats me,' he said.

So he told them everything he knew. Scorpion's origins, Harrison's vendetta – everything except the bit about Rosie. He figured they'd get on to that in their own good time.

'What you're suggesting is –' AJ let her thoughts trail off. 'But we can't just leave Harrison out there on the loose even if it does get us to Scorpion. Can we? We need to find both of them, and soon.'

'The one thing we do know is that the operation is going to be big. And big means expensive. No one could mount something like this without planning and stockpiling and spending on infrastructure.' Chip was thinking aloud. 'Follow the money.'

'Well, we haven't turned up anything so far,' AJ said. 'There are plenty of busy Hawala brokers and aid organisations sending money to the Middle East through Turkey. We're on to them as usual. But there hasn't been any mention of a scorpion. Ever.'

'Scorpion. Alaqrab,' Chip said – using the Arabic name for it. 'I've never heard it mentioned. And I've known just about all of them over the years. Or I knew of them. All the old al-Qaeda guys. All the pseudonyms. All the noms du guerre. Abu Hafs al-Masri, Abu Abdul Rahman al BM – he was called that because he was good at using the BM chemical weapon. And all the young ones as well. We kept track of them.

'After the Soviet invasion we knew Osama was funding the Afghan Jihad and the fight against the Syrian regime. We knew pretty much everyone in the Muslim Brotherhood. We followed bin Laden and other Yemenis when they settled in Afghanistan. We knew about al-Qaeda. We didn't do enough about it but we knew them all. I've studied every one of them. But I've never heard anyone called Scorpion. Maybe he was freelancing. It's possible. There was plenty of that happening. People working for various Taliban factions and warlords.'

'Shalomar?' AJ asked. 'Could he be Scorpion?'

'I've asked him already,' Chip said.

'I see.' AJ didn't need him to spell it out. 'And?'

'He's a tough bastard no doubt, but he didn't confirm or deny. He's into something though. I'm convinced of that.'

'Well if he is Scorpion, we'll know about it,' AJ said. 'We've got him wired up like a Christmas tree. In his home, his car, the office. We know where he is and what he's doing all the time now. Shalomar farts, we'll smell it first.'

24.

'The Butcher of Lakemba'. Brian Williams picked up the paper from the top of the pile on his desk. 'What are we doing about this? We've got all these pointy heads, we've got all the fancy technology that the Federal budget and the Five Eyes intelligence network can provide and we still can't find one former soldier with a knack for chopping off hands and blowing people away.' His blood pressure was up.

'The people out there in Lakemba are screaming for us to do something.'

'Here.' As was his habit, Williams continued reading to his audience although both of them – the ASIO chief and Andrea 'AJ' June – had already read the reports of what they already knew.

'*Two more young Muslim men were found murdered in Sydney's western suburbs yesterday. Both had their hands removed and both had been killed with a small calibre shot to the head in what police described as a "professional" manner.*'

'And this – "*'I was tortured,' claims sheikh.*" By Jenson fucking Burton. "*The head of Lakemba's Croydon Street mosque and the leader of the al-Ma-ana Muslim education centre has claimed he was questioned for many hours by Australian intelligence agents at an undisclosed location. Sheikh Wissam Shalomar says he was questioned about the disappearance of a police officer and was subjected to unlawful torture.*

'"*They tied me down and used the 'Waterboard' technique to try and get me to confess to terrorist activities. This is the sort of behaviour that has enraged Muslims around the world,*" *he said.* "*Don't imagine it's just the preserve of smiling American soldiers at Abu Ghraib, this practice continues and is proof that the government sanctions the state harassment and intimidation of all Muslims.*"

'*A spokesman for the attorney-general told the* Daily Telegraph *that the nation's intelligence agencies would not comment on the claims but denied that so-called "waterboarding" or any other form of torture or physical abuse had ever been used or would ever be used by them.*'

'I'll bet that's what you said.' Williams looked directly at Gray. 'But, in this case, is it true?'

'Was he questioned? Yes,' Gray answered directly.

'He was questioned, yes, sir.' AJ backed him up.

'Where? And is it true he was waterboarded? For Christ's sake.' Williams threw the paper onto the desk in front of him.

'At our facility in Clyde, sir. Yes, the intelligence officer used some forceful techniques as you would expect but waterboarding was not one of them,' AJ said. Williams thought she didn't seem entirely confident.

'No pictures, no evidence, I take it?' he asked.

'No. Of course not.'

'Of course not. Well at least you've done something right.' His contempt for the nation's spies was growing by the day.

How is it, he wondered, that they simply couldn't find this one crazed fuck-up of a soldier? They kept telling him they needed more equipment, more powers. Surveillance, surveillance. But what good was it if the person they were trying to find didn't play the game? No phone, no internet, no credit cards. No electronic or digital footprint at all.

'Maybe you should all go back to trench coats and old-fashioned shoe leather. That's how they kept track of the bloody communists and the ratbags. By sneaking around at protest meetings. Following people of interest. Why not a few compromising photographs?' Williams said, fuming. 'How many bloody jihadis have your lot turned? None. And how many of your own people do they have working for them on the inside? Not many. And certainly one less now thanks to the nutcase trained by our own military. And now you're coming at us with this story of someone called Scorpion who is apparently planning a series of attacks that would make 9/11 look like an argument at a convent picnic and all you have to show for it is a three-page plan and the word of the commando in the cuckoo's nest that, again, no one seems to be able to find. Incredible.'

He had to check himself there. But he so badly wanted to give Gray both barrels. He was sitting there in his three-piece suit all puffed up like some fucking Etonian out of a Le Carré novel. A three-piece suit. In this weather? Fuck off.

'Prime Minister, I do think we need to take this threat very seriously. The provenance of this is unquestionable and we are putting a great deal of effort into it,' the ASIO chief said, puffing himself up a bit more. 'I know I've said this before but you remember the alliterative ad campaign one of your predecessors put out with the hotline number warning the public to report any suspicious behaviour they might see to the authorities? To remain "Focused not Fearful", "Mindful not Menaced" that sort of thing? Well, as you know, I regard myself as the wailing personification of that campaign.'

You sure do. This bloke's the whole fucking alphabet, Williams thought.

'But other than this three-page plan,' Williams said, 'at this stage, we have no further confirmation of any of it?'

'No, sir. Not yet,' AJ spoke up. 'But we do have every reason to believe that something *is* coming. There has been an increased amount of internet traffic from Iraq and Syria, a lot of grooming of individuals. And we're certainly doing our best to engage with the community on that. But we believe an attack is imminent, almost inevitable, and we fear it won't just be a fourteen year old with a death wish and a pressure cooker full of explosives. This could be the first really coordinated plan made here that we've had to confront.' AJ paused, she looked at Gray, then back at the PM. 'Sir, at this stage the fact is Harrison is our best bet of finding Scorpion.'

'It's like a fucking Hollywood script,' Williams said. 'But even they couldn't make this up.' The PM looked first to

Gray, then to AJ, then back to Gray. He took his time and then he spoke slowly but deliberately.

'We – I – cannot sanction leaving a killer out there to do a job you lot don't seem capable of doing. You. Need. To. Bring. Him. In.'

AJ remained calm but determined. They all knew their roles here. This was the dance they knew they needed to do. Plausible deniability. No trail.

'We're working on it, sir. But the reality is he is still out there,' she said.

Williams looked across the desk at his security chief. The desk had first been used by Prime Minister Robert Menzies at the start of World War II. How different and how much simpler things were then, he thought. Menzies never had to face shit like this – the perception that the government, that he as prime minister – was losing control of the situation. They seemed to be in danger of national security actually becoming a negative politically. Incredible. As if the soft-cock critics on the left would have done any better. Another small-scale attack, another hostage crisis, would be devastating. And a big attack – a coordinated mass attack of the kind that was being suggested? Unthinkable on every level.

Brian Williams lowered his voice. He picked up the *Telegraph*, turned it so his two security chiefs could be in no doubt and pushed it over towards them.

'You know what has to be done,' he said. Gray and AJ simply nodded.

'As far as I'm concerned,' he said, 'this conversation never happened.'

•

The two spooks left the room. Confidence wasn't usually a quality Brian Williams was short of but he had been unnerved, there was no denying it. He was playing with fire but what choice did he have? No one had any better ideas. There was a plot out there to bring on mass casualties and chaos. A list of roads, bridges, oil refineries – the fucking Opera House? Everyone saw what happened with one gunman and a cafe in Martin Place. The whole city shut down and they were still sifting through it all, looking for who to blame for not being able to protect people who just wanted a cup of coffee.

He got up from behind the desk and began pacing the room. He pulled his phone from his pocket and hit the redial for Barry Angel, his lanky good-for-nothing party director.

The phone rang once before it was answered.

'Baz? This shit is starting to strangle us. What are focus groups saying?'

'On the terror stuff?'

'Yes, for fuck's sake. The fucking terror stuff.'

'They're coming back loud and clear. The more we talk about it the less convinced they are that we can do anything about it.'

'That's never happened before.'

'No. Pretty hard to talk about tackling Muslim radicalisation when a descendant of the First Fleet is out there blowing people away.'

'Mmm.'

'We've got to think of some way to take back the initiative, get on the front foot.' Angel was thinking aloud. 'Why don't we set up a prime ministerial commission to engage with the Muslim community? "National security is about security for us all". Let's have a "National conversation about what it means to be tied by a set of common beliefs and values". Put Hakim Hourani in to head it up.'

The PM smiled for the first time that day. He had an even better idea.

'Baz? Have we offered Hourani a seat yet?'

25.

The flight from Sydney was smooth enough despite the small shuttle planes they used on the short route. They were always more susceptible to turbulence and Hakim had never liked them. The weather in Canberra was hot and still. If nothing else, he always enjoyed coming to the capital for the climate, it had a certain harshness that appealed to him. Cold and bright in winter. Hot, dry and even brighter in summer. It was certainly hot and bright this morning and even he was relieved to get into the terminal after the short walk across the tarmac.

He adjusted his tie carefully and brushed the shoulders of his suit coat to remove any signs of dandruff as the escalator took him and his fellow passengers to the ground floor. He liked to be neat. He walked past the baggage collection area and noticed, as usual, the huge advertisements for arms contractors, like Raytheon and BAE systems, that plastered the walls. Pictures of submarines, helicopters and the new joint strike fighter with captions like 'Mission ready', 'For security, for jobs, for Australia', and 'We're proud to train Australia's future military pilots'. He assumed these were put up in the hope of influencing the politicians who crawled through the terminal day after day. There was a lot of money in war.

They said they would send a car to collect him but Hakim had decided he wanted as much time alone before the meeting as he could get. It was an important day. He'd been told the prime minister wanted to see him and had something to put to him. A seat in parliament perhaps? That had certainly been rumoured for some time now. He'd told them he was more than happy to get a taxi from the airport to Parliament House, but he was regretting that now. The queue for the taxis was long.

He thought about the meeting while he waited in the queue. It was a big step and it had to be handled carefully. The problem he had was how to ride the perceptions in the Muslim community that the Williams government had been formulating policies that were traumatising them. People were worried about the laws designed to tackle extremism. What was the definition of radical they asked? It seemed the definition was first to be Muslim and then to be unpredictable. Everything from planning to fly to Syria and join the fight to appearing to be overly moody at school – anything could get you noticed and watched. Were there any other immigrants in this country's history who had suffered the same sort of discrimination?

It was easy for those in positions of power to pretend that the flaws in society were the fault of those who looked different or worshipped differently. There were many faults in this society but Hakim's message to his community was that the answer was not to shy away from engagement but, rather, to embrace it. That would be his challenge and he was more than ready for it.

26.

Damien Murphy was scrolling through a number of websites and social media pages he had up on the screen. He was wearing board shorts, thongs and an old Nirvana concert t-shirt. He looked like he hadn't shaved in days.

'There are 45,000 Twitter accounts connected to Islamic State in some way, that we know about, and around 400 are active here. Then there's all the Facebook shit. Finding anything amongst all the kitten pics, fashion tips and food photos . . . I mean, it's like trying to find a tick on an elephant.

'But guess what? Yours truly here has something you all need to look at.'

He turned and smiled at the room.

'There are a number of charities we've been keeping an eye on. Most of them are legit – they send medical supplies, some send doctors, some just send money for reconstructions, others send funds for the camps. But there are a couple that funnel their money through other regional organisations; money that ends up eventually funding other things. By far the biggest and most active here is the group known as the Muslim Relief Fund. They're very effective.

'Now, here's where it gets interesting.' He put up a PowerPoint with arrows and boxes linking the MRF Australia to branches in the UK and in the US.

'MRF is an international charity. It has strong links with the Muslim Brotherhood and Hamas, and through them the Islamic Relief and Development Fund based in Turkey.'

'Ring any bells?' Chip said, standing up now to join Murphy at the front of the room. 'The Islamic Relief and Development Fund was deemed to be funding terrorist activities in the United States, Germany, the UK and the Netherlands, and they were proscribed here in Australia way back in 2009. Their funds and assets were frozen in the United States under the Patriot Act and the investigation into their activities is still underway. We know through Israeli intelligence that MRF's British director met with Abu Alaa al-Afri, IS's second in command, nearly two years ago. And my friends in the CIA have also identified a further nine individuals from IRDF with links to IS. Just last month, a couple of IRDF offices in Kosovo were closed down after it was found they were organising the undeclared transfer of funds to Iraq and facilitating travel for some European jihadis. We know as well that the IRDF was used for the delivery of supplies on behalf of MRF into Syria and Iraq as recently as last year.'

Chip threw it back to Murphy who changed the screen.

'So we have picked up mention of the development fund in a number of the conversations we've monitored. But there's more to it. Stick with me it's a bit convoluted,' Murphy said.

Like everyone else in the room, Sid was struggling to follow the links. He was still having trouble with headaches and dizziness as it was. And to add to his general frustration, Haifa was still playing it cool with him as well. Actually more than cool. She was avoiding him completely. Not answering texts. Not returning calls. When he asked her why, she simply said she needed time out. Time out from him and time out from K block. She said she was becoming increasingly uncomfortable with the tactics and methods K block was using. She had asked AJ for some leave.

'Now, none of this is particularly new,' Murphy said, flipping forward to another slide. 'For the last eighteen months or so MRF have been active out at shopping centres collecting money, holding donation rallies and the like. You can see them almost every day of the week at Bankstown Mall with their donation buckets. They ask individuals to give them cash and to sign up for regular donations in the form of direct bank debits.'

Here he threw up a slide of a collector in the mall to illustrate his point.

'But the majority of the fundraising happens online. We don't really know how much money has been collected. The money trail is pretty hard to follow.'

'It always is with these charities that have offshore connections,' Chip pitched in again.

'But look here. Six months ago MRF established a trust account that started banking money – lots of it. The money comes in from overseas – in dribs and drabs, mostly below the $10,000 line that would be picked up as an alert. But, as you can see, it's been a steady stream – almost $15 million. But it's also been going out of the account at a pretty rapid rate and not all of it has been going overseas as far as we can tell. We'll get to that in a minute. But first here's our friend Shalomar who also happens to be a director of MRF. As well as directing charity funds through the IRDF we know he has been channelling big sums through this Somali Hawala broker.'

Murphy put up a shot of Shalomar emerging from a travel agent's shopfront in Greenacre.

'Through some of our colleagues in Mossad, we've established that the money is in the first instance going to Mogadishu and from there to who knows where or what. But here's something fascinating.'

He pulled up another slide. This one showing the MRF website and a photo of a man holding up what looked like emergency food pack rations on the back of a truck.

'You'll notice the logo for the IRDF charity appeal in the corner here. It's just a pointer to another charity raising funds, but the connection is there.'

He scrolled the page down and clicked on the photo.

'This is Adnan Taleb. He's a dual Lebanese Australian national. According to Lebanese intelligence he is the religious leader for IS in the northern Lebanese city of Tripoli and he is thought to be an active recruiter. He features in a video that's doing the rounds online thanking Australians for their fundraising efforts and their donations. He was arrested last week trying to cross into Turkey carrying a suitcase full of money – $250,000 to be exact. He says the money was destined for legitimate aid but we know the route to IS front lines in Syria is via Turkey and we know that's where the money and resources are going across. Taleb's arrest comes just a month after the release of this man – Ibrahim Shalomar. He's also a dual national and, yes, the name's familiar, he's the first cousin of the Lakemba preacher, Wissam Shalomar. Ibrahim spent about a month in Lebanon's Roumieh prison charged with "funding jihadist groups" but the Lebs couldn't get the charges to stick and he was released. He has since travelled back to Australia – he's thought to be living back here in Sydney but unfortunately we seem to have lost him. You still with me?' he asked.

Sid wasn't sure he was. His head was throbbing. He'd been scribbling notes onto a sheet of paper as Murphy had been talking, hoping that might help him connect the dots.

'So,' Sid said, putting his pen down. The note taking hadn't really helped. 'We've established that MRF is raising money here. We've established that some of it's being sent overseas, we think to fund jihadist activities. But you're saying millions of dollars is being pushed through the account. Presumably not all of that is leaving the country. Right?'

'Spot on,' Murphy said. He paused to let this sink in. 'What we've also established is in the last few years Wissam Shalomar – our humble cleric – has been amassing a real estate portfolio that LJ Hooker would be jealous of. And he's been flipping them pretty fast too.'

He put up half-a-dozen examples.

'Here's just a few. A three bedroom house in Greenacre bought by Shalomar eighteen months ago for $800,000. Sold a little over a year later for $1.2 million. Keep in mind property prices in this part of town have increased by nearly twenty-five percent. Here's another – a shopfront in Lakemba bought for just over a mil; sold three months later for $1.5 mil. Two warehouses in Clyde bought and sold for a $600,000 profit. It goes on and on. Quite a portfolio.'

'Impressive,' Sid said. 'Classic pea and thimble money laundering trick.'

'Yeah, but messy too. Some of the properties are being bought from Shalomar by other directors of the MRF charity.'

Five mug shots appeared on the screen.

'There's Shalomar, of course, and there's Dr Mohamad Altahami; Keyser Mohamed, a local builder; Mohamed Ibn Mahlek, who you all know is the big deal in Leb restaurants; Dr Ahmad Humaydi there; and Masood al-Zahiri to his left.

'We suspect some of the money is being ploughed back into other charities and used for legitimate aid work – that's certainly possible – but we also suspect some of it is being washed through for other purposes and that's the trail that's proving to be hard to follow but – well, we're giving it a go.'

Murphy stretched across to the laptop and clicked on another file. A logo appeared.

'There does seem to be one distinguishing feature that all the directors have in common – all of them are also connected to this organisation – the Sunni Progress Association.' He cast a glance around. It was obvious he was looking for Haifa. It wasn't widely known that she had asked AJ for leave.

'The Sunni Progress Association is run by this man.' Murphy clicked again. Another mug shot came up. 'Dr Hakim Hourani.'

Sid felt himself take a sharp intake of breath.

'Are you sure?' he said. 'Hourani's connected directly to the money trail? Or is it just coincidence? It's a close-knit community out there.'

'Here's a photo taken at the annual charity function at the end of last year,' Murphy said.

The directors were all lined up in a row. Wissam Shalomar was shaking hands with Hakim Hourani. Both men were smiling.

'It turns out Wissam Shalomar is also one of the directors of the Sunni Progress Association. And here's something else. It's taken a bit of digging but we've found that Dr Hourani himself has also bought and sold a few of the MRF properties,' Chip spoke up, underlining the connection.

'I thought they were enemies?' Sid was really struggling now.

'Yeah, didn't we all.'

27.

Sid still had AJ's warning about Hakim Hourani ringing in his ears.

'Be careful how you move on this,' she'd said. 'To say Dr Hourani has powerful connections would be to understate things considerably.'

Then there was Chip's advice on seeing Haifa. Which was pretty much summed up as 'Don't ask me for advice. I've failed at that game all my life. I've never been able to figure women out.'

Chip had been married once. Sid knew that at least, although he'd never met Mrs Walker.

'She liked living with the blinds down, I liked living with the blinds up. She liked mustard, I liked ketchup' was all Chip had said about it. 'These days I prefer hookers. You don't have to talk about the future or the furniture with them.'

After days of ignoring the empty hole in that corner of his life, Sid had finally decided to act. He toyed with the text for most of the morning but eventually just hit the button – a moment of assertive no return.

Fancy catching up? I really need to see you.

Nothing for nearly two hours – then this:

Okay. My place tonight. You can bring dinner.

Not for the first time, he wondered how it was that a piece of technology could so determine his mood. Suddenly almost everything seemed sharper, brighter.

'Dinner' in so far as that related to food was at least one of Sid's stronger points. He considered making a crab curry but then thought that might seem a little try-hard. Perhaps a pasta and some salad? But even to do that well required more effort and concentration than he thought he was able to cope with at the moment so he decided a walk down to Chinatown to pick up a roast duck and rice and some Chinese broccoli with oyster sauce would probably hit the right note.

Anyway this dinner wasn't about the food.

His momentary brightness began to fade as he pondered just how difficult the evening might get. Haifa didn't seem especially close to her brother but, as everyone knew, siblings didn't need to be close to instinctively protect each other. On the other hand, she could get closer to the source – if that's what Hakim was – than anyone else in K block could.

Sid wanted this relationship with Haifa to be more than just work, it already was of course, but that just made things all the more difficult. Hakim Hourani's entanglement with the charity and with Shalomar surely wasn't coincidental. But was Sid's entanglement with Haifa preventing him from fully exploring an obvious avenue of investigation? Not yet. But perhaps it could if he didn't act soon.

Haifa's distance and coolness was confusing and grating away at him. Was he the problem? Was it K block? He assumed 'the methods' she was growing troubled by referred to Shalomar's claims he'd been waterboarded. Chip had denied it, but Sid wasn't sure his friend was telling the truth. Chip wasn't known for his sensitivity.

As conflicted as Haifa seemed about some elements of her own community, he could see working for K block was taking a toll. Who could blame her?

She knew just how big the potential problem was. There were fourteen-year-olds sitting in their suburban bedrooms talking about beheading people and blowing things up, for fuck's sake, getting their instructions from someone on the other side of the world through Twitter.

But a few crazy brainwashed kids, fanatics and criminals was all it took. And when you saw sophisticated plans for coordinated attacks, like the Scorpion list, it was hard not to feel totally overwhelmed. Everyone was overwhelmed. The list was the focus of everyone's attention now. K block still had primary carriage of the investigation but the NSW counter terrorism squad had been brought in on it too. Broader sections of the AFP had also been drawn in and the commissioner himself was now part of the planning and decision-making process. Security on public transport had been stepped up and patrols around iconic buildings and the targets on the Scorpion's list were now scheduled around the clock.

Sid knew working on the inside could create a weird obsessiveness and anxiety about what could be – what could happen. When you were immersed in that world of irrational ideological hatred. When you had to watch the videos, the damage and the suffering and the online bragging. It was like dancing with shadows in the dark. When your job was to second guess an adversary that was as tangible as smoke you often had to fight to stop angst blooming into panic.

He walked on down Goulburn Street towards Chinatown. The streets were buzzing. An energised few blocks pulsing with life, but all the more fragile for it. It could all come unstuck so easily.

BBQ Palace was packed as usual with people who probably never thought twice about their safety. The shopfront window was a dripping menagerie of ducks, char siu, roast pork, chicken and squid. The smell was intoxicating. Whether it was 3 am or 3 pm didn't matter, there was always a noisy crowd in BBQ Palace. This was what Sid liked most about Sydney – the multicultural dynamism of the place; so different from the suffocating country town of his childhood. Sure they'd had the Italians and Greeks back then, but he didn't remember them making much of an impact, apart from the constant talk about the Mafia and the occasional strange name in the school playground. The Griffith of his childhood was a world that seemed stuck in time, dominated by the Masons on the one side and the Catholics on the other.

In the city the dull rhythm of stifling country Australia was finally shaken off: the afternoon teas, the meat and three veg – all that seemed like another country.

But he knew all that life, all that pulsing optimism, could be shattered in an instant. The Scorpion list had everything needed to shut the city down, to cause panic and destruction. Hit the transport network first then cause maximum fear. The transport ops here in Sydney had been war gaming it for years but really there was nothing anyone could do against a determined individual. What was it they said? 'We have to be right every time, the terrorists only have to win once' – any one of the things on the Scorpion's list of thirteen targets could do it.

That was the deal though, wasn't it? Sid thought as the queue at BBQ Palace moved forward and the fat man behind the counter quartered ducks with a precise and rhythmic swing of a heavy cleaver. That was what this society was all about. A level of trust. And trust was what was being lost. Trampled by terror and by politicians whose only answer seemed to be to fight against the threats by trusting people less – a double negative. In his good moments, Sid could kid himself that the real answer was to fight terror with intelligence and optimism. But he knew, they all knew, it would only take one big attack.

•

Cronulla could look a bit like Griffith in the 1980s too, Sid thought when he eventually got there. Sure it wasn't that bad, nice place to grow up probably, but fuck it was white. He joined the commuter crowds streaming off the train and into the shopping strip. The sun had pretty much gone but it was still light and the air was soft and velvety warm. It was only just after six, too early to head to Haifa's so he hiked it up the hill to the RSL club looking for a beer.

'The Club by the Sea' the sign said. More than a club, Sid thought – more like a lifestyle. Out the front two old blokes were practising their lawn bowls technique on the grass bowls court – it was a scene that transported him back to his childhood, to his grandfather in his lawn bowls whites, his little Mason's bag full of small town secrets and deals. Inside though, the RSL was all modern 'clubland' – pokies, schnitzel nights and a glass wall with a view that took your breath away. There was nothing like this in Griffith.

From up here you could see the full arc of the bay – all the way to Kurnell.

As if to reinforce Sid's uncomfortable nostalgia, the Johnny Nash hit from the 1970s was playing as he positioned himself and his beer to take advantage of the view. He could see clearly all right but the bright sunshiny day had begun to fade. Two men were fishing off the point at the southernmost end of the beach. There weren't too many people on the beach. A gaggle of school girls in bikinis, a few families. A dad teaching his kid to surf on a soft board in the small waves, and a few people swimming laps in Haifa's rockpool. One of them looked like it could even be her. Long, lazy, efficient strokes. Some older folks were out strolling along the path.

That's when he saw him. He almost choked on his beer. Mick Harrison making his way along the waterfront path towards the pool. He was moving slowly but the shuffle and the stoop were unmistakable even from this distance. What the fuck? What was he doing here? One of the swimmers stopped at the southern end of the pool. Haifa? Harrison walked towards her – stopped momentarily as if trying to decide what to do next – then walked on. That was it.

•

There was no sign of either Harrison or Haifa by the time Sid made it down to the pool. He ran up to her apartment block and hammered on the door.

'Did you see him?' he said when she answered. He was too loud and urgent, he realised.

'Good to see you too,' Haifa said. She was still in her swimmers and was drying the ends of her hair with a beach towel.

'Harrison. Did you see him? Down there at the pool?'

'What are you on about?'

'He was fucking there. Watching you. He walked right up to you in the pool. Harrison did.'

'For real? That was Harrison?' Her mouth fell open. Her eyes wide. She stopped drying her hair and put the towel over her shoulder.

He could see he had shocked her.

'Yeah. It was him. For sure.' He spoke more slowly and without the sense of alarm and urgency he'd been conveying.

'Wow, that's creepy. I wouldn't have recognised him from the photos I've seen. Where were you then?'

'Up at the club. I – don't worry. Anyway, did he say anything?'

'No. Nothing. He just looked at me a bit weird and then kept on walking. I just assumed he was a nutter.'

'He is.'

'You okay?' she asked, over the shock now. She smiled.

'Not really. No. You?'

'No, pretty shit actually.'

'Anything I can do?'

'Oh I don't know. How about containing that mad American? What the fuck is he doing going around torturing people?'

She moved forward and kissed him. Not long, but enough to say – nice to see you again.

He followed her down the hall and into the kitchen.

'You believe Chip really did that?' he said, dragging the conversation back.

'I have no reason not to. Even Shalomar wouldn't make that up. People have too much invested in that iconography. It's become the symbol of everything that went wrong. You know it has. What do you think? He didn't do it?'

'I don't know. He said he didn't.'

'And you believe him?'

'I don't know what to believe.'

Sid realised he was still carrying the four takeaway containers of dinner. He put them on the kitchen bench.

'I don't think I can keep working at K block,' Haifa said. 'It's fucking me up.'

'I gathered that much.'

'You know I'm no defender of extremists.' She put added emphasis on 'defender'. 'In fact, I've spent my life trying to run away from all the expectations and the doctrines of even the mildest form of that fucked-up religion I was born into. But I don't think I can keep doing what I'm doing.'

Haifa took some plates from the cupboard above the sink. She put them on the granite bench then gripped the edge of the stone. Her shoulders dropped. Her head bent forward. She looked exhausted.

'I just don't believe we're tackling it the right way,' she said after a pause.

Sid wasn't sure how to respond. He reached across for the food and started taking the containers out of the plastic bag. This was always going to be a difficult conversation. 'I know it's complicated. The politics of the Middle East. The wars. All the fucked-up things the West has done in the past few years but you can't deny it is Muslims, Islamic extremists, who are threatening to blow things up, to cut people's heads off and create mass destruction and confusion. Acts of terror.'

Haifa pushed herself upright and turned away to look out the window to the fading light, the sea and the sky melting into a purple summer haze. She kept her eyes focused on some distant point on the horizon.

'That's just the thing. Even thinking about it or talking about it has become dangerous for every Muslim. We listen to their conversations. We monitor them. But tell me who can define extremist? What are we really looking for? What is acceptable for people in a democracy to think, or say or read?'

'That's a big question. I'm not sure I'm the one who can answer it,' he said. 'I can't live your experience, I can only live mine. And I see young kids looking at manuals on how to make bombs and how to conduct jihad. That's not right.'

'Yes, but what do we do? Do we hold them without trial or rights because we think they might be up to something?

Because that's where we're at. We're just like them.' Haifa looked directly at him then with those wide smoky eyes. Waiting. Waiting for an answer that would satisfy the doubt and the contradictions.

Sid knew he couldn't give her the answer she wanted. 'So you think we should just leave them to go about plotting ways to blow up innocent people? That would really fuck us up – democracy or not.'

Haifa was coming to this from a place he'd never understand. 'And now we have a government and a prime minister designing laws that are specifically aimed at Muslims,' she said. 'Is it any wonder that they – we – all feel like we're under siege? I mean, let's be honest, the terror laws that allow us to hold anyone we have cause to suspect and then to question them as we like – let alone what fucking Donald Rumsfeld gets up to with his torture techniques – it's all designed to apply to Muslims – to my community.'

'Oh, come on. You know that's not how it is. Our intervention has already saved lives. If we hadn't acted –'

'Yes and they're criminals. Just like the other arm of my family. Lock them up, sure. Throw away the fucking key for all I care but treat them as criminals, don't go after them because they dress differently or don't eat pork.'

'That's a bit simplistic. It's not that easy and you know it.' Sid was starting to wonder where this was all going and how long it would go on for. Haifa seemed to be just warming up. It wasn't turning out to be the night he had expected.

'No, it's not,' she said almost sucking the words through a clenched jaw. 'But I tell you what, we're all being demonised by it. Every time you pick up a newspaper or turn on the TV news – there it is, this obsessive focus on "national security". I'm starting to agree with Shalomar. It is easy to see it as a coordinated attack on the Islamic community. And here I am working for the arm of government that's doing the most to traumatise my community. Even my brother – my fucking do-gooder brother – thinks I'm betraying my heritage and he's spent most of the past year turning himself into Mr Agreeable.'

Sid was struggling to follow her now. She was angry. Her mood had swung so fast. And what was she saying about her brother?

'What do you mean?' he said.

'Well, he obviously wants a seat in parliament, that's all I can think. Because he's working a new seam. He was never like this in the past. A few years ago I would have said he was as conservative as Shalomar on all this stuff.'

'Why didn't you say so?'

'Why should I?'

'What do you know about the Muslim Relief Fund?' Sid asked.

'The charity? What's that got to do with anything?'

'Shalomar is on the board. They're flipping real estate like crazy. We've tracked some of it and we know they've made profits. Not hard. We're in the middle of a real estate bubble. People are making fortunes out of rat-infested tunnels under the flight path in Tempe but the paperwork says this charity run by Shalomar and his mates is running at a loss. How does that work? Your brother's in on it too.'

This changed the tone. Haifa looked sceptical.

'What?'

'Yeah. He bought a few places from Shalomar. Hasn't sold them yet.'

'So? What would I know about it? Maybe he's just a canny investor.'

'It's a money-laundering exercise, Haifa. We know that much,' Sid said. 'And there's something big going down too. Not just a couple of kids with a camcorder and a sharp knife.'

Sid told her everything he knew about the Scorpion's list – the detailed plans.

'Someone's funding it,' he said. 'And we – well I – think it might be connected. And maybe your brother's involved too.'

Haifa turned away.

'Because he's Muslim? Because he's a community leader? Because he's my brother?' She didn't turn back to look at him.

'No. Because he's connected to Shalomar. Closer than anyone knew. Because he's involved in the money laundering somehow. Because – because we don't have a fucking clue who Scorpion is and at the moment it's the best lead we've got.'

Haifa still had her back to him. She didn't turn around.

'I think you'd better go,' she said.

28.

By the time summer came Ted Warburton had nothing left. Two years earlier the mortgage broker had convinced him to take out a million dollar loan to refit the milking shed. 'Why not buy yourself a nice bolthole up on the Gold Coast while you're at it?' she'd said.

She didn't even ask for much in the way of paperwork. Just proof that he owned the farm. Ted's family had been farming the flat 300 odd acres of dairy farm near Invergordon for more than a hundred years so no problem with that. But she didn't even ask for proof of income. A 'low doc' loan she called it and she just wrote down an estimate of farm profit at around $150,000 a year. He told the woman he'd be lucky to make half that in a good year but she said not to worry it was just so they could speed up the process. Seemed to know what she was talking about and he certainly needed the upgrade. There was no way he could carry on without getting some new machinery. He was turning seventy-three that year and he knew he couldn't keep going if he didn't do something. He and Audrey had no kids to hand it on to.

Ted had never actually seen the townhouse but it did look good in the brochures the broker had shown him. Anyway, turned out to be a complete dud. They couldn't even rent it. Then the repayments started piling up. A year later, Ted had to take out another big loan just to settle up on the arrears for the first mortgage. Things began to spiral out of control. Now the bank was circling the farm.

It all got too much for Aud. Ted had been a bit stressed about everything, he had to admit that. But he hadn't really hit the piss that hard. Anyway, it had been three months since Aud walked out. 'I'm going to my sister's,' she'd said. He hadn't seen her since. Funny, isn't it, how you think you know someone but even after fifty years of living together you find out one day you don't.

So he'd sold off most of the cows already by the time the fella from New South Wales rang him. He said he was running an operation up near Gerroa and had seen Ted had been selling off stock and equipment. Said he might be interested in anything Ted might want to flog off – milking stands, fertiliser. He said he'd pay good cash for any of it.

Next thing you know this bloke's knocking at the door. Young fella, just starting out. Looked like maybe a bit of Aboriginal in him, or Arab maybe. Anyway, good luck to him, Ted thought. This country's not the same these days. What with the halal food in the supermarkets and the bloody Chinese buying up all the land. Ted reckoned even he might have to sell out to the Chinese eventually unless the bank got to him first. He saw that show on the telly the other night too about the reffos from Burma who'd all gone out to Nhill over past Horsham. Saved the bloody town they reckoned.

The young fella had a look around. He seemed a bit disappointed in the near new milking stands but he was real keen on the fertiliser when he saw it in the shed.

'Eighty twenty-kilo bags. It's only enough for about five acres,' Ted told him.

The young bloke didn't have his farmer's licence with him, which by rights you should have if you're going out buying ammonium nitrate, but he offered cash – good money too. And the stuff had been sitting there a bit too long by then anyway. Probably wasn't that much chop anymore. You know how it goes after a while when the crystals start breaking down. You gotta use it fast or throw it out by the time it gets to that stage. And the bloody compliance costs for buying, trucking and keeping that stuff were killing farmers around here now. Bureaucracy gone mad, Ted reckoned. So many licences and different government departments to deal with, how was a farmer expected to pay for it all? Selling and carting the stuff had become a nightmare. Ted could understand why but it did make it hard for blokes.

Anyway this young fella didn't have his farmer's licence on him but he had a bloody big truck and – well, he was offering a good price. Ted's place obviously wasn't the first stop the young bloke had made either, there were plenty of other bags already in there. He needed all the help he could get Ted reckoned, starting out in this business now, and God only knew Ted needed help right at the moment too. So he told him he could have it as long as he kept quiet.

He did have his dangerous goods signs and his transport paperwork so that was okay. At least he wouldn't have too much trouble at the heavy vehicle inspections – although Ted told him he could never be sure when the bastards were open. If he wanted to avoid them, best to travel at night or on the weekend.

29.

Chip Walker had long ago stopped expecting life to be predictable. It took you wherever it wanted to take you. But having said that, within the randomness of the journey there were always a few constants. He had found, for instance, that it didn't matter where he was in the world, or what sort of regime happened to be in power in whatever country he happened to be in at any given time, there were always two certainties. Whether it was Riyadh, Kabul or Grozny you could always find someone to provide hard liquor and hard sex in exchange for hard currency. And here in Sydney there was certainly no shortage of either commodity, although the hard sex came at a premium price.

Almost any sort of kink was tolerated at Club Pigalle, a word-of-mouth establishment tucked away in a small warehouse in Francis Street, just down from Hyde Park. It had been serving a loyal clientele of well-heeled and powerful patrons for decades. A lot had changed about the neighbourhood in that time but it would take more than a bit of gentrification to force the judges, politicians and business elite out into the suburbs.

The 'Russian' twins were good. They were tall, blonde and athletic, and as he had requested, they were both wearing leather masks. They called themselves Olga and Masha – probably Moldovans or Ukrainians, Chip thought as they began tying his hands behind his back. One slipped the collar over his head and tightened it around his neck. The other one undid the top three buttons of her tight-fitting blouse to reveal more cleavage and began playfully striking him with the paddle. Chip wanted it to be slow. He'd paid good money. There was plenty of time.

The blindfold hadn't been part of his request. There was a certain amount of licence afforded to the girls in this business but he knew instinctively and immediately when it happened that this wasn't part of the floor show. His concerns were confirmed when the first punch hit him in the stomach and took all the breath from his lungs. The second came down over the back of his head and sent him crumbling to the floor. The gag was put on fast and it wasn't the gentle hand of a former waitress from Kiev doing the tying anymore. Chip tried calling out but all that did was earn him a kick in the ribs that sent pain shooting through one side of his body. More than one rib cracked, he reckoned. He held the scream in, not wanting to give whoever was doing the hitting any satisfaction. If the blindfold and the gag weren't bad enough, his head was then forced inside a sack. Two sets of hands, rough masculine-smelling hands, picked him up off the floor and carried him out of the room. Doors opened, fresh warm air enveloped him briefly as he was thrown into the back of a van. He thought of his mother. He hadn't thought about her for years.

•

When the phone rang, Sid was having one of those dreams where he was constantly having to overcome ridiculous obstacles to get somewhere on time. Doors opened only to reveal more doors, then fences that had to be climbed and stairs that seemed to go on forever but just came to an end way off the ground. He had no idea what the dreams meant but he'd been having them off and on for years. They were some of his better dreams.

It was 5.17 in the morning. Still dark.

'Sid? It's Cavan.'

'Huh?'

'Cavan. Maskey, for Pete's sake. Wake up.'

'What's up?'

'It's your mate Chip. He's been hit. He's alive, but only just.'

That jolted him awake. He was out of bed in one smooth motion.

'Jesus – where are you?'

He put the phone on speaker and started dressing in a hurry.

'Clyde. Outside Freeman's panelbeaters in Berry Street. The paramedics are here. They're taking him in now. Okay with you? He won't make it much longer without the professionals anyway.'

'Shit,' Sid said. What the hell was Chip doing there? Outside? 'I'll be right out.'

•

Despite the early hour, the flashing blue and red lights were attracting a crowd of interested onlookers in the pre-dawn gloom. Where did all these people come from? Sid wondered. There was nothing out here but half-empty warehouses, busted arse panelbeating shops and, of course, an on-the-quiet detention and interrogation facility that was certainly not on the list of local attractions. Cavan Maskey wouldn't have known about it either.

Maskey was over near the panelbeater's entrance, smoking and talking to a forensic. A flash was pulsing behind them. Someone taking photographs of the scene. Tape had been rolled out marking off a section of bitumen car park about the size of a basketball court in front of the entrance.

The front, of course, was a façade. The real entrance to the intel facility was around the side through an unmarked door.

'Hey, Cav. I got here as fast as I could. Where is he?'

'He's gone. They scooped him up about a half hour ago.'

'Is he okay?'

'He'll live. Probs. He was in a pretty bad way. Bashed hard and, get this, he's had his kneecaps shot out, like something from the Falls Road. I haven't seen anything like that for years. If he does live he may never walk again. I remember seeing guys like that at home. They had some big stories to tell but they never got out of their wheelchairs.'

Sid felt the air leave his lungs, his head began to spin. He reached out for the factory wall to hold some of his weight for fear he'd collapse. His own knees were weak and his legs felt like they were about to give way underneath him. He felt sick. Then angry.

'Anyone see anything?' he asked once he'd regained his balance and his breath.

'What do you think?'

'Yeah, didn't think so.'

'A young apprentice from the cabinet-maker's place down the road came in on the early train, found him on the drive there in a pool of blood. One thing I don't get,' Maskey said looking up at the panelbeater's sign, 'why here? What the fuck was he doing here?'

'I guess we'll need to ask him,' Sid said.

'It's a hit with a message anyway. S'pose you've got some idea what the message is. You don't need to tell me. Your business. You and the spooks. But this looks like you and the brothers are in some deep shit. The jihadis don't do this, the fuckin' gangs do. This is Brothers for Life – or at least what's left of 'em.'

'Yep. Deep shit all right.' Sid sighed. 'We'll handle it from here. You can tell your guys to go once they're through. We've made enough of a spectacle here already.'

'Uh huh. Whatever you say. Just get me some clearance.' Maskey paused.

'One other thing,' he said, 'he was having a lot of trouble breathing, he had nothing on but he was soaking wet, not sweat either, like someone had tried to drown him. Oh and this –'

Maskey signalled to the photographer.

'Gaz, show Sid here that thing on his chest.'

The photographer flicked through his photos on the camera. He found what he was looking for and handed it over. Maskey held it up for Sid to see the screen. It was a close-up of Chip's torso. Two claws stretched across his stomach and a recognisable tail wound its way up one side – a sting hung over the spot where his heart was.

'There. Looks like it's been drawn on with permanent marker – or maybe stencilled on. Someone's spent a bit of time on it. What is it do you reckon? A crab maybe – a spider?'

Sid didn't need to guess.

30.

'Thing is, because it happened where it did we've got fucking cameras everywhere. We've got this thing covered from every angle.'

Damien Murphy was pulling up the CCTV footage from the Clyde site.

'Here: 3.47 am. The van pulls up. Watch this.'

He clicked between four cameras all showing different angles of the driveway to the shopfront. The footage was pretty good considering how dark it was. The van was a late model tradesman's white Toyota. No windows behind the front seat. Two thickset men built like club bouncers got out dressed head to toe in black. They were wearing balaclavas. They were – easily – 130 kilos each. One opened the back door of the van, the other dragged Chip out by the feet. Chip's not small, plenty of burgers and Bud have gone in over the years, but the bouncer dragged him out like he was an inflatable doll. He was barely conscious, that much was easy to see. They dropped him on the ground. One of them delivered a kick. The other one pulled something out of his pocket. He lifted Chip's head up off the ground, shouted something at him then passed something to his mate. A flash went off. A camera or more likely a phone. They let Chip drop to the ground again.

'What are they doing? Taking photos?'

'Looks like they wanted a memento of the occasion.'

'Wait. Here it comes,' Murphy said. 'It's pretty brutal. Not PG viewing.'

The guy with the phone pulled something else out of his pocket. A small handgun. The gun fired. One shot directly into one of Chip Walker's kneecaps. The American twitched and convulsed on the ground. Then another shot directly into the other kneecap. Chip didn't move at all after that. The one without the gun delivered a final kick to the kidneys then they both got into the van and drove off.

'The numberplate?' Sid said. 'I don't suppose –'

'No. That came off a VW Passat reported stolen the day before in Lidcombe.'

'Yep. Figures. Any news from the clinic?'

'Um yeah. Here.' Murphy pulled up an official-looking email. 'Says he's stable but critical. Conscious.'

'Don't suppose it mentions visiting hours,' Sid said.

•

Chip had been taken to a private and protected ward at Royal North Shore Hospital. Sid got there just after 6 pm. The dinner must have just gone around because the place smelled like boiled chicken, broccoli and custard. The food in the rest of the country might have been changed by decades of interesting immigration but today's hospital food would look almost identical to the hospital food of a hundred years ago. Who eats fucking custard and jelly except when they're laid up in hospital?

It had been a long time since he'd eaten himself. It was only a bit over twenty-four hours ago that he'd been lining up at BBQ Palace looking forward to a night with Haifa. No point going over all that again, he told himself. Things were moving too fast now. The smell of the hospital food was making him feel slightly ill. How could anyone eat that shit?

Chip certainly wasn't having to suffer that indignity. He'd be eating through a tube for a while yet. He was almost unrecognisable. His face was a swollen mess and, even if he was awake, he'd have trouble seeing out of the slits that were left of his eyes. Big black bruises ran across his cheeks and his lips were like two sweet blood sausages. He was lying on his back. His legs elevated and heavily bandaged.

A monitor kept a constant beeping rhythm.

The doctors had said he was conscious but he didn't look it.

'Chip? Martini time?'

He grunted something indecipherable in reply and lifted one arm.

'Can you talk, mate?'

A bluish tongue emerged to dampen his two swollen lips.

'Vodka. With a twist. Don't put any fucking olives in it,' he said in a whisper.

Sid had to lean in to hear him properly.

'Can't get a decent martini anywhere in this country.' He grimaced in pain as his attempt at laughter was cut short.

'Yeah, well, we'll make sure we find you one when you get out of here. Who did this? Any ideas?'

Chip said nothing for a long time. Sid thought he might have passed out. Then he coughed, shuddered with pain and spoke.

'Has to be Shalomar,' he said. 'Why else would they have taken me back there?' Another long pause and another painful cough. 'But how would he know? He was packaged up the entire time. He wouldn't have known where he was.'

'Someone must know.'

'They wanted to know what we knew about Scorpion.'

'What the fuck? They wanted to know what *we* knew?'

'That's what I said to them. But they just wanted to know how much we knew. And they wanted to know where Harrison was.'

'And?' Sid asked.

'They got nothing out of me. You don't know anything, there's nothing to tell.' He paused again. 'Anyway, good luck to them. We can't even find Harrison so I doubt they will.'

Sweat was starting to break out across his forehead. The talking was taking it out of him.

'They also said it was a message from –' he trailed off without finishing the sentence.

'A what?'

'From Goulburn. Supermax. *Don't fuck with us.* One of them mentioned a doctor.'

'A doctor?'

'That's what he said. They kept taking fucking photos. "Smile for the doctor," he said one time. That was it. Probably nothing. Never mentioned it again.'

'Dr Shalomar?'

'Could be. They're all a doctor of something. Take your pick.'

Sid heard it coming before it hit the surface. A rumble of a cough from deep within. Chip started to shake, then heave. A thin line of yellow mucus rolled from the corners of his mouth. The colour of his face changed dramatically and quickly – first pale, then red, then turning towards purple.

'Shit. Chip? Are you –'

No, he fucking wasn't all right. Sid ran to the door and shouted for help. A nurse was already running towards the room. The constant low beep of the monitor had flatlined into a long drone. The nurse pulled off the sheet, checked the machine then hit a large red button just above the bed.

Within seconds the room was full of people urgently but methodically going through a drill. One big male nurse started CPR, another man, who Sid assumed was a doctor, flicked quickly through the paperwork at the end of the bed.

'Adrenalin,' he said, matter of fact.

Someone else began making up the intravenous go-juice.

'One, two, three.' The nurse giving the CPR was counting quietly. He looked up at the monitor. 'Still nothing,' he said.

'Okay, move.' Another pair of hands slapped defibrillator paddles on Chip's chest.

'Stand clear.'

The current surged. Nothing.

The big nurse came straight back in and started CPR again.

'One, two, three.' Pump.

Nothing was working. Nothing was fucking working, Sid thought, panicked now by the lack of response. *Do something. Try harder.* Chip was dying on the bed in front of them. The monitor was still a flat line.

He was starting to turn blue.

'Fuck. Fuck. Fucking do something!' Sid's thoughts burst to the surface.

'You shut up.' The response came back just as loud. 'What do you think we're trying to do? This isn't an episode of *CSI*, Sherlock. One. Two. Three.'

No. More like *The Wire*, Sid thought.

The paddles went back on.

'Stand clear.'

Another surge. Then a beep, slow but persistent. The purple colour began draining from Chip's face.

'He's alive,' the nurse said. 'He's breathing.'

'That's enough for one day,' the doctor said, looking at Sid. 'You can leave now.'

•

When he got back to Surry Hills, Sid went straight out to the back shed. His rusting old ten speed was under a worn plastic tarpaulin. It had been a long time between rides. The tyres were flat, there was no seat, but the combination lock was still wound around the crossbar and the code was the same as every four digit code he ever used: 1978. The year he was born. He wheeled it through the house and chained it to the front iron railing. He pulled the chain. It didn't break at least. Probably secure enough, although you'd have to be pretty desperate to want to steal this penny-farthing, he thought. He went back inside and poured himself a large Bushmills, followed by a few more.

31.

Sid woke early with an Irish hangover and questions raging through his brain. He didn't think he'd have to wait too long to hear from Harrison. But he really had no idea when that would be or where.

And what about Haifa? He could see she was upset but was she being just a bit precious? She knew the game. If she didn't like it, maybe she should leave. Where would that leave them though? His own feelings aside, Haifa was damn good at her job. She was the real deal. A thorough and determined investigator and of course an authentic Muslim entree into a community that was notoriously hard to crack. She could build trust quicker than any of them. And if she left? What then? Would that be the end of their connection? The end of whatever this was that had been happening. He definitely didn't want that. Above all else he didn't want that.

Unlike Haifa, Sid didn't really sweat the big ideas, the big constructs. She was right. He did view the world as a lot more black and white than she did. Maybe they'd never overcome that. But what was her brother playing at? It was clear he wasn't entirely what he seemed. What was with the real estate investments? The charities and the connections to Shalomar? Just coincidence? Just unavoidable community contacts? Funny then how they played it up for the TV cameras, like that evening on *Crossroads*. What did she say? 'He's working a new seam.' And what are they doing with the money? Where's that going? Who are all the others on the charity board? Are any of them who they really say they are?

•

He found the note pinned to the doormat under a brick. He nearly tripped over it as he was leaving.

'Ward Park. Alone. No funny business.' The note said in large, barely legible letters.

Ward Park sat on the edge of the old housing commission blocks at the top of Devonshire Street, across from the corner with Riley Street and just up from the Shakespeare. There were a few bench seats under a big eucalyptus on one side that afforded some shade and a good view of everyone coming and going. Sid sat on one of them. He didn't think he'd have to wait long. Only long enough for Harrison to make sure he was on his own and there was no 'funny business' about. At this time of day there was a steady stream of foot traffic through the park with houso residents coming and going, out for their first snifter of the day, and the cool young things on their way to the cafes on Crown Street for their lattes and green juice.

Sid smelled him first – well before he saw him. The dishevelled figure came from behind him and sat down on the bench.

'Sidney,' he said eventually, after making a big show of looking up and down the park.

'Fuck, Mick. Lost your deodorant?'

'You want my help or are you just going to sit there and insult me?'

'Good question. I don't know if I do want your help actually but it seems at this stage I don't have a choice.'

'No closer to finding the mysterious Scorpion then?' he sneered.

'Obviously not.'

'Well I'm all ears. How can I help?'

Jesus. How did he get himself into this situation? Sitting here passing the time of day with a fucking battle-crazed murderer who smelled like an old running shoe.

'Next time you get the urge to start chopping someone's appendages off I want you to ask a few questions for me,' Sid said.

'Uh huh. Such as?'

'The night before last a couple of thugs beat the crap out of one of my team. In between shooting off his kneecaps they mentioned a doctor – "smile for the doctor" they said. See if anyone knows who that is or what they were talking about.'

'Any ideas yourself?'

'Not really. Nothing substantial anyway. Look for connections Mick. Any jihadis talking about a Doctor, I want to know who.'

The parade continued in front of them. The air was still and humid. Despite the tang seeping from Harrison none of the passing traffic was paying them any attention.

'While we're at it, what's up with stalking Haifa? What the fuck, Mick? Leave her out of it will you.'

'Just wanted a closer look.' Harrison's stubbled, weather-beaten face broke into a wide grin. 'Haifa? Nice. You're on to something there, mate. I'd go for it too. Well – if I could.'

'You might need to take a shower first,' Sid said.

'Fuck off.'

The two of them sat staring out at the park, not saying anything for a while, watching the random inner-city life unfold before them. Commuters. Dog walkers. Gym junkies. Addicts. Old. Young. Some striding through the park with purpose. Others just ambling through their morning.

'Look at them,' Harrison said after a while. 'They wouldn't have a fucking clue, would they? They don't know what we did. They don't want to know what we did. They don't even care. And you know what? I'm with them. What was it all for? Tell me that. What was all this for?' Harrison held up the arm with the prosthetic hand. 'We went there. We blew the crap out of the place. We secured the villages. We paid off the war lords. We shot the Talibs to the shithouse. We built schools, we built hospitals. We gave them all hope. Then we just left and, apart from fucking ourselves up, what did we achieve?'

Harrison's good arm was waving about and his left leg seemed to be moving involuntarily.

'Yeah. Hardly seems worth it. Even I'll admit that,' Sid said.

'Something good is going to come out of it in the end. I'll make sure of that.' Harrison coughed and scratched nervously at the side of his neck. He must have been going at that for a while. Scabs had begun to form.

'What, by killing everyone you think is a fucking terrorist? Come on, Mick, you need help that's what you need.'

'Yeah and so do you. That's why I'm here, right?'

'So it would seem. Yes.'

'Okay then. If I'm going to keep assisting the authorities I need some money. You gotta put me on the payroll.'

'You know I can't do that.'

'Nothing official. Just some cash. A grand that's all. That'll get me through for a while.'

'What are you on? More than just the Oxys, that's for sure. Ice?'

'Anything that helps, mate. Anything that helps.'

Shit. That's just what Sid needed. Paying a fucking psycho Ice addict for information. If anyone found out – shit. Sid pulled out his wallet. Checked again that no one was paying them any attention, and handed over all the cash he had.

'Almost 200 bucks there I think. That's all I've got for now.'

'I'll need more.'

'Yep. There'll be more later, okay?'

Harrison grabbed the money and shuffled off.

'We'll talk,' he said as he was leaving.

Sid felt an uncomfortable anxiety creeping over him. He got up and continued the walk down Devonshire Street to the office. He couldn't shake the smell.

32.

THE OLD HOUSE WAS ONE OF THE LAST LEFT ON WILLEROO Street. Haifa had never understood why they called them California bungalows. Not that she'd ever been to California but she'd never seen anything like them in any of the movies. This was the house she'd grown up in – a small single storey dark brick three-bedroom cottage with a patch of lawn out the front and a driveway up one side leading to a single garage. A picture of suburban stability defiantly resisting the changing world around it. Most of the other houses had been demolished long ago and replaced with squat blocks of flats. After her mother died, Haifa rarely came back here. It felt claustrophobic just to be walking up the street.

Haifa knew enough about her brother's movements to know that he wouldn't be in at 10 o'clock on a Friday morning – he'd be out at work at Lucas Heights, then taking tea and preparing for Friday prayers.

She walked up the six tiled steps to the small covered patio area. Her father used to sit there and smoke in the evening.

The old chair had long gone but the small table with the mosaic top that she'd made in high-school art class was still there pushed up into the corner.

Something was different though. It took her a few seconds to notice but, since the last time she'd been here, the front windows had been barred and a new heavy security door had been fitted. She put her old front door key into the lock. It turned and opened – the new door had been keyed the same as the old one behind it. Security like this would have been unheard of when Haifa and Hakim were young. Back then this was one of the most respected – some would have said feared – houses in Lakemba, thanks to the notoriety of her two older brothers. No one would have dreamed of messing with the Houranis. Not that her brothers were home often. They were much older than both Haifa and Hakim – almost a different generation. Certainly their parents treated them that way. Taleb and Tariq were always welcomed and lavished with love and attention but their lives were set on a different course. For Hakim and Haifa, home was a strict environment of study and family responsibility. As the youngest child and the only girl, the boundaries for Haifa had been stifling. She couldn't wait to get out, to get away from the expectations. If her father hadn't died when he did she may not have ever been able to. It was only when he was gone that her mother accepted her need to break free. Her brothers, Hakim in particular, had never been entirely comfortable with it and they certainly weren't comfortable with where she'd ended up – with what she'd become.

That was what puzzled her the most about Hakim's transformation. She remembered him as a devout and strict Muslim. When they were younger, he'd become more and more intolerant of her refusal to accept what he considered were her responsibilities as a young Muslim woman. He railed against the clothes she wore and the people she mixed with. He lectured her about how the West was the root cause of Muslim grievances. He prayed, he studied, and he was constantly in search of a theological answer to everything.

Haifa fled to university looking for her own answers at about the same time Hakim went abroad.

And now he'd become the pin-up boy for modern, moderate Australian Islam, feted by politicians. She didn't get it. All the while, according to Sid, Hakim had also been buying and selling real estate with Shalomar, a preacher who'd been running an Islamic centre that helped groom young boys into radicals and funded and organised their trips to the jihadi front lines. And he was now linked to a dodgy charity that was laundering money for the same purpose. It just didn't add up. Sid was right about that. But Haifa needed to see it for herself. And what did it mean? She knew what Hakim's motivations were. She knew how he and others in the community felt about what had been happening. The constant ratcheting up of the terrorist rhetoric. It was driving some of them further towards the radical end of the spectrum. They didn't feel welcome here anymore and they were so easily influenced. She could see that but she couldn't sanction the violence. That was never the right answer.

She stepped into the hall. The smell of rose water still lingered in the musty air just as it always had, even all these years since her mother had died. With it came the rush of nostalgia and suffocating memories. Not all of them bad. Her childhood had been isolated but she had been loved and, when she was young at least, had wanted for nothing. It was only as she grew older that she found she was questioning more. And the answers were never enough.

It was a simple house. Three bedrooms, a lounge room, a small bathroom and a kitchen. The lounge room had barely been touched in years and looked as formal as ever. An old couch, two comfortable armchairs, a small coffee table, a fake log gas heater in the fireplace and a black-and-white portrait photograph of their parents on the wall.

Hakim had taken her parents' bedroom as his own and what had been the 'boys' room had become an office of sorts with a desk and a computer, bookshelves and Hakim's many framed degrees, awards and achievements on the walls. She pushed open the door to her old room expecting to see it as she remembered – a single bed, a desk for study, the posters of Savage Garden and the Red Hot Chili Peppers, the shelf of stuffed toys, pictures of girl friends, the old lava lamp and the beanbag that she used to sit in for hours on end reading. All of it was gone. She took a deep breath. The walls were instead plastered with passages from the Qur'an. A prayer rug sat on the floor and there was a basin for washing. A huge picture of the al-Aqsa mosque in Jerusalem covered one wall.

The corner by the window, the spot where her bed had been for all of her childhood, was now taken up with a small desk and a large three-drawer filing cabinet.

The transformation shocked her but she regathered herself and walked in, still hoping to find some familiar reminders of herself. Hakim hadn't ever told her he had removed the remnants of her childhood from the house but then she hadn't been back to ask either. She was tempted to turn around – walk out and never return. She still wasn't entirely sure why she'd come but part of it was to see how her brother was living and to unravel some of the uncertainties that Sid had planted in her mind.

She walked to the desk. There were files piled neatly in one corner. She opened the one on the top. Inside were dozens of newspaper clippings. 'Teenage Terror', 'Suburban Jihad', 'The bedroom bomber', '#global Jihad'. Articles on how a generation of young Muslims were being groomed by Daesh, calls for stripping 'Aussie terrorists' of their citizenship. Some passages were underlined for emphasis. One article spoke of the split emerging within the Sunni community, driven by overseas preachers coming to Australia espousing a stricter interpretation of Islam and seeking to influence young people. There was apparently a 'power struggle' at the top of the national peak Islamic council. It looked like a research file, but why would Hakim want to keep such stuff?

She opened the top drawer of the filing cabinet. It was neatly packed with old religious texts and some small wooden boxes with beautiful mother-of-pearl inlay which held what looked like old handwritten religious passages. There were a few maps as well, neatly folded. Maps of Afghanistan with inscriptions in Farsi, place names and dates. She unfolded one. Uruzgan province. Shaded areas marked Taliban-held territory. Crosschecked areas – smallish islands of territory – were marked as ISAF. Date – March 2010. Under that was another map with a vast area stretching from Yemen in the south through Egypt, Jordan, Syria and Iraq and all the way to Hungary and Moldova shaded in red. 'The Ottoman Caliphate' was stamped across it in flowing Arabic script.

The second drawer had more files. Some of a technical nature. Much of it in Arabic, some in English. She picked one up. *The Art of War*, volume three. She flicked through it – a slickly produced, thorough technical terror manual. There were chapters on interrogation techniques, sniper training, instructions on bomb making and chemical weapons. A sick feeling was rising in her stomach. She dropped the book carefully back in its place.

She closed the drawer. Her breathing was heavy. Her hands were shaking. There would be an explanation. There must be. She opened the third drawer and almost closed it again without looking further. There were two plastic Coles shopping bags in there. Puffed up like two stuffed pillowcases. She lifted one out and eased off the elastic bands that had been wound around it. She opened the top of the bag and took another sharp intake of breath. The bag was stuffed with money neatly packaged and stacked in denominations. Bundles of notes – five, ten, twenty and fifty dollar bundles. There must have been thousands of dollars, tens of thousands, hundreds of thousands. Haifa had never seen so much money.

She was so taken aback, so preoccupied, she didn't hear the front door open. She didn't hear the creaking in the hallway, and she didn't hear the door being pushed open.

It was the click of the safety catch being released from the Glock that dragged her back. Hakim was pointing it directly at her.

'Hakim?'

'Haifa?' Her brother lowered the gun. 'What the –'

'Exactly.' She gestured around the room. 'What the fuck, Hakim? What have you done to my bedroom? What is all this?'

Their relationship in the last few years had become more and more formal – more his doing than hers, Haifa thought. But all of a sudden the easy quarrelling banter of their childhood came rushing back. Hakim was speaking to her in English like they used to. The only thing different was that Hakim was holding a gun.

Haifa looked down at the pistol in her brother's hand.

'What's with the weapon?'

'What's with sneaking around in the house while I'm not here?' Hakim responded.

'Last time I was here this room was mine.'

'Yes, well, you haven't been around for a while.'

'But what's it all about, Hakim? What's with the maps . . . the quotes – the fifty ways to blow yourself up manual – and all the money for fuck's sake?'

Hakim's look hardened.

'What are you trying to say?'

'You know what I'm getting at. All this bullshit you've been going on about. All this "we need to deal with the terror threat" and "we need to deal with the radicals", the TV appearances, the public profile. That's not you. You might be fooling some people, but you're not fooling me. And here.' Haifa picked up the file of clippings. 'What's this? Are you doing a research paper on Australian jihadis?'

'Know your enemy, Haifa. Isn't that what they tell you at spy school?'

'No. What they taught me at spy school is look beyond the obvious. Look for the unusual. Look for any behaviour that seems different or out of the ordinary. And right now, Hakim – right now, that's what I'm looking at. How do you square the circle? That's what I want to know. How do you go from refusing to let your mother and your sister leave the house without their faces covered to defending "Australian" values? How do you go from shaking hands with a cleric we all know has been facilitating recruitment and travel for the jihadis to standing next to the prime minister and calling on Muslims to do more to tackle the extremism? You think no one's watching those contradictions?'

'I'm doing more for this community than you are. Running around listening to people's phone calls. Tracing their movements. Finding bombers under the beds when there are none. These are your people . . . our people.'

'Yeah, maybe that's the difference. I'm not doing this for us – for the Muslims. I'm doing it for everyone. Yes, some of the politicians are exploiting the fear. But you'd know all about that, wouldn't you? Standing there next to Williams, nodding for the cameras. And then we find out you're also working with Shalomar on the board of a charity that's funnelling money to the jihadis.'

Hakim put the gun down but he took a step towards her. 'What are you saying?'

'I'm saying what you know. But I don't understand. I need an explanation. I need to know you are not as mixed up in it as some are starting to think you are. Because I come back here and I find all this?' Haifa threw her hands wide. 'Maps of Uruzgan province 2010?' she continued. 'Isn't that when you were in Geneva? Were you in Geneva? I don't know anymore. I just don't know what to believe, Hakim.'

Haifa waved her arm around the room. She reached in to the filing cabinet and pulled out one of the bags of cash.

'And what's this? There must be tens of thousands here.'

'Put it back, Haifa. It's money tirelessly collected from good people who want to do nothing more than help. You've seen us. Well, maybe not – we don't do much collecting in Cronulla,' he sneered. 'But we are out there every day, talking to people, collecting money from those who haven't much to give. There is suffering and pain. People want to help. They are not blind to what is going on. And the quickest way to get the money to where it's needed is through the Hawala. In cash. That's what that is. That's a truckload of medicine. It's a week's food for a refugee camp.'

'But you wouldn't know where it's going,' she said. 'In the end how can you maintain credible accountability? Questions will be asked. Questions are being asked.'

Haifa was more confused than ever. Hakim moved closer.

'Listen, sister. We do things differently, okay? But essentially we are both working towards the same end goal. We need leaders in the mainstream. That is what I am trying to do here. I'm trying to become part of the system to protect our rights within it. But I'm being more honest about it than you. At least I haven't thrown away my identity and my culture.'

'Bullshit, Hakim. You're coming apart. You haven't convinced me.'

'And perhaps I never will.'

'What about the brothers? Have you convinced them? Have they thrown it all away too? Or is that a culture you can identify with too? Another culture of violence. It's all so fucked up, Hakim. What all this has done to us. It's all so fucked up.'

'Haifa. Don't talk like that.'

He tried to reach out to her. She pulled away.

'I have nothing to do with them,' he said. 'I haven't seen or spoken to them for years. They are a stain on our family.' He almost spat the words out.

'And, anyway, don't you talk to me about violence. Waterboarding, Haifa? Waterboarding? What sort of message is that?'

'Is that true?'

'Shalomar says it is.'

'He says a lot of things. Not all of them are correct.'

'He wouldn't lie about this. Why would he?'

'And I suppose you think the retaliation was in order. That is what it was, wasn't it?'

'I don't know anything about that. But you can see how these things spiral in the wrong direction.'

'Did you tell the prime minister that?'

That one hit a chord.

'Yes, I walk a fine line, I admit that. But I do it for the greater good.'

'You're a contradiction all right. I just hope you know where you're going. You need to know though that not everyone is as convinced of your intentions as those who want to use you for their own reasons.'

'None of us know where we're going, sister. Only Allah knows. That is the truth.'

'Fuck off, Hakim.'

She turned and stared into the inky black of her brother's stern eyes, searching for some hint, a clue to who he was, what he'd become and what was driving him. She thought she knew him. Now she knew she didn't. Haifa walked out more afraid than she'd been in a very long time.

33.

IN THE PRIME MINISTER'S OFFICE, BRIAN WILLIAMS WAS SIPPING his first espresso of the day. He was feeling good, energised.

The news had begun to unfold live on the 24-hour news channels just after 5 am. As usual, tip-offs had been made to the hacks and when the bomb disposal and counter terrorism units got going their every move was recorded and broadcast to the nation. There was no stopping it once it started rolling. The quiet suburban street was overrun in minutes with armoured vehicles, police cars and TV broadcast vans. The front door of the two-storey brick veneer house was broken down with brutal efficiency, the sleeping residents were wheeled out into the street and a dazed teenager cuffed and rushed into a waiting custody van. As expected, the family was stunned. They stood around looking shocked and unsure of what to do. Police liaison officers were trying to explain what was happening even as the house was being sectioned off and teams of police in heavy armour and bomb detection equipment filed through the front door. Within minutes, a crowd of neighbours had gathered to watch the drama unfold and they were immediately set upon by reporters searching for personal details of the 'ordinary, polite, quiet family that kept to themselves'.

A big operation. A rolling drama broadcast to the nation. Impressive. These were the days that made him. Days when the government got out on the front foot. Brian Williams was pumped. He loved this end of the day. Sure, he was pretty good at the other end of the day too. He could stay up talking policy, drinking red and arguing with all comers for hours on end but nothing gave clarity like 5 am. That was thinking time.

The press conference he'd called was a good six hours away yet. Williams walked over to the Menzies desk and picked up the day's red folder full of briefing papers prepared overnight by the media team. They usually came up with some talking points, some prepared lines and even a full speech if it was needed. Today wasn't one of those days. Today Brian Williams would be writing his own speech.

The police operation was still unfolding live on the TV. He picked up a pen and scrawled 'Fear' across the front of the briefing paper.

Fuck the AG's department. They'd been sending memos asking for the rhetoric to be turned down. Seemed some of the spooks thought the same too. It was too inflammatory, they said – counterproductive. Bullshit. They were fucking public servants. What would they know? In fact, fuck them too. This was an opportunity. Just what he needed. Get all the top brass there too – all the commissioners. And bloody Gray would have to earn his money today as well.

The PM was relaxed now, confident. He put another pod in the Nespresso machine and hit the button. He looked up again at the television.

'This is your government keeping you safe,' he said.

•

'This is your government keeping you safe.'

Here we go, Sid thought, Brian Williams in full flight. He was addressing the nation from the safety of the AFP's high security conference room in Canberra behind a lectern with the reassuring, sparkling AFP shield emblazoned on the front, polished up for the TV cameras. Williams had Gray standing next to him and the Minister for Justice, the clean-cut young James Morris, on the other side, looking like the young self-assured suburban solicitor that he was. They were flanked by the AFP Commissioner and the NSW Police Commissioner with all the epaulets shining on their shoulders. Williams was announcing a new public terrorism alert system. The current four levels – low, medium, high and extreme – were going to be replaced with a more nuanced five-step system – not expected, possible, probable, expected and certain. 'Not expected' and 'possible' already seemed so last century, Sid thought. Truth is it would never get below probable ever again. Might as well have a three-step system – 'probable', 'likely', 'bang – we're fucked'.

'What happened this morning is another example of how vigilant we need to be in the face of this increasing threat,' Williams said, looking straight to the camera. 'As Commissioner Bryant has already detailed, the young man detained this morning will be charged with conspiring to commit a terrorist act. A second man is also due to be arrested and charged with weapons offences relating to the same plot. These two men were planning to target officers at this year's Anzac Day commemorations. A blatant and brazen attack on the very soul of this nation. Now, I don't want to prejudice proceedings any further. It must be said these are allegations only at this stage but it's not spilling state secrets to acknowledge that the planning was well underway and was extremely sophisticated. Anzac Day is, of course, still some months away but the Australian public can rest assured that security will be stepped up at all public events.'

The commissioners, the ASIO chief and the minister were all nodding along in agreement like a row of puppies.

'I've said it before and I'll say it again,' Williams went on. 'They are coming after us. Every one of us. They are coming after every democracy and every society that values freedom and liberty.

'This arrest this morning is proof yet again that the murderous frenzy that has gripped the Middle East has, and will, continue to reach out to us. We are not immune to the long grip of evil. The intent here was to murder innocent people, innocent Australians. These are troubling times but this vortex of evil will not prevail.'

The PM gathered up his notes and moved to walk away from the lectern but the assembled media was bursting with questions. They began shouting over the top of each other, the usual pissing contest to see who could get the leader's attention first. The cameras didn't cut away but Sid heard the odious Jenson Burton's voice rising through the melee and eventually into free space.

'Prime Minister, can you comment at all on the reports today that money is being channelled through Australian charities to terrorist organisations?'

'No. That is an allegation at this stage. An investigation is underway I believe but I have no further comment.'

Sid recognised the booming voice of the veteran television correspondent Phil Bertram cut through next.

'Prime Minister, congratulations must go to the security agencies here for intercepting and preventing an obviously dangerous development but why is it that they seem incapable of hunting down the killer who is still working his way through the ASIO watchlist? Was this young man on the list? Are the police any closer to finding and detaining the killer?'

The prime minister and his flankers ignored the hubbub and continued making their way out of the room. The PM's press secretary, pushed herself in front of the cameras.

'No questions.' She glared at the cameras. 'No questions. As you were all told. No press conference here. There'll be time for that later.'

Sid hit the mute button. All this for a fucking kid with an internet bomb kit and a chip on his shoulder. There were kids out there – hundreds of them possibly – being groomed online, willing to do anything. Deluded, fucked-up teenagers mostly. The 'lone wolves'. K block had no idea how many. This guy wasn't even on the list. Totally out of the blue. And, meanwhile, Sid was trying to figure out how to deal with a much more coordinated, sophisticated attack on a scale no one here had ever experienced. Well, it wasn't just him, but it sure felt that way now that Chip was out and Haifa had all but disappeared.

But what if there were connections? It couldn't be discounted. The Scorpion was going to have to enlist a horde of crazies, lone wolves and nutjobs.

Sid went back to the translations that had now been done of the Scorpion's list. The only clue to timing anywhere was in the connection to something it referred to as 'the great defeat'. 'We will rub their faces in it. We will humiliate the infidels. The day of the great defeat will be marked and, praise be to Allah, justice will be served.'

Maybe it wasn't a great defeat for them but a great defeat for the infidel. Maybe 'the defeat' was talking about Anzac Cove? It seemed unlikely but they didn't have anything else to go on at this stage. It made some sense, Sid thought – strike at the heart of the national commemoration. Like a lot of those who had actually served in conflict zones, Sid was of the opinion that the whole day had been hijacked by political opportunists. A solemn occasion that had become a chorus of cheap patriotism and sloganeering. But not everyone felt that way. The politicians loved it. The media circus filled it full of sentiment and portent, and a generation of kids who'd never seen war seemed to find in it a sense of identity and purpose – however warped – that they obviously couldn't find elsewhere. It made it an obvious target.

He looked at the calendar on his iPhone. Twenty-sixth of February. If Anzac Day was the target they had less than two months to find the Scorpion.

He held that thought for less than twenty-four hours.

34.

Goulburn only had three industries. Farming, the jail and the welfare cheque. But since the end of the Wool Board and the guaranteed floor price, there was no certainty in the only sort of farming the dusty marginal paddocks around here could support, and the only certainty about the welfare cheque was that it would never get any bigger than the first day you signed up for it. No, the jail was the only thing that was keeping this three-pub truck stop alive. Actually, Sid noted, as he took the turn off the freeway into town, since the highway bypass a few years ago even the trucks didn't stop anymore.

Sydney Road was quiet. The Heritage motel was offering rooms for forty-nine dollars a night, broadband and breakfast included. The green 'Vacancy' sign was flashing in desperation. No kidding, Sid thought. Even the big Maccas was all but empty. Just a few cars in the car park. Auburn Road was dead too. It was only seven thirty though and Sid remembered from his days as a probationary constable that Goulburn's main street didn't get lively until the pubs started to close. But it wasn't the sort of lively suitable for family viewing.

He pulled in to one of the nose-to-kerb parking spots just in front of the Paragon Cafe as instructed. He turned the Hyundai off and waited. The Paragon had been there for decades, one of the original Greek cafes that the post-war migrants opened in countless country towns all across Australia. When Sid was a boy in western New South Wales every town had at least one. You could always get a mixed grill with chips, bacon and eggs, a burger with the lot and a cold milkshake in an aluminium container. Occasionally even a moussaka, although eggplant was mostly reserved for the Greeks themselves back then. There weren't that many Greek cafes left anymore, killed off by the drive-through Big Mac. Still the Paragon in Auburn Road seemed to be defying the trend. There was a steady crowd of what passed for Goulburn high society along for their Friday night out. The sons and daughters of graziers with their finely checked blue and white dress shirts and their jeans and moleskins, families in from the bush for a rare treat, and a large group of young women out for a hens' night. One of them was wearing a tiara and a satin sash declaring herself to be the 'bride'.

Sid cast a professional eye up and down. The street itself was pretty quiet. A few down and outs shuffling along in their track pants with no perceptible intent, a young guy in shorts and a torn t-shirt checking bins and looking agitated – another advert for the benefits of Ice, he thought. They'd started calling Goulburn the 'South Pole' of late and it had nothing to do with freezing winters.

Eight o'clock rolled around. Sid turned on the news. They were still running the Brian Williams press conference from earlier in the day. The reaction to it had been cool from some in the Muslim community who were complaining they were being singled out. A new research paper claimed as many as eighty percent of Muslims felt they were being unfairly targeted by the government's counter terrorism laws. Sid listened as the radio reported that the leading Sydney Muslim community leader Dr Hakim Hourani said many Australian Muslims were starting to feel as if they were 'under siege' but he continued that the community had to accept that it had a problem and had to engage with the authorities to prevent a small group of extremists tarnishing them all. Meanwhile, steps were being taken to increase security around monuments in the lead-up to Anzac Day, and serving soldiers were being warned not to wear their uniforms when they weren't on base.

Sid thought of Haifa. 'Under siege.' They were the words she had used too. And if she felt that way then it had to be true that there were plenty of others who felt the same. As for her brother – well, Sid didn't know what to make of him. He was sounding like the voice of reason. What the fuck?

He was so wound up in his own thoughts he jumped when the passenger door opened. Mervin Cole, sweating and puffing, squeezed his hefty frame into the little Korean car. He wasn't the fit prop forward he once had been.

'Jesus, Sid. Relax,' he said. 'Sorry I'm a bit late.'

'No probs, Merv, I'm just sitting back enjoying the ambience of a big night in Goulburn.'

'Yeah, well, we wouldn't want you to get too excited.'

'No danger of that.'

'No – guess not.' Cole took a handkerchief from his pocket and wiped away the sweat from his face.

Merv had played rugby league for Wellington and for NSW Country back in the 1980s. That was before the convictions for drugs, armed robbery and assault. His was an all too familiar Indigenous story. But in the last ten years or so he'd cleaned himself up and become an advocate and prison activist. He ran outreach programs, he broadcast a prison show on community radio, and he engaged with young Indigenous offenders, helping them into training and reform programs. For the most part, he didn't have much time for cops but he and Sid had known each other for more than twenty years. Sid had intervened in a case involving the rape and murder of a young white woman on a property near Yass. It was the bad old days. Merv was being verballed by a lazy and undoubtedly corrupt local sergeant. Sid made sure the young footballer knew his rights, remained silent and got the legal representation he needed. The intervention was never forgotten. Not by Merv or the local sergeant.

'I've got something I think you need to know, seeing as you're working with the Arabs and all,' Merv said.

'Yeah I figured. You don't call unless you do.'

'There's a young fella. He's heard some stuff. Stuff you might be interested in. He's been mixed up with the Lebs. A convert. There's a lot of us blackfellas now growin' their beards and talkin' about Allah in there.'

'We've noticed. Can't see the attraction myself but then who knows what happens to people in that place.'

'They like it 'cause the mullahs talk about it being a religion for the oppressed and the downtrodden. You grow up oppressed and disenfranchised with no prospects, no jobs, and you hear that message at close quarters all the time – it's not such a big step, you know. And they're tough, too, those Lebs. For sure. Almost as many of them in there now as us blackfellas.'

Merv was still sweating heavily. He wiped his face again.

'Geez, haven't you got any air-con in this shitbox? Is this what happens when you move up the ranks? You'd think they'd give you a proper car, Sid.'

'I don't like to stand out from the crowd. You know that.'

'Ha ha. You've changed. Was it Afghanistan that did that?' Merv joked.

'Maybe,' Sid said, coming across more serious than he intended. Merv got it.

'Must have been a shit sandwich over there. Rosie and everything . . .' he trailed off.

'Something like that.'

'Anyway, this young fella. He wants to talk, but he says once he does he can't go back. He'll need protection. It's big. Really big, he reckons. And he's scared shitless.'

'That's a big ask, Merv. You know that. What's he in for?'

'Armed robbery, vehicle theft, drugs. The usual. But he says you really need to know what he has to tell you.'

'What if it's not good? What if he's making it up? I have to go all the way up the chain to do what he's asking. You told him that right?'

'Yeah, I told him. He knows. But he had one word for you that he reckoned might convince you.'

'Oh yeah? And what was that?'

'He said tell him it's about "Scorpion". I don't know what that means but he said you –'

Sid tried not to react but his bad poker face must have given him away. He instinctively looked up and down the street, as if he was worried that someone might have heard.

'Shit,' Merv said, looking across. 'That's hit a nerve.'

'Leave it with me.' Sid was trying to hold his breathing steady. 'I'll work something out for first thing in the morning. What's his name?'

'James. James Brown.'

'Like the soul singer?'

'Yeah that's it.'

'Right. That's easy to remember then. Thanks.'

'No problem. You make sure you look after him though. That's a scary place in there. And you look after yourself too. You had your blood pressure checked lately?'

Merv reached across and took Sid's hand. He gave it a farewell shake.

'Good to see you again, brother. Keep cool.'

Sid turned the Hyundai back up Auburn Road and on to Sydney Road. He headed for the Heritage motel, pretty sure they'd still have a few of their forty-nine dollar rooms left.

35.

From the outside, Goulburn jail looked like a Victorian-era convalescence home. All convict brick and cast iron. Inside, it was one of the most high-tech prison facilities in the world. The old familiar jingle of keys could still be heard in some of the low-security areas but access to the maximum-security wings like Supermax was possible only with the whisper quiet buzz of retinal scans and fingerprint readers.

'Follow me, sir,' the young prison officer said once Sid had been relieved of his phone and put through the full body X-ray machine.

The young guard led the way through a high-tech wonderland of silently opening and closing heavy steel doors. Two other guards followed but kept a strict twenty metres behind them as they worked their way through unmarked corridors. Without the guides, Sid would have had no idea where they were.

The hallways were painted an almost comforting, sunny, light yellow and lined with numbered grey doors – a few had cards attached to them identifying the inmate and their food preferences. Even here, Sid noted, serial killers had orders in for extra fruit and brown bread.

After a few left turns and about 200 metres they came to a stop outside an unmarked door.

'He's inside. We have cameras on every angle and there's a panic button in there if you need it.'

'I didn't think he was such a high-security danger,' Sid said, only slightly alarmed.

'We don't take chances with anyone in here.' The officer punched a six digit code into the keypad.

Sid had checked in with AJ first thing that morning. 'Don't promise him too much,' she'd said. 'We might be able to organise some protection but we can't bust him out. No matter how good the information is.'

'Well, it must be good,' Sid argued. 'He'd know the risks and the consequences. He also knows how important it is to us.'

'We might be able to swing a slightly earlier release – but the information better be red hot, Sid. And Brown has to know protection means whatever he's got left to serve is going to be lonely.'

The room was small and windowless with a solid bench at one end the only seating. A metal cage big enough for a full-grown man to stand up in and turn around filled the corner at the other end of the room. James Brown was sitting in the cage on the floor dressed in an orange jumpsuit.

'G'day,' he said, quietly. 'You took your time.'

Brown was a small man in his early thirties. He had the shaved head and beard favoured by most Muslims doing time inside. The file Sid had been given on him detailed a litany of petty crimes and juvenile detention before he graduated to armed robbery and assault. The last offence was an attempt to hold up the Westpac bank in the Sydney suburb of Leichhardt. His weapons of choice had been a crude and cheap sawn-off shotgun and a crowbar. He'd been in Goulburn now for nearly seven years, most of it spent in the regular security wing but, like most, he'd spent time in solitary from time to time for bad behaviour. He'd been a big fighter in the early years. Involved in all the scraps and gang- and race-related turf battles. All that changed two years ago when he found Allah. Overnight it seemed he became a model inmate. Reserved and quiet, mixing only with the Lebs and the other Muslims and his Indigenous brothers.

'I only heard you wanted to talk yesterday. These things take time to organise. Merv sends his regards,' Sid said.

'Mm. I need some guarantees. Before – before I talk.'

Sid stood just inside the room. The door had closed with a heavy thud and the peculiar silence of a heavy walled jail cell filled the space between them.

'Well, I'm not so sure it works like that. You see it all depends on the quality of the information.'

'Yeah sure,' Brown scoffed. 'You wouldn't be here if you weren't interested. You know about Scorpion. I wasn't sure about that. That it was out. But I knew that if it was, if that was the word, you'd come running.'

'Yep. You're right about that.' Sid sat down on the bench and looked around the room.

'Not much of a place this, is it?' he said.

Brown stood up and placed his hands against the cage, his fingers poking through. He pressed his face up against the heavy-gauge wire.

'The walls in here have ears,' he said in a soft whisper. 'It'll get out. This meeting. And once it does Allah's not going to save me if I'm still in here. But if you don't hear what I've got to say hundreds, perhaps thousands, will die.'

Sid stood up and took a few steps towards the cage. Brown was smaller than him. Five foot eight at the most.

'You need to come a lot closer if you want what it is that I'm going to tell you. And believe me, I think you do,' Brown hissed. 'Closer.'

Sid hesitated. How close should he get? He could see Brown's fingers straining through the metal grille of the cage. How strong was it? He took three deliberate, slow steps towards the cage and stopped about a metre out.

'Closer,' Brown whispered again.

Sid looked around, checking the cameras, reassuring himself that they were at least being watched. He took another step – close enough now to notice the badly chewed nails at the end of Brown's fingers.

He turned his head but he had to stoop to get his ear close enough to James Brown's mouth.

'It's coming.' Brown spoke so softly that even with his ear almost touching the cage Sid could barely hear him. 'It's big. The heavy boys here are talking about it quietly. Like I said they call it "Scorpion".'

'Yeah, that much I know. So far you're telling me stuff I already know. Who or what is Scorpion, that's what we need.'

'That I don't know.'

'Well, fuck me, that's not going to get you out of here.' Sid straightened up. Disappointed.

'Wait. You don't have much time. You want to know when right? Will that get me clear? If I tell you I can't go back. That's it.' Brown was sounding nervous now. He was breathing heavily and shuffling from one foot to the other.

'Okay,' Sid said. 'The Scorpion's list. It talks about "the great defeat". Anzac Day? Is that what it means?'

'Faark. You have no fuckin' idea, do you?' Brown almost laughed. Then he pushed his face hard up against the wire.

'Let me tell you,' he said, serious now.

Sid lowered his head. He could feel Brown's breath against his cheek and the sweat and heat emanating from both of them.

'It's not *your* great defeat they want to mark.' Brown was whispering now, barely audible even this close. 'It's theirs. It's Islam's great defeat.'

'And that is?'

'They talk about the end of the last caliphate. A turning point in history and an event momentous for Islam.'

'And when was that?'

'1924.'

Brown paused. His shallow, stale breath brushing hot against Sid's ear.

'The third of March.'

36.

By nine o'clock Sid was back on the Hume Highway heading north. He had the little Hyundai's air-con pumped up full but he just couldn't seem to stop sweating. It was hot but even if Sid had had this morning's meeting in the Antarctic he'd be struggling not to overheat. It was March the first.

'It's coming,' Brown had said. 'It's going to be big.' Sid couldn't get that out of his head. Yet here he was in his little Korean shitbox heading back to K block for an emergency meeting, no closer to finding Scorpion and no closer to busting open the operation, if indeed that's what it was.

Before he left Goulburn he'd arranged around-the-clock protection for Brown and a transfer to Silverwater – new name, new identity, the works. Brown needed to be close enough to talk to again should they need to. Silverwater was just an hour or so from the office and secure enough, they said. Sid even promised Brown he'd see what he could do about an early release although naming those sort of promises was above his pay grade.

Sid was pushing the little car past 130 kilometres an hour as he approached Marulan. A highway patrol had pulled over a Subaru WRX with its chassis lowered and a 'come and get me' racing stripe. He instinctively pulled his foot off the pedal when he saw the flashing lights. There was no time to waste explaining things and pulling rank.

He pulled out into the right-hand lane to overtake a truck that was slowing down to take the exit into the heaving vehicle checking station.

•

It had been a quiet morning so far for John Graham. The older model Ford LTLA was the first prime mover that had turned in since his shift began nearly half an hour ago. You don't see too many of these around anymore, he thought as he watched it approach. His professional eye told him this one was a late nineties model – 1997 probably – and it had been well looked after. It was pulling an almost new Vawdrey Wingliner container trailer on the back – small, but good gear. John Graham knew most of the blokes who did the long haul up and down the Hume and most of the rigs. He hadn't seen this one before even though it had NSW plates. He'd never seen the young driver before either.

The truck was carrying two loads, the driver said. For delivery into a Clyde warehouse that afternoon. His dangerous goods certificate was all good, the rest of the paperwork raised no alarms and the young fella's licence was in order. John Graham had no reason to be suspicious and if it was someone he knew he would have just waved them through but after he'd been over the roadworthy checklist he did a once-over visual of the chemicals in the container.

That all looked pretty good too. Clean, tidy and secure even though the container was only a little over half full. That was odd. Blokes didn't usually bother hauling half-full containers up and down the highway. Anyway, not really his business to worry about how these guys made a buck but he did note it in the log and mark it with a red flag. Just procedure. An alert had come through that morning to red flag anything that seemed in any way out of the ordinary with chemical transport. That happened from time to time and John Graham didn't think too much of it.

'Have a good one mate,' he said to the young driver as he handed back the stamped paperwork. The young fella didn't say much in return, just a curt 'Thanks'. Seemed keen to get back on the road.

A few minutes later, Jimmy Chapman came rolling in with his Volvo pulling a refrigerated B double. John Graham and Jimmy went way back. He soon forgot about the red flag and the half-full trailer of chemicals.

•

Sid made good time. The traffic was light and it was just after 10.15 by the time he sailed into the first of the tunnels on the M5 – number one on the Scorpion's hit list. Yeah, it wouldn't be hard, would it? Drive the load down here, jack the vehicle, wait for the traffic to build up – then boom. Chaos, fucking chaos. Do it in the Harbour Tunnel at the same time. Hit the trains and the ferries. A few iconic sites like the Opera House. Then really go big with the fucking oil refinery in Rydalmere. Everything they'd heard. Everything they'd been warning about. Now they had to stop it before it happened. But even if only half of what was on the list went off the city would be paralysed, the place would go into panic, people would die. This wasn't just the 'lone wolf' Gray and all the others had been banging on about. This was a pack of lone wolves all blowing themselves up at the same time. And Brian Williams was still frothing at the mouth over a kid in a cul-de-sac with fast broadband and delusions of glory. Shit, you couldn't find enough 'senior law enforcement officers' or 'prime ministerial concern' for the sort of press conference you'd need to explain how they failed to stop this.

Can we stop it? Sid wondered. Where was Scorpion? Who was Scorpion? They still had no idea. But they were getting closer. They had a date. They had a motivation. They'd find him. They had to find him. Two days. Two days to solve the biggest challenge of his career. There were lives at risk, potentially thousands, and reputations too. They'd throw everything they had at it. It'd be a multi-agency operation but he had no doubt where the blame would lie. K block was the only unit working directly with Harrison – a drugged-up, stitched-up half-crazy special forces freelancer. No one had seen or heard from him for days. K block let him run and there was still hope he'd lead them to Scorpion. But now James Brown had given them confirmation – independent confirmation. 'It's coming. It's big.' No kidding.

The M5 spat him out of the second tunnel. The road looped around the airport and flew under the runway heading east towards Botany. A few 747s were lined up ready to take their passengers somewhere else. Somewhere else had a good sound to it right now. His phone rang. The screen lit up. It was Haifa.

'Have you heard?' she said. Just like that. As if they'd only yesterday been smoking weed together and watching the sun go down. No 'Hello'. No 'How are you?' Just 'Have you heard?'

'Heard what?'

'The news. Hakim. They've taken Hakim.'

She was calm. Matter of fact.

'What are you talking about?'

'Where are you?'

'Just heading into the Eastern Distributor after the airport. I'll be in the office in a few minutes.'

'Okay, see you there.'

'Haifa?'

She was gone.

It was 10.30. He flicked on the radio just as the news headlines began.

Making news this morning. The prominent Muslim community leader Hakim Hourani has been kidnapped at gunpoint by three unidentified assailants.

The kidnapping occurred as Mr Hourani was holding a press conference to discuss the recent allegations of the misappropriation of aid money.

The kidnappers were wearing black balaclavas and black paramilitary-style uniforms. No ransom has been demanded and police say they still have no idea where Mr Hourani has been taken or why he was kidnapped.

In a statement just released Prime Minister Brian Williams says security agencies will do everything in their power to find Mr Hourani and bring those responsible to justice.

'We have grave fears for Mr Hourani's safety,' the statement says. 'This is an assault on all Australians and on everything we stand for.'

Holy shit. You go off the radar for a few hours and look what happens. The radio switched live to a reporter on the scene who predictably knew nothing and had nothing to add. Sid turned it off, took the cross city tunnel exit and a few minutes later pulled into the garage under Goulburn Street. He raced out of the car park and up to the office.

Murphy, AJ and Haifa, were all huddled around a monitor.

She looked up as he came in. Expressionless. He couldn't read her. Later, he said to himself. Later. Plenty of time for that.

'Here,' Murphy said, setting the cursor over the editing timeline on the screen. He hit the space bar.

The vision rolled.

'Thank you for coming everyone.' Hakim Hourani moved up to the lectern looking a little nervous, as if he was uncomfortable in front of all the cameras. Sid looked across at Haifa. She raised her eyebrows as if to say, *'Really? I'm not buying that.'*

As usual, Dr Hourani looked like he just stepped out of a magazine shoot. Dressed in a fine tailored expensive suit and a narrowly knotted fashionable tie.

'I would like to address the reports in the media that have surfaced suggesting that money collected by the charity the Muslim Relief Fund is somehow making its way to terrorist organisations in Syria and Iraq, or that the body that I chair known as the Sunni Progress Association is somehow involved in this. I have been assured by the directors that this is not the case and I have been shocked by the reporting that suggests otherwise. Having said that, I do accept that the website carried the logo of at least one organisation that had been under investigation by the FBI in the United States. This organisation allegedly has links with what I understand was a Palestinian relief fund which it has been alleged was funnelling money to terrorist groups. I am shocked that the banner bearing the logo of that organisation was carried on the MRF website and we are still trying to ascertain how that came to be there and I want to reiterate the MRF has had no formal or informal connection to that group.'

Hourani was reading from a prepared statement. He looked up at the cameras from time to time. His face glistened under the lights.

'I can assure all Australians that all the money collected from the community on behalf of the MRF is for medicine and food for people in desperate need of help.

'I can, however, confirm that the Australian Federal Police have already interviewed a number of MRF staff members and, although I have little to do with the day-to-day running of the charity as one of the five board members, I am of course happy to cooperate with the authorities in any way I can.'

'Is that true?' AJ asked, looking at Sid.

'First I've heard.' He was genuinely puzzled. 'But then togetherness and cooperation aren't exactly buzzwords around here at the moment.' An expanded operation didn't always mean cooperation.

'Sshh,' Murphy hissed. 'Here it comes.'

'Now, I can answer a few questions but I really don't have a lot to add to what I've –'

The sound of automatic gunfire rang out. The camera jerked around. Everyone was screaming. Three men wearing balaclavas and dressed entirely in black, brandishing crude-looking automatic weapons, stormed into the room shouting, *'Allahu akbar.'*

Screams and confusion. The camera was locked off at an angle but was still rolling.

Two of the men picked Hourani up from the ground where he was cowering behind the lectern and started dragging him off to the right. The other raised his gun, looked into the camera, and let a few rounds fly into the air.

'Allahu akbar,' he shouted.

The gun had a short stumpy stock, a magazine and an even shorter barrel – like an AK47 sawn off at both ends. It looked just like the guns Sid had seen Palestinians making in Israel, modelled on the Carl Gustav machine gun. They were cheap and easy to make. All you needed was a blueprint off the internet and a good metal lathe. They called them the 'Carlo'. They looked amateurish but they spurted rounds that were just as deadly as a bought gun.

'Shit,' Haifa said, the colour draining from her face.

Murphy hit the space bar again and the image on the screen froze.

'Fucking, eh?' He whistled. 'Pretty dramatic.'

'Do you buy it?' Sid said, looking at Haifa.

'I don't know. I mean, yes. I mean, fuck, Sid, what am I supposed to say? My brother has been dragged off at gunpoint. And no one knows where to.'

'Yeah. We're in the shit all right. Two days. Two fucking days. That's all we've got.'

'The Scorpion is talking about the caliphate, right? Or the end of it at least. I found some maps marking out the Ottoman Caliphate in my brother's house a few days ago.' Haifa sounded a little shocked.

'What's the significance?' Sid asked.

'I don't know. Nothing is making much sense right now.' She paused. 'But yeah. He – something's not right.'

'What's it really about? The caliphate? Do they just want to avenge the defeat? That's what Jimmy Brown said.'

'Maybe. But it's bigger than that. They want to redress the borders that the colonial powers drew up when they carved the territory into separate states. They want the territory, sure, but it's an idea they want. It's the idea of a homeland.'

She paused.

'That's the idealist's view of it anyway. Really it's about controlling territory so you can control oil and wealth. Just like every other fight for that area.' She looked over to the frozen image on the screen. 'This lot are motivated by money as much as radical theory. For that to work they need territory of course.'

Sid looked at the screen too. A raised gun. A captive. There would be worse to come.

'Yeah, well it's the "avenge" bit of the equation we've got to worry about right now,' he said.

37.

'It was here. It was all here.' Haifa pointed to the empty wall. She couldn't believe it. Everything was gone. 'The al-Aqsa mosque. It was over there.' She swept her hand around. 'The desk was there. The filing cabinet right next to it with the maps, the money. Shit.'

They were standing in her old bedroom. There was no sign of the private world of Hakim Hourani that had been here just the other day. All that was left was the prayer basin and a file of newspaper clippings lying on the floor.

'This is all pretty weird. I – I don't know what to think. Seriously, this place was decked out like bin Laden's cave. And now – now there's nothing.'

'Think it through, Haifa. Was there anything that might give us a lead?'

'I don't know. He spent a lot of time trying to justify his weird flip to accepting liberal Islam as a means to an end. All the while he's working his way through *The Art of War*. But then a lot doesn't add up about any of this. I hardly know him anymore – obviously. All that time overseas and –'

Sid picked a bit of Blu-Tac off the wall, brushing his hand across it as if hoping to feel evidence of what she said had been there. 'I assume you already know they've run a check on the years he spent in Geneva,' he said. 'Apparently there weren't a lot of contact hours at the university. People remember him at the nuclear research institute, they also remember him not being there much. The Swiss don't have anything on him. He didn't leave the country as far as we know – at least not on his own passport – but he did seem to lie low. Some might say he disappeared for long stretches.'

'And?'

'Well. Put two and two together. Might be totally on the wrong track, but he was in Geneva from when – 2008 to 2011? That's the same time we were hunting "Sabre" in Afghanistan.'

'Sabre?'

'Yeah, that's what we called him. We now know they called him "Scorpion".'

'Oh, Sid come on. What are you saying? Hakim is Scorpion? You're not serious.'

'I'm just – just suggesting. Just trying to make sense of it all. Clutching at straws, really. But it is odd, isn't it? His relationship with Shalomar. All this stuff that you say was here. His role in the charity, his public persona, his ideological inconsistencies?'

'Yes. It is weird. He says he's trying to work from the inside.'

Haifa bent down and picked up the manila file of news clippings.

'Speaking of disappearing . . . I know I haven't really been around much.' She looked up and held his gaze with those sharp smoky grey eyes. 'I'm sorry. I just – I'm just not sure where I fit in all of this anymore.'

Sid took her hand.

'Don't. It's okay. I understand,' he said, knowing he didn't understand at all. He drew her closer – but the clippings folder was still in her other hand preventing anything but an awkward half hug.

She opened the folder. Jenson Burton's report on the waterboarding was at the top. She started reading it – then stopped – cold.

'Did the hit on Chip ever become public?' she asked.

'What do you mean?'

'It never did, did it? The papers.' She waved the file.

'No. It stayed close. Very close.'

'He knows.'

'What?'

'Hakim. He knows about it. I said to him, "I suppose you think the retaliation was in order?" He didn't say "What retaliation?" Didn't say "What are you talking about?" He said, "Yes, things can spiral in the wrong direction" that's what he said. He knew.'

38.

'Where are you? Where are you right now?'

AJ was on the phone, sounding unusually stressed. Hard to blame her.

Sid had just pulled on to Canterbury Road. They were heading east back towards the city.

'We're just leaving Hourani's house in Lakemba.'

'Okay. Hang on.'

There was silence on the other end for a good thirty seconds.

'Still there?' AJ said eventually. 'Head for Bankstown police station. The PM's office is organising a conference call asap. You'll need a secure room. That's the closest we've got.'

Sid turned the car around and headed back to Bankstown. It wasn't far but the afternoon peak-hour traffic was heavy. Fifteen minutes later they drove into the car park.

Cavan Maskey was waiting for them as they emerged from the lift on the second floor.

'Jeez, you've got some friends in high places,' he said. 'We don't get calls like this every day.'

Maskey led them down a corridor and into a bland, windowless room. A conference call microphone and speaker were set up in the middle of a long table. Chatter on the other end of it suggested the call was already live.

'Here they are,' Maskey said loud enough for everyone to hear. He raised his eyebrows at them. 'I'll leave you to it,' he said more quietly as he left the room.

'Sid?' It was AJ.

'Yes. We're here.'

'Okay. In Bankstown we have Sidney Allen and officer Haifa Hourani, who as you all know is also Dr Hourani's sister.' She paused to let that sink in before continuing. 'Andrea June Evans and Damien Murphy here in Goulburn street. And in Canberra?'

'Yes. Yes. We're here in Canberra.' Sid recognised the voice – the PM's chief of staff, Ange Catano. 'Prime Minister Brian Williams, Drummond Gray from ASIO, CDF General Darwin and, from the AFP, Assistant Commissioner for Counter Terrorism, Andrew Fowler. Oh and Bridget Galston from the CDF's office taking minutes. And myself, of course, Angelo Catano.' Catano threw to Williams. 'PM?'

'Ange, thanks. Ahem. It seems from what we've been briefed on the situation may be a lot more urgent than we'd thought. Correct?'

No one jumped in to confirm it.

'Yes, sir, it would seem so,' Sid said eventually, filling the dead air.

He ran through in some detail where they were at, ending with the latest from the informant James Brown.

'– so, if he's right, the deadline for this thing is the day after tomorrow.'

Nothing but an electronic crackle came through the speaker. Sid looked at Haifa – he figured it was taking them some time in Canberra to digest it all.

Eventually the PM spoke up.

'Not to mention the fact that we've all just witnessed a kidnapping almost live on TV.' He paused. 'The media's going nuts. We're about to have a full night of prime-time panic on our hands. Any news on that front?'

'Not yet, sir, no,' AJ said.

'So the question for the moment is how do we approach this right now? Andrew?' He threw the question to the assistant commissioner.

'We've gone right through the list – the Scorpion's list we're calling it, are we? You should all have it there in front of you. Thirteen points as you can see.'

Sid and Haifa didn't have the list in front of them in Bankstown and Sid was sure AJ and Murphy didn't need reminding either but obviously the Canberra end had been given some form of it.

'It's definitely detailed on intent but, apart from suggestions of a few trucks and chemicals, not so much on delivery. None the less we've got everyone watching everything. We've raised the internal alerts with the NSW transport boys. Everything is being crosschecked and doublechecked. Nothing is flying into or out of Bankstown that we haven't looked at more than twice. We've got constant patrols around the refinery at Rydalmere and I recommend we put a ban on heavy vehicle transport through tunnels – at least for the next few days.'

'Really? That's hardly going to reassure the public,' Williams said.

Fowler ploughed on. 'Can I also suggest we shift the public alert to the highest possible level?'

'Oh come on.' Williams was sounding more and more nervous. 'We can't do that, we'll have widespread panic.'

'Sir. There is a real danger that quite a few members of the public might not be around to be reassured if we don't put measures in place to prevent at least what we know.'

'Okay, but no unnecessary frighteners. We can put the truck bans in place. We can keep our eyes peeled but we don't need to raise public concern to the level of terror attack "Certain". Do we?'

'Perhaps not sir. No,' Fowler answered.

Sid was pretty sure he wasn't the only one wondering what the fuck they had the levels for if they weren't ever going to use them for fear of scaring the public. If there was ever a time . . . Anyway, those weren't his decisions to make.

'Um one thing.' Drummond Gray's plummy querulous tone. 'What have we made of number thirteen on the list. "The switch". Any ideas?'

'No, sir. That one's still a mystery.'

'Just a point then. We don't entirely know all of their intentions. Could be a few surprises they haven't told us about.'

Silence.

'Um, right then.' Williams broke in again. 'We will meet again first thing in the morning. Let's get those transport bans in place. We want a workable explanation I assume, Ange? At least one of the reptiles in the media will get on to this.'

'Agreed. We'll work on it.'

'As for the rest of it,' Williams continued, 'I want this solved. I want this out of the public eye. It's your job. If we – if you – do it right, it won't be noticed. If not we'll see it on TV. That'll be it for today.'

A shuffling of papers came down the line. Sid was about to hit the hang-up button.

'Oh by the way, Ms Hourani.' The PM hadn't quite finished. 'I meant to say. Your brother's a good man and I certainly hope we have a lot of work together ahead of us. We'll find him. I'm sure.'

'Yes. Thank you sir.' It was the first time Haifa had been asked to speak.

Sid and Haifa started to leave, walking down the corridor towards the lift, when Cavan Maskey came barrelling towards them.

'Come with me,' he said. 'There's something you need to know.'

He was flustered, red-faced. His shirt was hanging out the front of his pants and his tie was loose around his neck and listing badly to the right.

'That's a good suit gone to waste,' Sid said.

'Fuck off. You need to see this. No fucking joke. You might not like it but you're going to need to see it.'

For a big man he was already moving fast. They followed him down the emergency stairwell one floor. It smelled musty and damp with the faintest whiff of cigarette butts and stale fast food.

The first floor was a big open-plan office space. A typical detectives' office. Desk after desk – only half of them occupied. Most covered in disorderly piles of paper and old coffee cups. Your run-of-the-mill Ds looking after weekend break-ins and insurance jobs up one end, homicide over to one side, and an operations desk down the far end. That's where Maskey was heading with a purpose he didn't often display. It almost made Sid nostalgic.

'We've found your mate,' Maskey said, barging ahead.

'What?'

'Your mate. The fuckin' crazy hand chopper. We've found him.' He pushed through the swinging gate that separated the operations desk from the rest of the room. Sid and Haifa followed. A big district map took up most of the wall. In front of that there was a long bench with a number of file trays and a few computer monitors. The police radio crackled in the background.

'Dave. What's the latest?' Maskey addressed a young Asian constable.

'Wheeler and Kelly have just got there, sir. Four dead 'uns. The older guy, Harrison? He's alive, Kelly said. Not good but. Ambos are there too now.'

'Shit,' Sid said. 'Tell them not to touch anything. Don't let the medics in until we get there, okay? Seriously. Where are they?'

Dave got up from his seat.

'Might be too late for that.' He pointed to the map on the wall. 'Here. Corner of Haldon and Grace. You'll have to fight your way through the fireys and the bomb squad first. The only reason we found the bodies was because half the building was blown off. Looks like some sort of gas explosion.'

'When did it happen?' Sid asked.

'About twenty minutes ago now.'

'Shit, Cav, you're supposed to tell us about anything like this the moment it happens.'

'What do you think I'm doing? We're not discussing the fuckin' footy results here now are we?'

The three of them piled into Cavan Maskey's patrol car. He hit the siren and they blazed their way down South Terrace and on to The Boulevard but the traffic was already banking up big time. Even with the noise and the light show they were clearly not going to get anywhere fast. Maskey swung the car off the main road and started tearing through the back streets. Eventually they hit King Georges Road, scattered more traffic left and right, took a few more creative turns and ended up stuck in a pile-up of frustrated drivers in Croydon Street one street back from Haldon.

'Fuck it,' Maskey said, still red-faced and frustrated.

'Come on. This way.' Haifa got out of the car and started running west. Sid followed, Maskey came panting up the rear. Croydon Street was like every street around the area, a mix of four-storey red brick flats built in the 1970s and smaller 1950s bungalows with easy-care concrete gardens.

Haifa veered off to the right at one block of sad-looking apartments and hotfooted it up the driveway. There was no fencing to stop them and nothing blocking their access through an adjoining block. They came out on Haldon Street just near the Aldi supermarket. Haifa turned right.

'Come on,' she shouted. 'Put some muscle in it. It's up here.'

'No kidding,' Sid said. The traffic wasn't moving on Haldon Street. Cars were trying to pull off the road to let rescue vehicles through. A hundred metres further along, a large crowd was starting to gather.

They pushed through the curious rubberneckers. Maskey shouting all the way, 'Move. Police. Police. Out of the way.'

Once through the police line they could see there'd been one hell of a big bang. A small building, four units maybe, not much bigger than a large two-storey house, had been torn apart. A Hazmat team with masks on was already scouring the scene of the blast itself, which Sid guessed must have been a garage. The smell was overpowering. A mix of acetone and hydrogen peroxide – like sticking your head in a bucket of nail polish remover and hair bleach. Sid recognised it. Triacetone triperoxide, or TATP. Also known in some circles as 'the mother of Satan'. The latest in homemade jihadi bomb technology. It had become the go-to terrorist's explosive in Europe in the last year or so and had started turning up in Sydney only recently. Once it was made, it was hard to detect and could be used in small amounts. Perfect for suicide vests. The ingredients were easy enough to source but it was highly volatile, required expertise and a fairly sophisticated network in place to make it.

'Sarge. Over here.'

One of the Bankstown detectives waved them over.

'What's the go, Kelly?'

'They're up the stairs. We've taped it off. Haven't touched a thing as yet. Pretty grim. One dead down here in the garage, three more stiffs upstairs. One bloke alive, still breathing – just. They've put him on oxygen but they haven't moved him yet.'

The detective pointed up the stairs. Sid noticed the young D's eyes following Haifa as she filed past. Of course.

Grim was an understatement. An empty apartment, bare floorboards, thick vinyl blinds on the windows. Strips of old cheap fluorescent tubes cast a stark white light into the room. A few books, instruction manuals of some sort, lay in one corner along with a haphazard pile of scientific-looking equipment. It could have been the start of a meth lab but the stench outside told them these boys wouldn't have been learning how to cook up Ice.

One body was lying across an old couch, blood seeping from a gaping head wound. Another in a similar state was spread out on the floor, a pool of blood oozed across the floorboards. A third body closer to them was an even bigger mess. It had been hacked at. Deep wounds to the neck and face. There was a severed hand lying next to it – separated from the wrist.

'You've been busy, Mick,' Sid said.

'Jesus,' Cavan Maskey wheezed.

The paramedics were standing back from the scene.

Harrison had been propped up against a wall. He had an oxygen mask on. His eyes were closed and he looked more dishevelled than ever. He was covered in blood. Not his own, Sid guessed. More dead bodies. He felt his stomach churn.

'Can he talk?' he asked the medic closest to him.

'Yeah. He's stable enough for now. Doesn't know who he is though. Or he wouldn't tell us anyway.'

'No probs. I don't need a verbal. I can ID him from here even amongst this mess.'

Sid felt Haifa standing close beside him. She wasn't saying anything but she was breathing heavily. He could sense her shock. The scene was bloody and confronting.

Harrison's good arm moved. The paramedics jumped. He gingerly removed the oxygen mask but he kept his eyes closed.

'Someone has to do your job for you,' he wheezed. 'These cunts are on my list but they're the foot soldiers for yours. The Scorpion's list. They were just about to move out. Seems they didn't get the chance.'

He coughed and wheezed, held the oxygen back over his mouth, took a few deep breaths then put it down again.

'This one. He gave it up after a bit of a fight.'

'What?' Sid said.

'He spilled the beans. The Scorp. It's the preacher – the mufti. Dr Shalomar, would you believe? The other guy – Hourani. He's got nothing to do with it.'

'Really?'

'Well that's what that one said just after I cut off his ear.' Harrison raised a lazy finger towards the body closest to him. 'He was under some duress you might say.'

Haifa left the room without saying a word.

39.

Sid found Haifa out the front of the building scrolling through her phone.

'I don't know what to believe,' she said, not taking her eyes off the device in front of her. 'I don't know what to think. I –'

He wanted to wrap her up, hold her tight. He knew she wasn't given to public displays of emotion but she was struggling to keep the tears from her eyes.

'Fuck it. Fuck him. Fuck it all,' she said.

'It's all going off like crazy on Twitter.' She was still scrolling. 'This and the kidnapping.'

Twitter. Shit. And the PM and his flunkies were worrying about trying to contain the prime-time media frenzy.

'The truck ban's getting a big run too. The public seems to be connecting the dots all by themselves.' Haifa's voice was dripping with sarcasm.

'Yes, the panic seems well underway,' Sid said. 'Check it out.' He tilted his head towards the crowd of onlookers that had grown considerably in the short time they'd been there. There were hundreds of people behind the police line now. Some were starting to shout out. An angry mood was developing.

He walked over to what was left of the garage. Cavan Maskey was talking to the Hazmat team.

'Not much left to identify here,' he said. 'This fella was blown apart. Bits and pieces everywhere.'

Sid nodded towards the growing crowd.

'What do you think?'

'Doesn't look good. It's going to be a long night, I reckon.'

They could barely hear each other now over the noise. Kelly had started calling into his two-way for back-up.

Some in the crowd were aiming their anger at the police. 'What are you doing to keep us safe?'

But others were directing their anger elsewhere. Australian flags and banners had begun to appear along with placards declaring 'Ban the Burka' and 'Patriotism is not racism'. Sid spied a group of thickset men with heavily inked bald heads – tattoos of Nazi swastikas, the Australian flag and the number eighty-eight. Another one was wearing a red, white and blue plastic ski mask – the flag again – covering his face. A table had been dragged into the middle of the street. Chants of 'Aussie, Aussie, Aussie. Oi, Oi, Oi' started up.

Haifa came over. She looked worried.

'What does that even mean?' she said, scowling.

They watched as a blonde woman got up on the table with a megaphone in her hand. She started ranting about sharia law creeping into the country.

'The Muslims are coming here to our country. They're taking over. They're not assimilating. This is what happens. We have terror here in our streets.'

She was whipping up the crowd and the numbers were growing fast. People were pouring into the street. Another group had formed now and they were starting to call back. 'Racist scum. Racist scum.'

Sid could see the uniforms were getting anxious. He could still hear Kelly calling for back-up. Screaming into his two-way.

The reinforcements were finally starting to arrive.

'Shit. How did this spread so fast?' Sid said to no one.

Haifa held up her phone.

'Yeah, fair enough.'

Women in hijabs, young locals in jeans and t-shirts, Muslim men, young and old, were now yelling back at the Reclaim Australia crowd. They were joined by another group of younger demonstrators, many wearing hoodies and scarves across their faces. They were holding placards that said #NO ROOM FOR RACISM – a Twitter handle that was obviously starting to draw in even more people. Sid recognised them – the anarchist crowd. The anti-fascists or Antifa as they liked to call themselves. They were at everything like this. Drawn to a political fight like jackals.

Fights were beginning to break out. The situation was deteriorating badly. There were probably a thousand people on Haldon Street now and the police looked like they were about to totally lose control. In amongst them all were a couple of TV crews. The lights from their cameras highlighted pockets of violent confrontation in the moonlit night. People were shouting and screaming. A huge roar went up in the middle of the crowd. The fat boys with the flags and the Nazi tattoos started hitting out at anyone who looked vaguely like an anarchist or a Muslim.

The uniforms linked arms and started working their way further into the crowd, trying to push the two sides apart. Plumes of orange capsicum spray rose up from the melee. An orange cloud strobed by TV lights.

'Holy shit,' Maskey said. 'Who's running this show?'

People were being carried out of the crowd unconscious and injured. Some wailing and covered in blood.

The police reinforcements had begun to arrive in big numbers now. They included horses; Sid counted eight of them. There may have been more.

The horses started moving into the crowd and quickly proved a lot more effective at separating the factions. The police began targeting some of the worst troublemakers and pulling them out – cuffing them and throwing them into vans.

Haifa couldn't disguise her disgust. Her scowl revealed a deep chasm of loathing. Sid could see she was about to go off at someone, anyone. Don't get in her way, he told himself.

'There's something truly wrong with this country right now. Some stain deep in the core. How did it come to this?' She spat the words out.

Sid wanted to tell her it was human nature. He wanted to say people were complicated. People could be led. People didn't always think about what they were doing. And, yes, there was always an element of xenophobia under the surface but it was a minority; a preoccupation of small minds with even smaller ambitions. Still, you stir it up and this is what could happen. And the politicians had been stirring it up all right. There were votes in it apparently. How did that work? The politicians thought uncertainty and instability worked in their favour, obviously. And that made people less inclined to want to change. How fucked up was that? But he didn't say any of it. Now wasn't the time. Instead he just said, 'Yeah, totally fucked up.'

The cops finally started to get the upper hand. An impenetrable barrier of stomping, foaming horses was now keeping the two sides apart, the worst of the provocateurs had been removed and the crowds were starting to dissipate. The heat and danger of the situation had gone almost as quickly as it had come but there were injured protesters everywhere. Some overcome by the capsicum spray, others with more serious injuries being attended to by paramedics.

A few windows had been smashed as well. 'German Scum' had been spray-painted across the front door of the Aldi supermarket. No doubt put there by the fuckwits with the Nazi tattoos, Sid thought. Go figure.

Within half an hour the crowds had drifted off and Sid, Haifa and the others trapped in their positions by the rioting could now think about getting out. It was after midnight and Sid could feel a wave of fatigue starting to surge over him. It had been a long day but it was far from over. Not by a long shot. His phone was vibrating in his pocket. It was AJ. Sid looked at the time – 12.23. Less than twenty-four hours to go.

'Hey,' Sid tried to conceal his exhaustion.

'James Brown,' she said. 'He's dead.'

Sid almost dropped the phone. How could that be? A black cloud of guilt, despair and anger engulfed him.

'I thought he was going to be put in isolation.'

'It happened in the transfer. There were two others in the van. He went in alive and came out dead.'

'Shit.' No, he didn't want to know the details. They didn't matter now. He was gone. Fuck it. Dead. Sid had failed him. They had all failed him. They couldn't even protect an informant. If they couldn't protect someone they had under surveillance in the prison system how were they, how was he, going to . . .

He could feel the panic start to rise. The beginnings of a sort of out-of-body experience, as if he was looking down on what was happening – detached. He had no control over any of it and he felt like he was being tossed around in the current unable to resist the flow. Fuck he was tired.

'Listen there's something else.'

'Chip?' Sid asked, fearing the worst now. How much bad could they cram into one day?

'Say what? No. Um, well, Chip isn't too good but he'll live. The shots blew out the back of his legs. They may have to amputate. Like I say, he'll live, but it'll be a long haul.'

The phone went quiet. Sid was struggling to take it all in. A low chemical stench still hung in the air. The forensics were well into their work dividing up the scene and combing it for anything that might reveal a clue and lead to a conviction. Who did it? How did they do it? What did they use? But as usual Sid was more preoccupied with why.

Harrison was finally stretchered down the stairs and off in an ambulance.

'Sid?' AJ dragged him back. 'There's something else. A truck was red flagged at Marulan earlier loaded up with nitrogen fertiliser. Damo picked it up. Numberplate recognition cameras on the M5 around Liverpool tracked it in. It's ended up at Rydalmere. A warehouse.'

'Okay. And?'

'The warehouse is owned by the MRF.'

'The charity?'

'That's the one. Shalomar's charity.'

40.

Maskey cut the lights as they turned into South Street. Detectives Kelly and Wheeler did the same. Sid, Haifa and Maskey were in the patrol car. The two Ds from Bankstown were following in an unmarked Commodore. South Street was the main artery of the jumble of warehouse-filled streets that made up the industrial end of Rydalmere. Older-style panel-beating workshops and welding joints, small engineering and auto repair shops next to bigger, slicker warehouse operations and storage facilities. One of the newer places they passed had even been turned into a happy clappers Presbyterian church. 'Sunday. The lord sings in Rydalmere' the sign said. The place they were looking for was a big, modern grey building. The only signage on it was a 'For Lease' sign banged into the small garden bed that ran around the car park entrance. A nineties model Camry was parked in one corner and a windowless white van next to it. Sid recognised it immediately.

'That's the van from our little street movie. The fuckers who took out Chip over at Clyde the other night.'

Sid could feel his temples throbbing.

'Keep going,' he told Maskey.

The big cop turned the next corner and drove on slowly for about 200 metres.

'Okay, this'll do.'

Sid went to climb out of the car but Maskey stopped him.

'Wait.'

He opened the glove compartment and pulled out two Glocks – a standard NSW police issue 22 and a smaller Glock 27.

'I can't believe they let you guys loose without one. Here. You never know, it might come in handy.'

He checked the magazine on both weapons to make sure they were fully loaded and handed them over to Sid and Haifa. Sid felt the cold metal and the weight of it in his hand. It had been a while since he'd had to carry a gun let alone use one. He noticed Haifa took hers without hesitating. She displayed a confidence that suggested slipping a firearm into a pocket was a fairly routine activity.

Maskey checked his own weapon. Also a Glock 22 but his was fitted with an Osprey 40 sound suppressor. The silencer doubled the length of the firearm. He slipped it in to a holster strapped on to his belt.

Kelly and Wheeler would be armed too. Kelly was also carrying a huge set of boltcutters and a small jemmy bar.

Sid could feel sweat running down his back as they stepped out into the night. There was barely a breath of wind. Was it the heat or the nerves? Probably both. It was hot and still. His body and his mind were aching and he could smell the adrenalin leaching through the pores of his skin, fighting off the waves of exhaustion.

Haifa was as cool as ever. She gave Sid a reassuring smile. She must have been tired too but she didn't look it.

The street was empty and badly lit.

Sid led the way, sticking close to the walls of the adjoining buildings. They moved cautiously and slowly, turning down South Street. A hundred metres or so from the corner they came to the unmarked warehouse. There were no street lights near the building but the almost full moon cast long eerie shadows. They had no difficulty seeing, but Sid realised anyone looking would also have easily seen them advancing towards the building. Not much they could do about that.

The office entrance was on the left-hand side of the front wall – two reinforced glass doors – locked. In the middle was a huge roller door, big enough for big trucks to come and go. It was locked too, they discovered, with three heavy-gauge padlocks. There didn't appear to be any other way in.

Maskey signalled a cutting motion to Kelly. The locks came off easily. They stood back as Wheeler lifted the roller door as slowly as he could. He was trying to keep it quiet but there was never anything subtle about rolling metal doors. Any element of surprise they might still have had would be gone by now, Sid thought.

The control panel for the security alarm was blinking on the wall just inside the entrance. It was flashing a battery warning sign. Had the power been cut? There were no lights on.

Maskey signalled to Kelly and Wheeler to go in. They had their weapons out now. Wheeler peeled off left, Kelly went to the right. Maskey, Sid and Haifa waited.

Inside it was a typical warehouse. A concrete floor and soaring cantilevered roof. A line of skylights at one end of the building, high up just under the roof line, some opaque plastic, some clear, some glass, a few broken. Moonlight was streaming in. It was a huge open space. Big enough to easily accommodate the two trucks parked on the right, two steel shipping containers on the left and a series of metal storage cages stacked one on top of another along the back wall.

Kelly got back first. 'No one there,' he said quietly, 'but you want to see this for yourselves. This place is tooled up.'

They followed him back to the cages at the far end of the space.

'Holy shit.' Sid exhaled hard.

Dozens of homemade 'Carlo' automatic rifles were lined up on racks against the wall. There was a metal lathe, a drill press and some welding equipment. Ammunition boxes had been neatly stacked on the floor and a collection of what looked like handheld rocket launchers lay across a wooden pallet; a few metal drums and a collection of gas masks and chemical suits topped off the arsenal.

Sid noticed the back of one of the trucks was open but it was too dark to see inside.

He took Maskey's Maglite and flashed it into the trailer.

More metal drums were stacked at the rear of the cargo bay. Bags of ammonium nitrate fertiliser – some of them open – formed a barrier against the aluminium siding on the driver's side. A collection of plastic buckets and a set of scales sat on a small bench that ran along the other side.

'Shit. It's a fuckin' explosives factory,' Maskey said.

Plastic tubing snaked from two sets of blast caps that had been taped to a bathtub-sized pile of tubes of plastic blast gel. The blast gel had been placed next to the metal drums.

'Jesus.' Kelly sounded both shocked and a little impressed at the same time.

'Crude but effective,' Sid said. It was a simple set-up but it was sure to blow big. He recognised the layout. Counter terrorism forces the world over would have recognised it. No TATP here. This was old-school explosives technology, a lot like the rig Timothy McVeigh used all those years ago to blow up the Federal building in Oklahoma. A white boy. A true American patriot. The biggest terrorist attack in US history before 9/11.

'Sid?' Haifa sounded alarmed.

'Sid,' she said more urgently this time. 'Quick.'

She was over by one of the shipping containers, pressed against the metal siding with her hand cupped against her ear.

'Listen. There's something in there.'

They all stood still. Nothing. Then a bump, and another. Then a muffled sound, unmistakably human.

'Shit. There's something in there all right.' Maskey moved to the front of the container, looking for the way in.

'It's bolted. Give me those fuckin' cutters.' He motioned to Kelly.

The lock was tougher than the three on the front door. Maskey was a big man but he couldn't get it off on his own. By wedging one of the boltcutters' handles against the container, and with Kelly getting in to apply pressure on the other handle as well, the two of them eventually broke it.

The door swung open. Kelly shone his torch in. At the far corner of the container was a body – a man, tied to a chair, bound, gagged and wide-eyed. His mouth had been clamped shut with packing tape and more had been wound around and around his shirtless torso. He'd been badly beaten. Blood was seeping from a split above his right eye, his face was puffed and bruised.

'Hakim,' Haifa shouted. She rushed in.

'Oh Hakim.'

She threw her arms around her brother.

'Quick, do something. Find some water. Hurry.' She was screaming now.

Sid swivelled around looking for something, anything he could do to help. But if there was a tap or a sink anywhere close by he couldn't see one. He followed her in to the container empty handed and helped free Hakim from the chair and lead him out into the open.

'It's okay,' Haifa was saying. 'It's okay. I'm here. We'll get you out. You're safe now.' She was speaking in English and Arabic, trying desperately to reassure him.

Hakim grunted back, unable to communicate.

Haifa started tearing at the packing tape. But she was working too fast, panicking, Sid thought, and she couldn't find the end point. He tried to help. She was crying now. Sobbing.

'Hakim. Hakim. Why? What have they done?' she was saying over and over.

Kelly moved in to help as well. He pulled out one of those multipurpose tools that seemed to have an answer for every problem and started cutting away at the tape. He eventually worked the tape free from Hakim's torso and then gave the tool to Haifa to get at the tape around his head.

Hakim started ripping at the tape too now his hands were free.

'Stop. Hakim. Stop. I'll get it,' Haifa said trying to calm him.

Once an initial cut was made it came off with a rush. Sid watched as Hakim sucked in great gulps of air. He collapsed, racked with an uncontrollable cough that eventually became the contents of his stomach on the floor. He was mumbling almost incoherently in Arabic.

Sid noticed Hakim carried a lot of scarring on his back and across his chest. Small burns and lacerations. They'd been there a long time by the looks of them.

They were all so focused on the drama playing out in front of them that at first they didn't hear the roller door clatter shut behind them. But they sure heard the weapon as it spurt forth a quickfire blast of rounds.

Everyone hit the ground instinctively. Haifa and Hakim fell backwards, back into the mouth of the container from where they'd come. Sid rolled to the left and kept rolling. Maskey did the same, pushing his bulky frame across the concrete floor with surprising speed. They pulled themselves up into the back of the truck loaded with the explosives.

Kelly had jumped right and disappeared behind the second container. The bullets had made a mess of Wheeler. One arm was barely hanging on to a shoulder. The colour had drained from his face and the shock spread as he realised what had happened. He started screaming.

'*Allahu akbar.*' The shout came from somewhere at the front of the warehouse. Another burst of fire silenced Wheeler's screams.

From their vantage point in the truck, Sid and Maskey had a pretty good view. Wheeler's body was sprawled out in front of the metal cargo container, Haifa and her brother were still inside. Maskey had lost his Glock with the silencer in the chaos. It was lying on the ground a few feet in front of Wheeler's body. Two men dressed entirely in black with their heads swathed in black cloth moved quickly. They were each armed with a Carlo. Belts of extra ammunition draped across their shoulders glinted in the half light. The air was thick with the smell of cordite. Shafts of moonlight streamed in from above and picked out wafts of smoke.

The two goons pulled Haifa and Hakim out of the container. Sid tensed and went to move forward. Maskey pushed him back down. Now wasn't the time for heroics. One of the goons had Haifa by the hair, the other almost had to drag her brother out into the light. Another black figure stalked slowly around the second container, gun raised, looking for Kelly.

'Come out, fucker. Hands high,' the man said in a low growl.

Kelly did as he was ordered. He pushed his weapon out onto the floor and held his hands above his head. A fourth, smaller man walked over to the young detective and spat squarely in his face. At first Sid didn't recognise him. He'd only ever seen him wearing robes, but tonight Wissam Shalomar looked like he'd just stepped out of a Lowes catalogue. He was wearing brown brogues, camel-coloured chinos and a pastel-coloured polo shirt, as if he was about to take the yacht out for a Sunday afternoon sail around the harbour. The personification of evil in comfortable shoes. Without saying anything more, he bent down and picked up Wheeler's Maglite torch and Maskey's Glock. He raised the gun to Kelly's forehead, looked intently at him, muttered something indiscernible under his breath, and fired.

A dull click.

A look of shock spread across the young detective's face, his head blew back, his knees buckled and he fell to the ground. Dead.

Sid choked back a shout of alarm. His stomach retched. Maskey expelled a violent and involuntary rush of air, as if he had been hit himself. They'd given themselves away.

Shalomar turned his head in their direction, walked slowly towards them and stopped under a shaft of light about two metres from the rear of the trailer. His face was expressionless but small beads of sweat began to run down his temples.

'Out. Or the girl gets the same,' he said softly, almost as if it was a job he had to do but had no stomach for.

Sid pulled his own gun out and pointed it towards detonator caps sitting on top of plastic rolls of tovex explosive gel.

'Let her go,' he said. 'Or I'll take us all out.'

'You wouldn't have the courage,' Shalomar sneered. 'You wouldn't have the conviction or the character.'

Sid tensed his finger on the trigger. He could do it. Blow them all to shit. The whole thing would be over. No more caliphate's revenge. No more threats. It would be just another factory blast, a big one, but just one more careless industrial accident. But Sid knew Shalomar was right, he wouldn't have the courage. He didn't have the strength, or the character, if that was what was needed. He looked across at Haifa, on her knees next to her brother – a homemade automatic rifle pointed at her head. She was dark with anger, fear and frustration.

'Just try me,' he said, turning back to Shalomar.

'Come out. I want to look you in the eyes as I shoot you.'

'I don't think that's how it's going to happen.'

'Okay, your choice.' Shalomar raised his gun.

'Hey. Now that would be courageous. One spark in this cracker box and we'll all go sky high. You know it. This is a bigger Roman candle than the finale on the harbour on New Year's Eve. We go up with it. All of us. Look at this. Nitromethane. Blast caps. Tovex. I don't really need to tell you that though, do I?'

It was a gamble but it was all they had. They'd just seen how cold-blooded Shalomar could be. Was it their turn now? Is this how it all ends?

'Fuck.' Maskey swore with a finality that suggested that was exactly what he thought.

They waited for an answer. None came.

'Shut the doors on these pathetic infidel cowards,' Shalomar said eventually. He sounded almost disappointed.

41.

Sid and Maskey waited in the darkness listening to the goons locking up. They were efficient. Within a few minutes, the silence was overwhelming.

Here I am again, Sid thought, locked up in another hot, dark, airless box. It had been quite the season for it. At least he wasn't alone and hallucinating this time. No, this time he was just dog-tired. Bone-crushing fucked. How long had it been since he'd slept? A lot had happened since that pissy little room at the Heritage motel in Goulburn. What he wouldn't give now for a room with floral curtains and a minibar fronting Sydney Road.

'Fuck this,' Maskey said using the glow of his phone to shine some light on their predicament.

'It's amazing, isn't it, how even thugs, murderers and criminals can forget about phones? No point locking someone up if you leave them with their phone.'

'Are you going to use that thing or do you just want to

waste the battery confirming our current good fortune?' Sid said. His own phone had long ago run dry.

'Second thoughts –' he said. 'Hand it over here. Call your lot and we'll be an online feature on BuzzFeed before the first patrol car gets here. "*Nine clear signs the Vortex of Evil has won.*" Your people leak faster than Brian Williams' cabinet.'

'Jesus. I swear you speak another language sometimes. I don't understand a word you just said.'

Maskey handed over his phone.

'Do you reckon those signs they have at petrol stations are right? You know, the ones suggesting if you use your phone too close to the bowser the whole thing could blow?'

Maskey just stared at him.

Sid dialled the number to his desk back in the office. The only one he could actually remember. That was another thing about mobile phones. He could never remember numbers anymore. These days they went straight to the contacts file and not the old-fashioned brain memory.

It rang once.

'Yep?' AJ answered, sounding stressed.

'AJ? It's Sid.'

'Sid? Where the fuck are you? What's happening? Did you find anything at the warehouse?'

'Yeah, we found something all right. We're still here. Locked in the back of a truck loaded up with enough nitrogen fertiliser and tovex to blow a hole to China. Two detectives are down and Shalomar's just taken off. Fuck knows where. They've got Hourani and Haifa.'

'What do you mean they've got Haifa?' AJ's stress turned to alarm. 'Where have they taken her?'

'No idea. Like I said, we're stuck in a truck bomb.' Sid tried to sound matter of fact, cool, while his mind and his pulse raced away from him.

'You need to get someone here now.'

'Okay. We're on it. There'll be a team there as fast as we can get them there.'

'Okay but don't broadcast it too widely. There's enough panic out there as it is at the moment.'

'You're not kidding. All the chiefs are lined up in the SCIF. They've got their maps lit up on the wall and they're complaining they've got nothing to put on them. I've had Williams' office at me every hour. Looking for "announceables" they say. Something to calm things down. A sign that we have this thing under control. Clearly we don't.'

'No – we don't.'

'Shit.'

42.

Within fifteen minutes the doors were being broken open by a squad of three special forces boys from the domestic counter terrorism unit – 2 Commando. They were wearing balaclavas and helmets with GoPro cameras mounted on them. They moved fast and didn't say much. A quick round of 'Hello, all right?' And then down to business.

'We've got them,' was all that was said. They were all wearing headsets, presumably wired up back to base, but only one of them spoke.

'Okay. We're yours.' He was looking at Sid.

They'd brought with them spare weapons, comms and an eagerness to get mixed up in something serious.

Sid called the office again. Murphy answered.

'Hey. I finally managed to get a lock on Haifa's phone but I've lost it again. They must have wised up. Looks like they're heading down the A6. South.'

'Speak English, Damo. The A6? Which fucking road is that?'

'It crosses the M5 and goes through Menai – that's where I lost her signal – then it keeps going towards the Princes Highway and down south to Wollongong.'

'Shit.'

'What?'

'That's the road that runs past Lucas Heights right?'

'Yep.'

'Jesus. They're heading for the fucking reactor. The Lucas Heights reactor.'

'Shit.'

'That place is watertight. More secure than – they'll never get past the first gate.'

It had been about half an hour since the circus left. Sid reckoned they'd probably already be there.

'Find out if Hourani's checked in,' he said.

•

Maskey hit the siren and the lights as they gunned the patrol car south. It was just past 4 am, still dark. There was already a bit of traffic about and they had to navigate their way through a crush of trucks that had backed up in the streets around the M5 junction. From the flyover they could see the long line of semis heading back west along the double-lane tollway.

Once through that mess though they got a clear run. The special forces boys were sticking with them – driving a black Audi. They were all flying down the A6 but to what exactly they still didn't know.

So much was racing through Sid's mind. How long had it been since he'd had a good night's sleep? His aching tiredness crackled with sharp adrenalin edges, anger and frustration. It seemed like months since he'd pulled out of the Heritage motel in Goulburn but it had been barely 24 hours. So much had happened in that time. Harrison was finally off the streets, Chip was barely alive and a murderous terrorist threat had become a rolling, unpredictable hostage crisis and Haifa was now in the middle of it. Sid felt sick and vaguely guilty. It happened. Things went wrong. People got hurt. But Haifa was now more than a colleague. The hunt for Scorpion had been personal from the start. It wasn't just Rosie he'd taken away. Now it was Haifa too. Sid wasn't going to let that happen.

Maskey's phone rang. It was sitting in the well between the front seats. Sid picked it up and answered. It was Murphy.

'Sid?'

'Yeah.'

'Shalomar is fucking tweeting.'

'What?'

'Tweeting. He's fucking taken to Twitter. "Announcement to come" it says. "Lucas Heights goes live. Inshallah" Hashtag Lucas Heights. Hashtag Auspol. Hashtag Vortexofevil.'

43.

Alaska Pulu had been a contractor with the security firm Risk Control for the past eight months. He thought the job was going to be more glamorous than it had turned out to be. They told him in the interview process that the company worked contracts all over the world, protecting diplomats, politicians and sensitive embassies and government complexes. But he ended up on the night shift at Lucas Heights checking the badges of employees as they drove in and out of the car park. He wasn't impressed. He'd worked for the Fiji border patrol when he was younger. He knew his way around firearms and difficult situations. He thought he was getting a job with an outfit that was like Blackwater. Travel, danger, adventure and money, that's what he was after. How wrong he was. It would be more fun to go back to club bouncing, he reckoned. At least you got to knock a few heads in that line of work.

It had been a quiet night. Just a few coming and going. Cleaners, a few technicians. The Feds were pretty regular as usual. They drove around every fifteen minutes or so just to check. They never stopped for a chat. They looked down on the contractors.

Occasionally a scientist or two turned up. It didn't happen often. The reactor worked twenty-four hours a day and the shift changes were regular and predictable, but it wasn't a total surprise for one of them to be called in at odd times. So he didn't think too much of it when the old Camry drove up and Dr Hourani flashed his credentials. Alaska barely looked up. He didn't look into the car and he didn't get out of his air-conditioned box and do the mirror check under the car either. They'd stopped doing them a long time ago, when they cut the night staff from two down to one.

He was a bit surprised though when the phone rang in his box. He was even more surprised when the guy on the other end swore when he confirmed Hourani had turned up for work. He was more surprised still when he saw what was happening on the monitors above his desk.

Alaska Pulu had been told he was strictly not allowed out of his box for any reason so he hit the emergency button and got on the radio.

There were five of them. How the fuck were there five of them? He switched the cameras manually so he could get a better view. They were outside the entrance to the reactor building. Two big guys who looked like they'd been dressed by the IS wardrobe department – black combat gear and black balaclavas. One of them was pointing what looked like a gun directly at Hourani and a woman. The other one was setting up lights on a stand. A fifth, smaller guy was fussing around with something on another stand. It looked like an iPad or a computer tablet of some sort. When he had secured it, he turned it towards himself and started pacing back and forth in front of it.

The two-way in the box burst into life.

'What's going on Blue 10? We can see the breach. Any idea who they are?'

'No idea,' Pulu said.

'What's going on? What are they doing?'

'I – I don't know. I –'

What could he say? I didn't check the car? I didn't look? I didn't do my job? Red emergency breach lights were flashing all over the console in front of him. The two-way crackled back.

'The lockdown's in place. They won't get any further.'

'Doesn't look like they're even trying. They've stopped just outside the entrance.'

Still they got that far. Not a good look for Alaska Pulu. He was trying to think of something to say that might save his arse, but before he could figure anything out a police patrol car came screeching to a stop at the boom gate. Two cops got out. A black Audi came in fast behind them and three heavily armed dudes, military of some sort, burst out in full operational mode, scouring the car park, weapons high.

Was this for real?

'Where are they?' The smaller of the two from the patrol car was holding up his badge now and screaming at him through the glass.

Alaska Pulu looked up at the six monitors above him.

'Outside the reactor building.'

'How the fuck do we get there?'

He pointed down the road.

'Two hundred metres. You'll see a roundabout. Turn right. Another two hundred or so. You'll see them. They're out the front of the reactor building.'

Before Pulu could finish the sentence, the military boys set off. The two cops bringing up the rear.

44.

THE MOOD IN THE SENSITIVE COMPARTMENTED INFORMATION Facility at the ASIO headquarters in Canberra was quiet and efficient. Half-a-dozen technical specialists and analysts were tapping away at their computers or turning on bits of electronic hardware. Drummond Gray looked like he hadn't slept all night. Unusually for him, he'd taken off his jacket. His shirtsleeves were rolled up – he looked as untidy as he felt. The prime minister was looking fat and red-faced but his discomfort was being contained as ever by his expensive wardrobe. All that attention to detail. And did the guy ever rest? Gray wondered. Brian Williams was more engaged and excited than Gray could ever remember. Fowler from the AFP was there too as was Hurls, stuffed into his uniform tighter than marbles in a stocking. The veins on the CDF's neck were pumping. They'd all been in and out all night waiting for something to happen, waiting for someone to tell them that it was all going to be okay. Now it was finally clear something was happening. This whole mess was going to come to an end somehow. From what they'd heard so far from AJ, it seemed as if the danger of a multi-pronged terror event had at least been contained but now they were watching something else unfold, something totally unpredictable.

They were sitting in front of a bank of monitors. Beyond that there was a large electronic map showing the site at Lucas Heights. Gray had almost scoffed when he heard that was the target. There couldn't be a more secure complex in the entire country. The agencies all knew the nation's only nuclear facility was a target – it had been before and no doubt it would be again – but the new reactor had been reinforced so much that even if some mad fucker decided they were going to fly a plane into it, it still wouldn't blow. After 9/11 they'd put what they laughingly called a Cessna net over the top of the reactor dome. It was no birdcage. That thing would stop a 747. And the lockdown procedure was so effective that there was no way anyone would be getting through on the ground either. None the less it seemed someone was at least attempting to give it a red-hot go.

Three green dots were blinking on the big electronic map on the wall. The counter terrorism commandos converging on the reactor building. The soldiers' microphones were live and streaming into the room over the speakers. They could all hear them panting as they ran, an occasional order to 'go low' or 'take the right' coming in. One of the monitors was showing the six squares of the Lucas Heights security cameras. Others were monitoring social media feeds.

'Monitor two,' one of the analysts shouted. 'Check out the Twitter feed.'

Monitor two switched to the main screen.

'Hashtag Lucas Heights is trending. So is hashtag vortexofevil. There, look, "Lucas Heights goes live". There's a Periscope up already.'

'Oh Jesus. That's just what we need.' Brian Williams understood immediately what was happening.

'Sir, they're live streaming on Twitter. Periscope, it's –'

'Uh huh. I know. I can see what's happening,' the PM said, dismissing the young operator's assumptions.

'He's live on Facebook too, look,' Drummond Gray chimed in looking from the small screen on his phone to the big one in front of them.

'The whole world can watch if they want,' Fowler added. The shot on the monitor was wide enough to show the whole scene. Shalomar was brandishing a knife, Hakim and Haifa Hourani were kneeling in front of him and two masked gunmen stood on either side pointing their weapons directly at the siblings.

'What are they doing?' Williams asked.

'There's no sign anyone there is trying to breach any of the secure areas. All the lockdowns remain secure. No attempted entry anywhere,' one of the techs said.

'They're not interested in the nukes. It's the message – the backdrop. He wants to make a statement.' Gray stated what everyone had now come to realise.

It was further confirmation of the breakdown of the old order. Anyone could control the airwaves. Anyone could say anything they wanted to anyone else and there would always be a record. This little show wasn't just for now. This was for all time. It'd be replayed everywhere. It would live on forever in Google searches in bedrooms all over the world.

The green dots were closing in now. The commandos were about a hundred metres away from the reactor building. Gray could hear them pounding their way towards the scene but his and everyone else's eyes were locked on to the live Periscope vision. The tech had switched it to the big screen on the wall.

Shalomar looked directly into the camera and then started reading from a text.

'*Allahu akbar*. I deliver this message to you, the people of Australia.' He pointed his knife towards the camera. 'I say this to you. As a government you have been at the forefront of the aggression towards the Islamic State. You have played your role as the obedient lapdog of the United States. Today your military is attacking us daily in Iraq and in Syria but you are no longer fighting an insurgency, you are fighting a state. We are an Islamic army. The caliphate has risen again. And yet you continue to try to squash us, to drive us out of our land. We will not rest. To deny us our rights to live under an Islamic caliphate will result in the bloodshed of your people. These two are just the first.'

Everyone in the SCIF was transfixed. No one knew what to say.

'Left. Go left,' one of the soldiers on the ground said.

Another voice.

'I've got him. I've got a bead on the little guy. You two take the others. Ready?'

'Ready.'

'Okay. Settle.' There was a pause. Heavy breathing only. Then, 'Do we have the all clear?'

In the SCIF no one said anything. Silence.

'Are you reading us back there? Are we taking them out? Are we good to go?'

Again, no response.

45.

Sid was running hard behind the special forces guys. Cavan Maskey was making it up the rear somewhere. It was still the half gloom just before dawn. He could see a couple of lights on stands had been set up on the concrete forecourt in front of the entrance to the reactor building. Half-a-dozen tiled steps led up to them. Shalomar was there, standing behind Haifa and her brother who were both kneeling on the concrete in front of him. There was a black-clad goon either side of them, both pointing their guns down at their heads.

The commandos fanned out as they approached the building. They were on a grass verge in front of a circular driveway now. There was nowhere to hide or take cover but Shalomar and the men in black didn't seem to be interested in their arrival in the least. It was like a stage – an execution platform.

'Hold up,' Sid said, not sure how to proceed. Shalomar was presenting a sermon. He was addressing it to an iPad set up on another stand a few feet in front of him.

'. . . The caliphate has risen again. And yet you continue to try to squash us, to drive us out of our land. We will not rest. To deny us our rights to live under an Islamic caliphate will result in the bloodshed of your people. These two are just the first.'

Maskey finally arrived, panting and sweating.

'What the fuck sort of pantomime is this?' he said.

'He's beaming it out live,' Sid said. 'Fucking Twitter.'

'What?'

'Never mind.'

Shalomar hadn't dropped a beat. He and the goons knew the cavalry had arrived but obviously couldn't care less. The preacher kept reading his prepared rant. The thugs in black were still pointing their guns directly at Haifa and her brother. The sermon wasn't going to last forever. Something was going to happen soon. Haifa's head had dropped towards her chest. Sid couldn't see her face. Was this how Rosie died too? The official reports of that day in Afghanistan simply stated an ambush and an intense firefight. She would have known she was in a fight for her life but did she see her killer or was she caught in the crossfire?

Haifa was shaking but her brother was as defiant as ever – holding his head high and still. His eyes were closed, like he was meditating. So still. So calm.

Sid looked across at the special forces. They were talking to each other through their comms – he couldn't hear what they were saying. There are three of them, he reasoned. They can coordinate the action. They can take out one each. He could see that was what they were thinking too. They started to move in. It was risky. Haifa and Hakim were in the line of fire. But this was what these guys were trained to do.

Sid weaved his way up to the one he assumed was the commander. The only one who'd said anything to him so far in this whole sorry saga.

'Do it,' he said. 'Take them out.'

Nothing happened. The commandos had stopped moving.

'Do it. Now,' Sid said. 'Get it done.'

The commando spoke without lowering his weapon.

'We haven't been cleared.'

'You what?'

'We're still waiting.'

'For what?'

'The security team. The PM, the chiefs. They're in the SCIF. I've requested an authorisation to fire. Still waiting.'

'What? What the fuck is going on?'

He didn't get any further response from the trained assassin. He pulled out his phone, now showing some life after a short recharge on the race here. He punched in AJ's number. In the few seconds it took her to answer it he considered trying to take them out himself. But how? He and Maskey only had two shots and with Glocks from this far away there was no chance they could aim them well enough to be sure to take anyone down. What then? Surely if it wasn't done quickly and cleanly Haifa and her brother were dead. The only way to do it was with these guys and their sniper rifles. What the fuck was going on? All that collective wisdom but no direction. No decisions.

AJ answered. Sid walked back, away from the action.

'They're all in the SCIF room,' she explained. 'They're following it all.'

'Yeah, I figured that much. We have to take him out, AJ.'

'Yep. I –'

Sid stopped. It hit him.

'They want this to happen, don't they? They want a fucking live execution.'

Could he be right? They wanted this to keep rolling?

Sid started to shake. He felt like he was about to burst but he had nowhere to direct his anger and his shock. He was almost crushing the phone in his hand. His throat was dry. He could barely speak.

'Tell me it's not true.'

'Sid. Don't.'

'Tell me that's not the case.' He was hot with rage now. 'Is this really what it's come to? Here's a national emergency unfolding right now. Here's a political opportunity. Is that what they're thinking? Really? Let me talk to them. Put me through to the room.'

'I can't do that, Sid. You know I can't.'

•

Drummond Gray was so taken aback by the speed of what had been happening he was momentarily paralysed. They'd been up all night. No one was thinking clearly, he concluded. Someone should put a stop to this. They should shut it down, but ultimately it wasn't his call.

'There are thousands following this now,' the tech said, still tracking the social media feed. 'From everywhere. This is going viral fast.'

On the big screen Shalomar was still in full flight.

'Send your fighters . . . it means nothing to us. Send your planes and your bombs, send everything you want to us because you will not harm us. Why? Because we have Allah with us. And this is something you don't have. The caliphate has risen again.'

He spat out the last phrase at a high-pitched frenzy. Then he stopped. He'd been reading from a text. Now he stared directly into the camera.

'This is how vulnerable you are.' His delivery now slow and deliberate.

'This is supposed to be one of the most secure sites in this country. But look we're here . . . To you Brian Williams, so-called prime minister, I say this. These weapons we have, we will not put them down until we've taken the head of every one of your foot soldiers and until the black flag is flying high. Until we put the black flag on top of Parliament House. We won't stop. *Allahu akbar.*'

Williams was sweating. He was staring, fixated by the drama unfolding in front of him. Gray looked across at General Darwin. They were both thinking the same thing. This had to stop. The CDF went to speak. Williams stood up.

'Okay,' he said quietly. 'That's enough. Take them out.'

He left the room.

•

The shots rang out as soon as the order was given. Sid saw the three men fall to the ground. Shalomar was hit through the neck. He saw Haifa rock forward and collapse. Had she been hit too? Her brother remained unmoved. Sid raced up the steps. There was a slow-motion feel to what was unfolding now. Haifa was on the ground. She wasn't hurt but she was in shock, shaking. Hakim still hadn't moved. The only sound was a soft gurgle coming from Shalomar. He was still breathing – a long way from dead. Sid walked back to the iPad on the stand. He turned it off and he turned it away from the scene just in case. Then he walked back to Shalomar, put his Glock close to the preacher's head and pulled the trigger. His anger and his pain, the years of loss and loneliness, were all invested in that one moment, that one action. He felt calm and certain. It was the only killing he'd ever done that he was totally at peace with.

'That's for Rosie,' he said.

46.

'Yep, that's the way it is these days. Hysteria rules. Anyone can get online and the rest of the media laps it up.'

They were in the waiting room outside the prime minister's office in Parliament House. AJ was on one of her rants about 'the decline of media standards' since the glory days when she was a working journalist. When 'checks and balances' were important. When 'verification' was considered essential before going to print. Now the 'Twitter tail wags the dog'.

The dog barked solidly for a week and was still barking. In the few hours after the Periscope went live it was retweeted relentlessly. More than 200,000 tweets with the hashtag 'vortexofevil'. It was a digital media frenzy that spiralled into a firestorm of self-affirmation for the finger-tapping activists on all sides of the political spectrum.

'Social media is no place for the faint-hearted or for fence-sitters' was her other pithy observation.

If it was coverage Shalomar was after, if it was publicity he wanted, Sid had to agree he got it. The whole country had been talking about nothing else ever since. The shock jocks got into it. The tabloids dubbed it a 'Nuclear jihad'. The broadsheets pontificated.

Shalomar and his boys were digital suicide bombers. Their mission had been to get publicity, to ratchet up the fear and to undermine community confidence. In that sense then, a victory.

'This is a vortex of evil. They're coming to get every one of us.' Brian Williams' mantra was now a potent reality. All week Williams had been pledging new tougher laws to deal with the 'evident threat of extremism'.

And what of the list? The nation was still on high alert. They might assume the operation detailed by the Scorpion was no longer an immediate threat but they had no way of knowing for sure. The weaponry and the explosives at the warehouse had been contained. All they could do was keep vigilant. Keep monitoring. Keep hoping. If not this one, then there would be others. High alert was the new reality.

Sid was still trying to process what had happened at the reactor. Why had the chiefs let the show continue? Was it just a fuck-up or did they do it deliberately? How long would they have let it run?

He had his suspicions but he didn't know the answer. Probably never would.

'The prime minister will see you now. This way please.'

Sid could martyr himself at this point too, he reckoned. Strap on his own suicide vest and pose the question direct to the PM. Not a good career move. Better to just take the accolades for a job well done. Accept the award that's about to be pinned on his chest and get on with it. Other than the special forces commandos and those who were in the SCIF at the time, he and AJ were the only two who knew how long it had taken for the shoot order to come. He hadn't told Haifa, and he knew he wouldn't. What good would it do? The one thing he could take away from it all was that justice for Rosie had been delivered. The Scorpion was gone.

47.

Sid took the four o'clock flight from Canberra. By five-thirty he was in a taxi watching the meter tick over as they fought the peak-hour traffic heading south.

He had barely left Cronulla since Haifa had been discharged from the hospital. After two days of medical checks and observation she'd been sent home with a schedule of future bookings with the psych doctor and a Serepax prescription. But, as she said to Sid, she preferred to self-medicate and he was happy to join her. Therapy seemed to consist of long sessions in the pool and frequent and enthusiastic sex. Sid cooked fish almost every night. They smoked a lot of dope, drank whiskey and watched the light fade into the velvet autumn evenings.

She had continued his musical education. The latest on the play loop was the haunting Sufi-inspired ambience of Arooj Aftab from Lahore in Pakistan. Haifa said it transported her to a better place. Sid couldn't deny it. After a bit of weed from the magic box and a few Lagavulins, the music, the warm breeze and the breaking surf outside made him feel he was totally out of harm's way – above everything.

Sustained by sex, food, music and a few soothing substances, the week since the Lucas Heights drama had gone by fast. Sid was in no hurry for the recovery period to end and he sensed Haifa was hardly ready to move on either. She still hadn't approached her brother about what she'd found in her old bedroom. The maps, the religious texts that he called research material. Did she believe him? Did Sid believe him? He wasn't sure. Something wasn't right. What had happened to it all? If it was there as Haifa said, why did Hakim remove it? There was more to it but maybe that was a job for someone else.

And Chip? He'd live and he'd walk again too. They'd given him two new knees.

'They tell me there isn't a more painful operation than knee replacements,' he'd boasted. Sid told him he'd shout the first martini once he was back on his feet. 'You don't need to be standing up to drink,' Chip said. Still, it would be a few weeks yet before he'd be back in a bar.

Sid paid for the taxi. Walked to the kerb and looked up at the apartment. It felt good. Being here, with Haifa. He had no idea what the future would look like but he was determined to hold on to the present.

They had both tried hard to ignore as much of the white noise of the media frenzy as they could so it was a bit of a surprise to see her sitting in front of the television when he walked back into the apartment. The prime minister hadn't wasted any time getting back to Sydney either. There he was on the screen. More talk about the need for community engagement 'here in the heart of Sydney's Muslim community'.

'Haven't you heard enough?' Sid asked.

'Ssshh. Look,' Haifa said without turning away from the screen.

The camera had reframed to a wider shot. Hakim Hourani, dressed in one of his fine tailored suits, was standing beside Brian Williams, nodding in agreement as the prime minister hit important points of emphasis.

'As Dr Hourani here knows only too well, the risks of radicalisation are real,' he was saying, 'but this is not a matter for governments alone. We can't do it alone. We need to bring communities along with us. We need schools engaged and parents. That's why we're reaching out with funding for grassroots organisations. Millions of dollars. And we need local community leaders like Dr Hourani working with us. That's why I'm pleased to announce that Dr Hourani has accepted my request to run as our candidate here in the seat of Watson at the next election.'

Hakim looked as serene as ever but he couldn't help but display just a hint of self-satisfaction.

'Of course it won't be easy,' the PM said. 'This is a seat the opposition has held for more than thirty years. But we believe it is winnable, especially with a quality candidate like Dr Hourani. A quality community leader, and if I might add, a top bloke, like Dr Hourani. We can do it and we can continue the great work to make our communities and our country safe and secure.'

•

' – we believe it is winnable, especially with a quality candidate like Dr Hourani. A quality community leader . . .'

Hakim Hourani heard the words slip by. A soft zephyr-like breeze had picked up carrying the last hint of summer. Wiley Park had just been mown and some of the pine trees had been freshly trimmed. The air smelled of eucalyptus, cut grass and pines. It was the smell of the future, of a new beginning. Fate was such a fickle thing, he thought. What lay around the next bend may not be what was expected. A good fighter knows that. A good soldier knows that. A good politician knows that.

It had been a long journey. There was plenty more to come. He smiled for the cameras.

'Over to you, Hakim.'

'Thank you, Prime Minister. Thank you.'

He turned to look straight at the cameras fully aware of the significance of the moment.

He began.

'I am deeply humbled by the opportunity presented to me to represent the people of this electorate.'

•

Mick Harrison had been drifting in and out of consciousness for days. A mess of wires and tubes were the only things keeping him alive. He knew the end was coming and he welcomed it. He had nothing left. His job was done.

Time seemed to be standing still. Every time he looked up at the TV stuck on the news channel on the wall it was deja vu all over again. Nothing but Brian fucking Williams or some other cunt banging on and on about terror. Had they thanked him? No. Yet he was the one who had uncovered the plot. He was the one who warned them. Now Scorpion was gone. Good riddance.

There he was again. Williams. He was in a park now. And who was that standing beside him? The doctor? Yep, Dr Hourani. Both of them trussed up in their fucking suits.

'– we believe it is winnable, especially with a quality candidate like Dr Hourani,' Williams was saying. 'A quality community leader, and if I might add, a top bloke, like Dr Hourani. We can do it and we can continue the great work to make our communities and our country safe and secure.'

Harrison looked up at the screen.

Hakim Hourani said, 'Thank you, Prime Minister. Thank you.' Then he turned his full gaze towards the camera.

Harrison was transfixed. The deep black eyes stared back at him, the prominent almost feminine nose and the lean face. He saw it now. The terrible mistake. The terrible miscalculation. Panic swamped him. His heart began to race. Pain gripped his chest and his head. He gasped for air, desperate to suck the life back into his convulsing body.

Acknowledgements

THANKS TO VANESSA RADNIDGE FOR EMBRACING THIS BOOK with such enthusiasm, and to Justin Ractliffe, Daniel Pilkington, Fiona Hazard and the rest of the incredible, professional team at Hachette Australia who made it such a pleasurable and rewarding journey. Thank you to Claire de Medici and Deonie Fiford for their thoughtful editorial advice.

Thanks also to Grace Heifetz at Curtis Brown for taking me on and backing the manuscript with such conviction and energy.

Thanks to my patient friends and critics who read the early drafts. Particularly Nic Cherbuin and Nicola Meares for their medical and technical advice. To Sam and Jill Holden for their encouragement and support, and to my tight group of mates Paul Daley, Chris Hammer and Jeremy Thompson who read, critique and encourage often and with gusto.

Special thanks to my great friend and travel brother Louie (Levent) Eroglu for sharing his knowledge of Western Sydney and his street smart wisdom. Few people know the ins and outs of Auburn and Lakemba like this proud son of Turkish immigrants.

Although this is entirely a work of fiction it can't help but be informed by my own experiences and by the generosity of many people.

Special thanks to the veterans of the Afghanistan and Iraq conflicts who have been willing to share some of their personal experiences, their technical knowledge and especially their post-combat struggles. We continue to send people to war but we still fail to fully understand and deal with the devastating personal cost of that decision.

Thanks also to those professionals who work in intelligence, policing and politics who have been generous with their time and willing to engage over the years.

Thanks to my amazing daughters, Ella and Neve, who have had to cope with my frequent absences and who most recently have occasionally had to deal with finding some confronting research on the family laptop . . . and finally, to my beautiful wife and partner, Tracy, for her continuing support and love.

Michael Brissenden has been a political journalist and foreign correspondent for the ABC since 1987. He began his career covering Federal politics and has been a correspondent in Moscow, Brussels and Washington. Michael covered many of the biggest international stories of the 1990s and early 2000s from all corners of the globe. He was the political editor for the *7.30 Report* in Canberra from 2003 to 2009, the ABC's Defence and National Security Correspondent and most recently he has worked as host of *AM*, the national radio program. This Walkley Award winner has just joined ABC's *Four Corners* as a reporter.

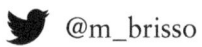 @m_brisso

If you would like to find out more about Hachette Australia, our authors, upcoming events and new releases you can visit our website or our social media channels:

hachette.com.au

HachetteAustralia

HachetteAus

HachetteAus

HachetteAus

www.ingramcontent.com/pod-product-compliance
Ingram Content Group UK Ltd.
Pitfield, Milton Keynes, MK11 3LW, UK
UKHW042000230426
12048UKWH00009B/445